ALL GIRL 6

LESBIAN EROTICA BUNDLE

EROTICA THEMED BUNDLES
BOOK 18

VICTORIA RUSH

VOLUME 18

EROTICA THEMED BUNDLES - BOOK 18

COPYRIGHT

ALSO BY VICTORIA RUSH

Adult Fairytales:

The Enchanted Forest: An Erotic Fairytale

The Land of Giants: An Erotic Fairytale

The Dragon's Lair: An Erotic Fairytale

Witch's Brew: An Erotic Fairytale

The Mage's Spell: An Erotic Fairytale

The Mermaid Lagoon: An Erotic Fairytale

The Coven: An Erotic Fairytale

Rapunzel: An Erotic Fairytale

The Seven Dwarfs: An Erotic Fairytale

The Land of Mutants: An Erotic Fairytale

The Erotic Temple: A Sexy Fairytale (Coming Soon)

Erotica Themed Bundles:

Voyeur: Lesbian Erotica Bundle

Public Affairs: A Lesbian Anthology

Futa Fantasies: The Ladyboy Collection

Threesomes: The Lesbian Collection

Threesomes - Volume 2: The Lesbian Collection

First Time: A Lesbian Anthology

Hedonism: An Erotic Anthology

Switch Hitters: Bisexual Erotica

Taboo Erotica: The Lesbian Series

BDSM: The Lesbian Collection

Party Games: The Erotic Collection

Party Games 2: The Erotic Collection

All Girl 1: Lesbian Erotica Bundle

All Girl 2: Lesbian Erotica Bundle

All Girl 3: Lesbian Erotica Bundle

All Girl 4: Lesbian Erotica Bundle

Erotic Fairytale Bundles:

Clover's Fantasy Adventures: Books 1 - 5

Clover's Fantasy Adventures: Books 6 - 10

Erotic Fantasy:

Pirate's Bounty: A Time Travel Adventure

Wild West: A Time Travel Adventure

Private Riley: A Time Travel Adventure

Cleopatra's Secret: A Time Travel Adventure

Bounty Hunter 2125: A Time Travel Adventure

Ninja Assassin: A Time Travel Adventure

The 300: A Time Travel Adventure

Arabian Nights: An Erotic Fairytale (coming soon...)

Steamy Time Travel Bundles:

Riley's Time Travel Adventures: Books 1 - 5

Lesbian Erotica:

The Dinner Party: Lesbian Voyeur Erotica

The Darkroom: Bisexual Voyeur Erotica

Naked Yoga: Lesbian Transgender Erotica

Nude Cruise: Bisexual Voyeur Erotica

Rush Hour: Taboo Public Sex

The Girl Next Door: First Time Lesbian Erotic Romance

Girls' Camp: Lesbian Group Sex

Wet Dream: Ladyboy Fantasy Erotica

The Convent: Taboo Sex with a Nun

Sex Robot: A Dream Sex Machine

The Personal Trainer: Getting Pumped at the Gym

The Dominatrix: BDSM Lesbian Domination

Webcam Chat: Lesbian Online Sex

Paint Me: A Kinky Bodypainting Workshop

The Toy Party: Girls Sharing Sex Toys

The Costume Party: Strapping One On

Swedish Sauna: Lesbian Group Sex

The Therapist: Taboo Lesbian Erotica

Elevator Shaft: Bisexual Threesomes Erotica

Ladyboy: Lesbian Transgender Erotica

Peep Show: Lesbian Voyeur Erotica

The Dare: Public Sex Erotica

Maid Service: Lesbian Threesomes Erotica

The Hitchhiker: First Time Lesbian Erotica

The Housesitter: Spycam Lesbian Erotica

The Spa: Lesbian Group Orgy

Parlor Games: Blindfold Sex Party

The Exchange Student: First Time Lesbian Erotica

The Hostel: Bisexual Group Erotica

The Harem: Lesbian Erotic Romance

The Orient Express: Lesbian Voyeur Erotica

The First Lady: A Forbidden Lesbian Erotic Romance

The Slave: Lesbian BDSM Erotica

The Masseuse: Lesbian Sensuous Erotica

Too Close for Comfort: Lesbian Forbidden Erotica

Naked Twister: A Wild Party Game

Lexi: The Sex App (Lesbian Fantasy Erotica)

Call Girl: Lesbian Bisexual Threesomes Erotica

Circle Jill: Lesbian Masturbation Workshop

The Viewing Room: Masturbation Voyeur Erotica

Spin the Bottle: A Kinky Party Game

The Hair Salon: Lesbian Voyeur Erotica

Tribadism 1: Girls Only Sex Workshop

Tribadism 2: The Art of Scissoring

Tribadism 3: Threeway Hookups

The Kiss: A Game of Oral Sex

Pledge Week: Sorority Sisters

Carny Games 1: A Wild Sex Party

Carny Games 2: A Kinky Sex Party

Carny Games 3: An Erotic Sex Party

Dreamscape: An Artificial Reality Game

Glory Hole: Guess Who's On the Other Side

Joy Ride: A Late Night Erotic Bus Trip

The Blind Girl: An Erotic Romance(Coming Soon)

Lesbian Erotica Bundles:

Jade's Erotic Adventures: Books 1 - 5

Jade's Erotic Adventures: Books 6 - 10

Jade's Erotic Adventures: Books 11 - 15

Jade's Erotic Adventures: Books 16 - 20

Jade's Erotic Adventures: Books 21 - 25

Jade's Erotic Adventures: Books 26 - 30

Jade's Erotic Adventures: Books 31 - 35

Jade's Erotic Adventures: Books 36 - 40

Jade's Erotic Adventures: Books 41 - 45

Jade's Erotic Adventures: Books 46 - 50

Fifty Shades of Jade: Superbundle

Standalone Stories:

The Polynesian Girl: A Lesbian EroticRomance

For the uninhibited...

WANT TO AMP UP YOUR SEX LIFE?

Sign up for my newsletter to receive more free books and other steamy stuff. Discover a hundred different ways to wet your whistle!

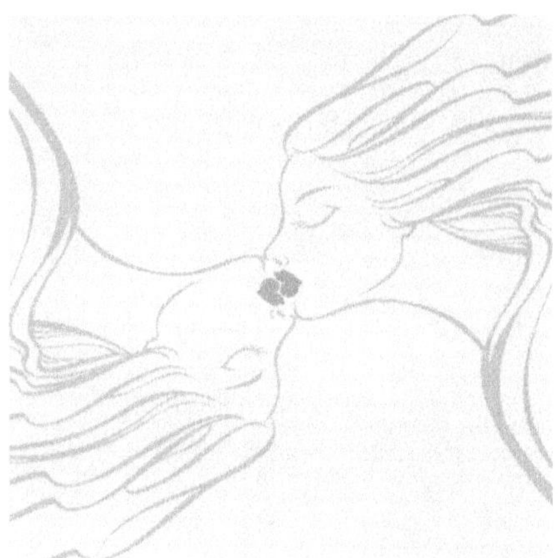

Victoria Rush Erotica

VICTORIA RUSH

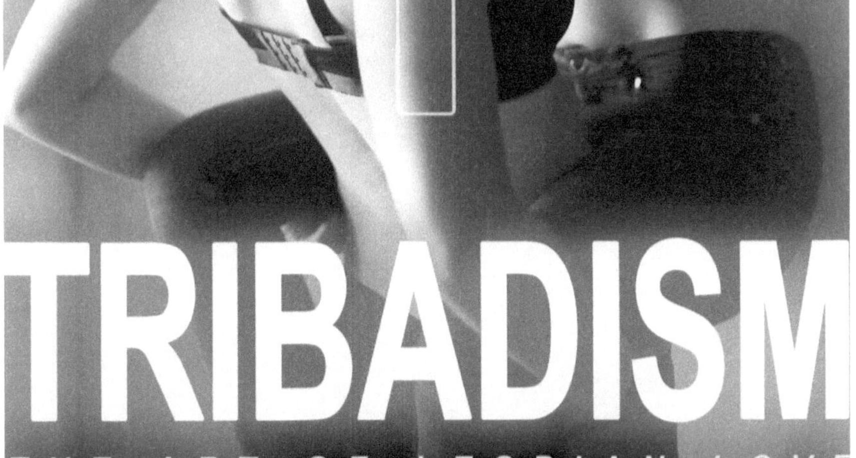

TRIBADISM

THE ART OF LESBIAN LOVE

1

When I received a message from my intimacy coach announcing a new all-girls workshop, my heart skipped a beat. But when I discovered it would be focused entirely on learning new tribbing techniques, a *different* part of my anatomy began throbbing. The idea of a group of naked women practicing new scissoring positions in full view of each other was impossible to resist. I booked a flight to New York for the next available session and was barely able to sit still the entire trip.

When I arrived at Laila's Upper West Side apartment on the scheduled day, she greeted me at the door with a soft kiss. Her co-op was decorated with the same tasteful Georgia O'Keefe and Japanese shunga art that I remembered, but instead of the reclining lounge chairs from her last session, this time her living room was set up with a series of large yoga mats arrayed in a circle around a single, vinyl-covered futon.

Some of the other workshop attendees had already arrived, and we introduced ourselves as we sampled hors d'oeuvres laid out on the buffet table, while soft instrumental music played in the background. I recognized a few of the women from the previous session where we'd learned how to squirt at her Fountain of Venus workshop. The pretty young redhead, Piper, had returned, along with the sexy blonde, Hailey, and the hot African-American lesbian, Trinity.

But the rest of the women looked unfamiliar and my pussy grew increasingly moist as I casually flitted around the room, sampling the buffet fare. Most of the girls had already changed into terrycloth robes laid out on hooks lining the entrance hall, and as we chatted amongst ourselves, Laila circulated amongst us making small talk, trying to ease the nervous tension in the room. With her long, silver-blonde hair, bright blue eyes, and taut, Madonna-like figure, I couldn't help stealing glances at her sexy body whenever her back was turned.

When the last attendee arrived and everybody had changed into their robes, Laila asked us to take a seat on one of the yoga mats and make ourselves comfortable. But with only half as many mats as workshop participants, each of us had to sit knee-to-knee beside one another in pairs. Whether this was by design or accident, I couldn't be sure, but as my exposed thigh brushed up against the young redhead's sitting next to me, I felt goosebumps beginning to spread over my body.

"Thank you all for coming," Laila said, sitting cross-legged on the futon while peering at each of the women arranged around the circle. "I recognize a few familiar faces from our last workshop. I hope you've been enjoying some of the new techniques we learned together."

"*Um-hmm,*" Hailey hummed, with a sly smile on her face. "It's a good thing these mats are made out of *rubber*," she said, rubbing her fingers softly across the surface of her yoga cushion. "Because ever since you taught me how to ejaculate, I seem to make a mess out of every place I have sex!"

"Well, I'm hoping that isn't always a *bad* thing," Laila smiled while clasping her hands over her lap as I tried to steal glances under her partially open robe.

"Absolutely!" Hailey said, leaning back on her outstretched arms to reveal the dark cleft between her parted knees.

"Our focus for this workshop is going to be a little *different*," Laila said. "Although if it involves a little extra waterworks, that should only add to the excitement. In this session, we're going to learn about the many different ways women can connect their bodies together. How many of you have touched another woman in this way?"

Many of the women around the circle raised their hands, while a few looked at Laila with puzzled expressions.

"Does kissing girls during middle-school sleepovers count?" a pretty brunette sitting on the opposite side of the circle asked.

"Yes, but I was thinking of touching in more intimate places..."

"With what *parts* of our bodies exactly?" another woman asked. "I went down on my roommate once after a drunken binge during college–"

"Those are all lovely ways to connect with your partner," Laila nodded. "But since the subject of this workshop is *tribadism*, I meant in a very specific way."

"You mean *scissoring*?" Piper said, bumping her knee excitedly against mine.

"That's another word for it, yes," Laila said. "Although technically, tribbing means to *rub*, so tribadism involves rubbing *any* two body parts together, though most of the time it involves stimulating the vulvas in one form or another. So, with that slightly more limited definition, how many of you have indulged with members of your same sex that way?"

A smaller number of women raised their hands and Laila nodded.

"And for those of you who've practiced the specific art of scissoring, how many different *positions* have you tried or discovered?"

"Five or six?" a pink-haired girl said, pinching her eyebrows together.

"Maybe ten or twelve," an attractive middle-aged woman suggested.

"How many different ways can two women *connect* that way?" the African-American girl, Trinity, said. "I mean, there's only so many ways we can twist our bodies and rub our pussies together."

"You might be surprised," Laila said. "Did you know there are over a hundred different ways two women can stimulate themselves without using their hands or lips? Even more if you add other partners into the mix."

"Will we be learning all of these positions at this workshop?" Piper asked, flapping her legs together in growing excitement.

"We probably won't have time to practice *all* of them here," Laila smiled. "But since this is a three-day workshop, we should be able to cover a lot of ground, in a manner of speaking."

"Including with multiple partners?" Hailey asked, peering around the circle with a raised eyebrow.

"On our last day, yes," Laila nodded. "But let's not get ahead of ourselves. We're going to take it one step at a time, starting with the basics and building up our repertoire of increasingly advanced positions while we go. Are you ready to get started?"

"Damn straight," Hailey said, pulling open her robe to reveal her firm, cantaloupe-sized tits. "I'm already starting to get pretty worked up with all this talk of pussy rubbing."

"Well then," Laila smiled. "Would you like to be my first volunteer? It'll be easier to demonstrate the positions with an assistant–"

"You're twisting my arm," Hailey said, rising up on her knees expectantly.

"Or your *legs*, as the case may be," Laila chuckled, patting the futon beside her. "Why don't you come join me so we can demonstrate the first position together?"

"Okay," Hailey said, prancing over to the middle of the circle and hopping down on the futon beside Laila. "How would you like me to position myself this first time?"

"As I said, we're going to work into this slowly," Laila smiled. "Partly to help those who've never done this before to get used to the idea of rubbing their bodies against another woman, but also so we can build up to more exciting and interesting positions. For our first demonstration, I'd like you to lie down on the mattress face up, with your legs spread a couple of feet apart."

"Naked, or with my robe on?" Hailey grinned, lying down beside Laila and looking up at her innocently.

"Whichever you prefer," Laila said, raising up and kneeling between Hailey's legs while facing her stomach. "Of course, it will be easier for the other women to see how we're engaging if we're both unclothed."

"I was *hoping* you'd say that," Hailey said, pulling off her robe and throwing it onto the floor beside the futon.

"For this first position," Laila said as nervous laughter spread around the room, "I'm going to demonstrate the *missionary* position with one woman lying on top of the other while we press our hips together."

Laila took off her robe and placed it on the floor atop Hailey's, and as everyone around the room stared at her impeccably shaped ass, she placed her hands on the futon beside Hailey's chest then lowered herself onto her body with her legs positioned straight behind her. When her mound pressed against Hailey's, Hailey tried to tilt her hips upward and spread her knees further apart to create friction on her clit, but she frowned peering into Laila's face positioned a foot above hers.

"This doesn't seem like much fun," she said, squirming awkwardly under Laila's pressing body. "I can't even rub my *pussy* against yours in this position."

"It's not designed to," Laila grinned, pulling her body higher up over Hailey's hips while she ground her vulva into her prone partner's mound. "This position is designed more for the superior partner's enjoyment."

She tilted her head to the side, looking back in the direction of the women seated in the circle behind her.

"For those of you at the six o'clock position behind me, can you see how I'm rubbing my vulva on my partner's pubis?"

The women behind her lowered their heads and nodded excitedly.

"Yes," one of them said, squirming slowly on her mat.

"This position is useful if one of you wants to assume the dominant position while focusing primarily on your *own* pleasure," Laila smiled, rocking her pussy firmly against Hailey's pinned hips.

She placed her hands on Hailey's big melons, squeezing them tightly while pinching her nipples.

"But you're also in a perfect position to stimulate *other* parts of your partner's body with this posture. And it's a great way to gaze into her eyes while you're pleasuring yourself and spreading your lubrication all over her stomach and mound."

"Mmm," Hailey purred, writhing her hips under Laila's gyrating ass. "I can feel you dripping on me already. This is *way* sexier than I imagined–"

"Plus," Laila said, lowering her face toward Hailey's. "You're also in a perfect position to *kiss* your partner while your rub your bodies together..."

Laila placed her lips on Hailey's and began kissing her passionately, moaning into her mouth. While everyone around the circle stared at the couple squirming in vicarious excitement, Laila began pressing her pubis harder against Hailey's as she flexed her buttock muscles in rhythmic contractions. From my perspective forty-five degrees behind the couple, I could see her wet slit sliding atop Hailey's glistening mound as her juices began to dribble out of her pussy and down between Hailey parted thighs.

"Oh my *God*..." Piper murmured beside me as her hand began moving softly under her robe while she watched the action. "That is *so* fucking hot!"

"Not bad for a seemingly boring position with one partner fucking the other in the traditional top-over-bottom position, is it?" Laila said, lifting herself off Hailey and sitting beside her on the futon in a cross-legged position.

"Hey!" Hailey said, peering up at Laila with a surprised expression. "I was just getting warmed up! Why did you stop so quickly?"

"This workshop is all about teaching you how to pleasure your *own* partners," Laila said, glancing over at the empty spot left on Hailey's mat. "There's a reason why I invited an even number of participants to the workshop. I'm guessing your seatmate would rather try this technique out for herself than just watch. If you guys feel comfortable, now's the time for everyone to pair up and try this position out for yourselves."

"Okay, but who decides who'll be on top?" Hailey said, returning to her position on her mat.

"That's up to the two of you," Laila smiled. "But don't fret about it too much. By the time we finish today, each of you will have multiple opportunities to position yourselves with different partners. I wouldn't worry too much about who goes where this first time. Just ease into it slowly while you savor the feeling of another woman's body caressing yours."

"I like the sound of that," Hailey said, lying down beside her partner and spreading her legs apart to reveal her glistening pussy. "I could use another shower after experimenting with the bidet in my hotel room last night. But I have a feeling *this* one's going to be even more exciting with a live person squirting on me..."

2

———

While the rest of the girls began to pull off their robes, Piper turned toward me looking like a deer caught in the headlights.

"How would you like to do this?" she said with a breaking voice. "Would you like to be the one on top or on the bottom?"

"Whichever you prefer," I smiled, becoming even more turned on by her apparent lack of experience in these matters.

"I suppose I should be on the bottom, with you being the more, um, *experienced* between us."

"That's the nicest way someone's told me that I'm old in a long time," I chuckled. "But I think I might enjoy it even more with *you* taking the lead. That way, you'll be able to learn what works best for you while I lie back and watch your pleasure."

I pulled off my robe and folded it on the floor beside me, then lay down on the double-wide mat, spreading my legs slowly apart. Piper glanced up and down my figure, lingering a little longer staring at my bald mound and glistening slit as a trickle of lubrication cascaded down between my crack.

"Wow," she said, darting her eyes back and forth over my exposed body. "You're stunning."

"You're very beautiful too," I said, peering up into her hazel eyes. "Take off your robe and let's see what we have to work with."

Piper pulled off her gown one arm at a time then placed it atop mine beside the mat. As she kneeled innocently before me, I ran my eyes up and down her slender, fair-skinned figure. Her skin had an alabaster, almost transparent tone, with tiny freckles on the top of her chest and upper cheeks where she'd had the most exposure to the sun. Her breasts were smaller than mine, but firm and upstanding with bright pink nipples, already hardening as her areolas puckered in obvious excitement.

Her pussy was shaved clean like mine, and as I peered between her splayed legs, I could see the bump of her clitoris protruding between her parted labia. I desperately wanted to jump on top of her and suck her button into my mouth and it took every ounce of my willpower to remain still awaiting her first move.

"Oh my God, Piper," I gushed. "You're absolutely luminous. Come lay that gorgeous body on top of me so I can feel your exquisite skin on mine."

I raised my knees a few inches above the floor and spread my legs wider apart inviting her to come closer, and as she stared at my dripping slit, she knelt in front of me, slowly lowering her upper body onto mine. When I felt her cool skin on mine, I moaned, throwing my arms around her back and pulling her closer, thrusting my tongue into her mouth.

"Mmm," I moaned, feeling her hipbones pressing against mine. "Rub your pussy against my mound. I want to feel your juices dripping all over me.

"Your breasts feel so soft," she panted, tilting her hips toward mine while she began to grind her cunny into my hard pubic bone. "I've never been with a woman this way."

"You're in for a treat then," I smiled, biting her upper lip softly. "There's nothing quite like the feeling of another woman rubbing her naked body against your own."

"So you've done this *before*?" she said.

"Maybe a few times," I smiled.

"Is there a right way to do it?" Piper said, swiping her mound awkwardly across mine.

"I'm not sure there's ever a *right* way for two women to caress one another," I said. "Just do what feels natural and pleasurable. There's no rush."

Piper turned her head to look at some of the other couples around the circle who'd already begun to moan and grind their hips together while writhing their bodies in unison atop their mats.

"It looks like some of the other women have found a way to stimulate their pussies more effectively than me," she said. "With my legs extended directly behind me the way Laila demonstrated, I can only seem to touch my bone against yours."

Overhearing her comment, Laila shuffled up next to the two of us, placing her hands atop Piper's buttocks.

"You've got to tilt your hips forward a few degrees to bring your sensitive parts higher up on your partner's mound," she instructed, peering into my eyes. "You might need to separate your stomach from Jade's while you arch your back in the shape of a camel's. Remember, you're the one in charge here, and you can do whatever feels best for you."

Piper did as Laila instructed, then she gasped when her nub slid over my bald mound.

"Huh!" she grunted, flinging her eyes wide open.

"Does that feel better?" Laila said, smiling toward me.

"Yes," she panted, beginning to rock her hips rhythmically over my hips as she rolled her clit over my skin.

"Let your *partner* guide you as well," she said, pulling my hands up over the back of Piper's flexing ass. "Her caresses and feedback will add to the excitement of the experience. Try to use *every* part of your bodies to stimulate one another while you're in this position."

As Laila pulled away to focus on other areas of the circle, I peered up at her and nodded. I appreciated her helpful guidance, but even more so I envied her role as the master of ceremonies being able to watch everyone as they engaged with their partners in such intimate surroundings. It must have been a feast for her eyes to take in the sight of all the couples grinding their naked bodies together while she sat back and took it all in.

"Lift yourself up on your arms a bit so I can see your face and play with your breasts," I said to Piper. "Like the lady said, being in the missionary position doesn't have to mean we're restricted to rubbing only our *hips* together. This will also give you a better angle to rub your pussy against my mound."

"Ungh," Piper groaned, propping herself up a few inches, tilting her pussy toward the lower curvature of my pubis.

"Better?" I said, holding her flexing buttock muscles in my hands.

"*Better*," she panted, gazing into my eyes while a soft flush began to roll over her pale cheeks.

I moved my hands up to her tits and cupped them softly, pinching her nipples between my fingers as I rocked my hips in concert with hers. Although the contact point between our hips negated any direct contact on my clitoris while lying prone on the floor, the movement of her wet pussy over the tip of my mound was driving me insane with desire as I watched her pleasure continuing to mount.

"*Yes*, Piper," I panted. "Fuck my mound with your pretty pussy. I can feel your juices running down my slit while I watch you getting more turned on."

"Yes," she grunted, placing her hands over my breasts as she humped my hips. "Squeeze my nipples while I fuck you. This is so sexy, making love to your beautiful body."

"You're *enjoying* being on top then?" I smiled, pinching her nipples harder as she began to rock her hips more rapidly over my hard pubis.

"*Fuck* yes," she groaned. "I'm going to come soon if you keep doing that. I'm getting close–"

While I watched her gaping mouth and the flush on her cheeks beginning to spread down over her neck onto the top of her chest, I couldn't resist touching her in more intimate areas, and as she began to tilt her head back, I snaked my right hand around the side of her ass, inserting two fingers into her sopping hole.

"Oh my God, Jade," Piper grunted. "That feels so good! Finger my pussy while I fuck your beautiful body. I'm going to come so hard–"

"Yes, baby," I purred, gazing up into her contorting face. "Let it go. Spray your juices all over my pussy. Let me feel you cum all over me."

"Huff, huff, huff," Piper gasped, approaching the turning point. Suddenly, she exhaled with a deep animal sound while mashing her vulva hard against the top of my pubic bone as she began jetting her juices all over my hand pressed hard against her contracting pussy.

"Ngah!" she hissed, peering into my eyes as her head jerked in spastic convulsions in tandem with the contractions she was feeling further below.

I pulled her head down toward mine and kissed her hard on the lips while she grunted into my mouth, jerking my hips hard against hers as we listened to the sound of other couples around the room reaching their own climaxes in blissful harmony. When the room finally fell silent and Piper collapsed onto the mat beside me, we peered around the room at the happy smiles on the faces of the other women who were panting and caressing one another softly.

"So, what did you all think?" Laila said, panning around the circle with a sly grin on her face. "Do you guys *still* think the missionary position is boring?"

"*Hell* no," Hailey panted, pinching her partner's nipples softly between her fingers.

"I'm glad you enjoyed it," Laila said, passing out some thick bath towels around the circle. "You might want to take a little rest while you take a few minutes to clean up. Because the *next* demonstration is going to ramp up the excitement to a whole other level."

While Piper and I began to mop up the puddle she'd left in the center of our mat, I smiled to myself thinking about how cleverly Laila had scheduled our workshops. As I peered at her juices dripping down the inside of both our thighs, I was happy to have paired up with one of the girls who'd attended the previous workshop where we'd learned to ejaculate stimulating our female prostate glands.

Laila wasn't kidding when she said a little waterworks will only add to the excitement, I smiled.

3

————

After everybody recovered from their orgasms, Laila asked for a new volunteer to demonstrate the next position. This time Trinity was the first to respond, and as she crawled over to kneel beside the workshop leader, Laila nodded at her with a smile.

"It's interesting that you chose to position yourself that way," she said. "Because in this next maneuver, there's going to be a lot of *kneeling*. I call it the *Praying Mantis*, not only because of the posture we'll be assuming, but also because in this case the one on top will be in a perfect position to gobble up the one on the bottom."

"Mmm," Trinity smiled. "It sounds delicious. Which one of us will be doing the gobbling?"

"As you're about to see, in this position we'll *both* get equal stimulation to the important parts, but it will be easier for me to demonstrate the many variations with me on top. So, if you'd like to lie down with your legs slightly parted, we can begin."

"It sounds similar to the start of the missionary position..."

"It might seem that way, but I assure you this will be a very different experience, one in which both partners can take an active role."

Laila crawled between Trinity's legs then she lifted one knee over the outside of her partner's hips while pressing the inside of her other thigh firmly against Trinity's pussy.

"Mmm, you're so *soft*," Trinity purred, rocking her hips gently against Laila's inner thigh.

"That's not the *only* soft part you'll feel in this position," Laila smiled, lying back on the mat as she pressed her left leg under Trinity's right thigh.

"In this variation of the classic scissoring position, we both have equal control over how we can stimulate our vulvas. It can be kind of fun when you feel like a slow, languorous fuck first thing in the morning."

Laila propped herself back up on her knees while tilting Trinity's body forty-five degrees toward her.

"But I find the *kneeling* position offers more opportunities to grind our pussies together while also providing a direct focal point to each other's upper bodies, where we can kiss and play with certain *other* erogenous areas..."

As Laila leaned forward, she began to gyrate her hips in a rotational movement over Trinity's angled pussy, creating some loud slurping noises. Those of us in a position to view what was going on behind them lowered our heads and gasped when we saw their two pussies gnashing together.

"Holy *fuck*," Trinity groaned. "I feel every inch of your pussy fucking me in this position. I'm kind of glad I'm on the *bottom* this time."

"It can be even *more* fun being the one on top," Laila said, grabbing Trinity's right knee and pulling it toward her chest. "You've got more leverage this way, and you can really dial up the action once you get properly warmed up."

"I'm definitely beginning to get warmed up," Trinity panted. "It feels incredible having your pussy touching me like that."

Laila smiled, tilting her hips forward a few degrees while Trinity uttered a deep, guttural moan.

"And in this position, we can also rub our *clits* together as hard as we want also."

"That is so hot," one of the girls behind the tribbing couple groaned, pressing two fingers into her pussy while she gaped at Laila's and Trinity's labia stretching and pulling while they rubbed their vulvas together.

"It can be quite a feast if you have a *third* partner in the mix," Laila nodded. "She can lie with her head at the junction of your two hips while she licks *both* of your vulvas."

"Were you looking for another volunteer?" I said, raising my hand.

"Maybe on our last day," Laila chuckled, pulling Trinity's foot higher in the air until her leg was pointing straight up, pinned tightly between Laila's plump breasts.

"Feel free to experiment with your partner's body in this position," she continued. "If she's *especially* flexible, you can really open up her undercarriage for a more direct attack."

While Laila gently pressed her upper body forward, Trinity's extended leg moved closer toward her chest, until Laila was leaning directly down over her abdomen with Trinity's foot pressed all the way beside her head.

"You're pretty flexible," Laila nodded, kissing Trinity softly on the lips while she rolled her pussy over her stretched gash.

"Holy fuck–" Piper muttered next to me, mesmerized by the sight of the two women locked in a wide-open scissor position with both of their dripping pussies clearly exposed.

"It's pretty hot, I have to admit," Laila said, lifting herself up while pulling back Trinity's pinned leg as she crawled off her partner and rested on the duvet in her customary cross-legged position.

"Oh my God," Trinity panted, placing her hands behind her back as she rubbed her slippery thighs together. "I haven't been fucked like that since my girlfriend tied me to my bedposts. Somebody better jump on me soon, or I'm going to burst a gasket."

"I'm pretty sure you won't have much trouble finding willing partners from the look of it," Laila chuckled, noticing half the women around the circle still moving their hands between their legs. "But in the interest of sharing the spoils, this time I'd like one person from each mat to move clockwise to the next position in the circle. That way, by the time we end our workshop, everyone will have had a chance to partner up with every other person in the group."

I peered around the circle, counting the yoga mats distributed like hour markers on a clock.

"If I'm doing my math right," I said. "That means we can look forward to ten more tribbing exercises before we finish the workshop?"

"I suspect it will be even *more* by the time we introduce some toys and multiple partners into the mix," Laila smiled. "But I wouldn't worry about keeping track at this point. There should be more than enough notches on your bedpost by the time we finish up here. So go ahead and shift one position to your left and give this new position a try. If you liked the missionary position, I have a feeling you're going to find this one takes your tribbing experience to a whole new level."

Piper suddenly turned to look at me with a wrinkled brow.

"Would you like to switch positions, or should I?" she said.

I peered over her shoulder noticing Hailey crawling toward our mat like a stalking cat.

"I feel pretty damn hungry about now," she growled. "Which of you two girls feels like getting gobbled up?"

"I have a feeling Piper might like being on the *bottom* this time," I smiled. "Why don't you guys enjoy yourself this time and I'll circle back a little later?"

"I'll look forward to that," Hailey grinned, grabbing Piper's hand and pulling her toward her, kissing her hard on her lips.

As the two women reclined onto the mat with Hailey in the superior position, I shuffled over to the next mat and smiled at a pretty brunette about my age.

"I'm Ashley," she said, holding out her hand awkwardly.

"Jade," I said, clasping her sweaty palm softly. "No need for us to be so formal, with us about to get all twisted up in knots in a few minutes."

"No, I suppose not," she chuckled, sitting back on her heels as she appraised my naked body positioned directly in front of her. "How should we decide who goes on top this time?"

"From the looks of it," I said, tilting my head toward the middle of the circle where Laila had just completed her demonstration. "I don't think it matters. But just to be fair, why don't we do rock, paper, scissors?"

"Aha," Ashley laughed. "Very clever. Winner goes on top?"

"Deal," I nodded.

We each held out our fists, then we pumped them together three times, straightening our palms on the last pump. I chose paper and Ashley displayed scissors, so that meant I'd be taking the superior position this time.

"I'm not really sure there'll be a loser in this instance," I smiled. "But I guess *one* of us has to play the role of the mantis while the other one pretends to be her prey."

"I'm ready to get gobbled up," Ashley nodded, lying down on the mat with her legs spread wide apart. "Feast away."

"Mmm," I hummed, peering down at her glistening pink labia. "Don't mind if I do."

I shimmied my body up between her thighs and lifted one knee over her hip while positioning my other one against her dripping pussy.

"So you prefer the *kneeling* position over the traditional posture?" Ashley said, gazing up at me.

"Laila named it the Praying Mantis for a reason," I grinned, glancing at her tits rolling softly to her side. "I plan on taking maximum advantage while you're pinned underneath me. There's a few tasty morsels I'd like to sample before I go in for the main course."

"As long as you don't bite my *head* off before you're finished," Ashley chuckled.

I leaned forward and pressed my lips against her face, biting her lip gently.

"Not right away," I smiled, pulling away temporarily. "At least not until I feast on your *other* your succulent parts."

"Yes," Ashley grunted, feeling my pussy pressing against hers as she tilted her hips to join our vulvas together. "Impale me with that weapon of yours. Split me open like a ripe melon."

"Fucking right," I growled, grabbing her thigh and pulling it hard against my stomach as I began to gnash my pussy against hers.

I could feel her puffy labia rolling over mine as I tribbed her slit with our gashes sliding over one another, intertwining like a sexy pussy kiss.

"Holy shit," Ashley panted. "You feel so *hot!*"

"And you feel so *juicy*," I groaned.

"Oh yeah?" Ashley grinned, staring up at me. "Do you think I've got enough to whet your appetite?"

"Fuck yes," I hissed. "I only wish I was wearing a *dildo*, so I could sink my cock deep inside those thick folds or yours. You feel absolutely delicious."

"Pull up a little higher," Ashley panted, reaching out to pinch my nipples. "I want to feel you rubbing on something a little harder..."

Understanding exactly what she meant, I tilted my hips forward a few more inches and placed my hand under her ass, pressing her pubic bone harder against mine. I felt our hard nubs touching together, and I mashed my pussy harder against her.

"*Yes*, Jade," Ashley grunted. "Right there. Fuck my pussy right there. Make me come all over your hot snatch."

Watching her face peering up at me with unbridled ecstasy was too much for me to resist, and as I lowered my face onto hers, I pulled her knee toward her chest, kissing her passionately while we ground our cunts together. There was something incredibly sexy about the lips of her mouth sliding in and out of mine while our lower lips gnashed and dripped over one another at the same time. As we both began to grunt louder into each other's mouths while grabbing each other's buttocks, I glanced over at the mat next to me watching Hailey hammering her hips between Piper's legs while she pulled one of the redhead's legs hard up against her chest.

"*Oh fuck, oh fuck...*" Ashley huffed underneath me. "I'm going to come, Jade. I'm going to come so hard all over your beautiful, wet pussy."

"Yes, baby," I grunted. "Gush all over me. I'm ready to take my prize."

"Ieeee!" Ashley squealed with one final powerful exhalation as her hips began quaking while she screamed into my mouth.

When I felt her jerking against our connected pussies, I couldn't hold back any longer and all the pent-up pleasure I'd been holding back suddenly exploded while I gushed all over her stretched slit like a dormant geyser. I must have squirted a gallon of juices over her upturned ass by the time I finished squirting in powerful contractions. When we both finished convulsing in each other's arms, I held her with her leg still pressed tightly over my chest, savoring the feeling of our sopping pussies pulsing and dribbling over one another.

"Where the hell did you learn to do *that*?" Ashley said when I finally pulled away.

"You mean that squirting thing?" I smiled.

"It felt more like a *waterfall*," she panted, still trying to catch her breath.

"I've been doing that for a while now, but Laila taught some of us how to really turn on the faucets at her female ejaculation workshop."

"I've got to learn that trick on my *own* some day," she said. "If you were a *real* praying mantis, I'm pretty sure you would have basted and sauteed me more than enough to finish the rest of your meal."

"Don't *tempt* me," I said, glancing down at her dripping folds. "If we weren't restricted to touching only our pussies together, I wouldn't hesitate to lap up the *rest* of you for dessert right now."

4

It didn't take long after Ashley, Piper, Hailey and I came for the rest of the girls in the room to reach their own climaxes. It was quite a sight watching all the other couples scissoring their figures together in a ring of twisted, shaking bodies. After everyone had a chance to recover and clean up, we took a break to enjoy a catered lunch of lobster rolls, potato salad, and Pellegrino. While we sat around the circle in our terrycloth robes, each of us couldn't help peering beside us to see who we'd be paired up with next.

On the mat to my left sat Trinity and a cute blonde girl who looked barely out of high school. As they nibbled on their food, they glanced in both directions, trying to guess which person from each pair would move to the next position. With four different potential combinations at each turn, the experience felt a bit like an erotic game of musical chairs.

I peered over at Laila who was making small talk with one of the couples sitting next to her and smiled at her ingenuity conceiving of another workshop that was equal parts stimulating and educational. I wondered how many of the participants had signed up to discover new techniques to spice up their love lives versus just looking for an chance to stare at a bunch of naked women having sex. Either way, I suspected her seminar had already exceeded many of their expectations, and I was looking forward to what she had planned for the rest of our session.

When everybody finished eating, we all sat back on our mats in the same cross-legged position as Laila, facing her expectantly. I couldn't help but giggle at how quickly she'd gotten all of us under her thumb, not to mention her sexy, naked hips.

"I hope everyone had a chance to rehydrate and recharge your batteries," she smiled. "Because this afternoon we're going to ramp up the action with three new exercises that will stretch your resources to the limit."

Exercises, I chuckled to myself. *That's one name for them.* Something told me I'd be feeling the after-effects of this workshop in more places than one by the time we finished.

"Are you guys ready to learn some more exciting new techniques?" she said.

Everybody nodded excitedly while she peered around the circle looking for a new candidate to demonstrate the next position.

"Any volunteers for our next demonstration?"

Everyone's hand flew up instantly, and Laila paused, glancing at the mat next to mine.

"*Becky*, isn't it?" she said, staring straight into the eyes of the cute coed sitting beside me.

The blonde girl smiled and Laila curled her finger in a come-hither motion toward her mat, inviting her to come to the center of the circle.

"We're going to test those quick reflexes of yours with this next position," Laila smiled, patting the futon beside her. "I call this one the *Reverse Cowgirl*, partly because one of us will be riding the other like a horse, but *also* because she'll will be faced in the opposite direction."

"Does that mean we won't be able to look at each other while we're doing it?" Becky said with wide eyes.

"Oh, we'll be able to *look* at each other alright," Laila grinned. "Just not at each other's faces. But I suspect we'll be able to find certain *other* body parts to keep ourselves entertained."

"Which of us will be the rider?" Becky asked innocently. "And who'll be playing the role of the horse?"

"Since you put it that way," Laila chuckled. "Why don't *you* be the one on top this time? It's a fairly simple procedure, and I can guide you just as easily from the bottom. But you might want to find something to hold onto. I can't account for how much *bucking* I might do once we get into the action."

Laila pulled off her robe, then lay face up on the futon with her legs extended straight out in front of her.

"How would you like me to position myself?" Becky said.

"This one's pretty straight-forward," Laila nodded. "You simply sit overtop of me facing my feet with your knees straddling my hips."

"Okay," Becky said, pulling off her robe and angling one of her legs awkwardly over Laila's naked midsection.

"Not so much on my *stomach* as my hips," Laila grunted, trying to catch her breath. "Unless you also want to *suffocate* me while you're fucking me."

"That wouldn't be much fun," the girl said, sliding her hips forward over Laila's lower abdomen, leaving a glistening streak down the middle of her stomach. "I don't think the rest of the group would like that very much."

While gentle laughter spread around the circle, Laila placed her hands on opposite sides of Becky's ass, pushing her forward a few more inches.

"In this position," she continued, "the trick is to tilt your hips at just the right angle and position your hips in precisely the right spot over my mound to get the best friction with your clitoris."

"Yes..." Becky grunted, rocking her hips softly over Laila's pelvis. "I think I found the spot."

"Now it's just a matter of you riding me to your heart's content," Laila smiled. "While trying not to fall off as your pleasure continues to rise."

"What about *you*?" Becky said, rocking her hips back and forth over Laila's hard pubis, leaving a wet slick on her lower abdomen.

"This position is mostly intended for the enjoyment of the one on *top*, but if you tilt your body forward a little further and shift a few inches lower down, you might be able to feel something a little *softer* for you to rub against."

Becky placed her hands on the floor beside Laila's knees, then she leaned forward about forty-five degrees, angling her ass up toward Laila's face. I smiled, beginning to realize that Laila hadn't chosen to be on the bottom by accident, having a perfect bird's-eye view of Becky's tight ass and exposed pucker.

"Yes," Laila panted, raising her head to stare at Becky's gyrating hips. "Do you feel anything different in this angle?"

"I feel your pussy rubbing against mine now," she nodded. "I like this position better. You're softer, and *wetter*."

"Mmm," Laila grunted. "I'm not sure which of us is getting wetter faster. I can already feel your juices running down over my labia."

The girls at the end of the circle lowered their heads to stare at the two women mashing their slits together while the women on the opposite end tilted their faces to peer at Becky's exposed rosebud stretching and puckering while she flexed her buttock muscles.

Unfortunately, in my position directly beside the tribbing couple, Becky's thigh was obscuring my view of their most interesting parts. But that didn't stop me from staring at her pretty tits shaking on her chest as she pistoned her hips over Laila's slit, approaching the peak of her pleasure.

"Okay," Laila said, grabbing the sides of Becky's ass, sitting up against her heaving back. "I wouldn't want you to drain *all* your energy before your partner gets to participate in this little rodeo ride. Why don't you go back to your mat to finish the demonstration? As before, I'd like one of you to move one position to your left to find a new partner. You might have to arm wrestle to determine who goes on top, but either way, I'm pretty sure you'll *both* enjoy the experience."

While Becky returned to her mat beside Trinity, Ashley and I peered at one another with lopsided grins.

"Rock, paper, scissors?" she said, unsure which of us should move to the next mat.

I looked behind her, noticing a full-figured girl looking like a dead-ringer of the pretty actress Christina Hendricks shuffling toward us.

"I have a feeling you're going to enjoy riding this next horse," I nodded, glancing behind me toward Becky's mat. "I'm gonna see if I can take a turn with that pretty co-ed."

"It shouldn't take long from the looks of it," Ashley said, peering down at Becky's dripping thighs.

"Catch you later, alligator," I smiled, crawling over to Becky's mat.

"In a while, crocodile," she nodded.

As excited as I was to mix it up with the pretty African-American girl, I was happy when Trinity chose to move to the next mat, leaving Becky all for myself.

"Hi," I said, stretching out my hand. "I'm Jade."

"I guess you know *my* name by now," Becky chuckled, clasping my hand with her slippery fingers. "Did you have a preference for how you'd like to play this one?"

"Something tells me *you're* in more of a hurry to finish this ride than me," I smiled, pinching her erect nipples softly between my fingers. "I have a feeling I'm going to enjoy watching you more from the *bottom* than with me on top."

"I was hoping you'd say that," she said, climbing on top of me as I lay down on the yoga mat. "Do you want me sitting up or leaning slightly forward?"

"Whichever way gives you the best stimulation," I smiled, caressing the sides of her ass.

"Mmm," she purred, rocking her wet pussy over my hard mound. "I'm already halfway there. This shouldn't take long, then I can focus on giving you some more attention."

"Let it rip baby," I said, squeezing her buttock muscles as she ground her cunt against my pubis. "Don't worry about me."

"Oh God," she panted. "That feels so good–"

"It *looks* pretty damn fine too," I groaned, watching her chest rising and falling as she began to breathe more rapidly.

"Oh fuck, Jade," she hissed. "I'm going to come. I can't hold it back any longer...."

She dropped her hands on top of my thighs looking for support, and I dug my fingernails into the side of her hips while her buttock muscles started quivering as she shuddered and groaned atop my hips. There was something incredibly sexy about not being able to see her face as I listened to her orgasm and watch the muscles in her back and buttocks twitching while she spread her knees wider over my hips.

Even though I'd barely had any time to begin getting worked up myself, I somehow found the experience even more gratifying than if I'd come myself. Fortunately, it didn't take long for her to resume her gentle rocking over my hips, and as she slid her vulva over the crest of my symphysis, she turned her head partly in my direction, revealing her flushed face.

"Would you like me to try this in a *different* position?" she said. "I'm ready for some more action if you are."

"Oh, I'm definitely *ready*," I growled, slapping the sides of her ass with both hands. "Ride me like a bucking bronco. You fit perfectly into my saddle."

"Mmm," Becky groaned, tilting her upper body lower as her cheeks began to spread apart, revealing her pink sphincter. "I think I can feel the *horn* of your saddle."

"Yes, baby," I groaned, feeling her nub sliding over mine as our slits meshed together. "Rub your clit against mine while I feel your juices dripping down my pussy. You're so warm and wet..."

"Not as wet as *you*," Becky said, tilting her head down to peer between her legs at my glistening slit. "Spread your legs a little further apart so I can see your juicy pussy. This is so fucking hot watching you this way."

Her dirty talk caught me be surprise, and I quickly spread my legs, pressing her knees further out to the side as her ass tilted higher toward my face.

"I've got a hell of a view watching *you* from this angle too," I moaned, feeling her wet vulva sliding over mine.

"Do you like watching my ass while I ride you from behind?" she said.

"Damn *straight*," I grunted, digging my nails harder into the back of her buttocks while I watched her pucker flexing as she ground her pussy over the top of my pubis.

"I'm going to come again," she huffed, gripping the top of my thighs tightly with her hands. "I hope you don't mind. This is just too damn hot..."

"I'm going to come too," I groaned, feeling my orgasm approaching like a freight train. "Keep grinding my clit just like that–"

"Oh *fuck*!" Becky rasped, pressing her chest down onto the mat between my legs while she humped my slit with her mound.

Suddenly, her rosebud began clamping in rhythmic contractions as she panted in muffled moans onto the mat. The sight of her pretty pucker flexing in powerful contractions while her buttock muscles quivered inches away from my face was too much for me to resist, and within seconds I felt the build-up of juices inside my pussy beginning to jet out in strong spurts all over her pussy and lower abdomen.

"What the hell...?" I Becky panted as I squirted all over our joined pussies while we shuddered in mutual pleasure.

I'd been so preoccupied staring at her pretty ass and focusing on our *own* pleasure that I hardly even noticed when the rest of the girls around the circle erupted in a cacophony of simultaneous pleasure, twisting and shaking their bodies together in the same position.

Holy shit, I thought to myself. *Just when I thought I'd seen and tried everything. Laila wasn't kidding when she said we'd learn a few new tricks when I signed up for her latest workshop.*

5

———————

While we all lay in a tangled heap on our mats panting and heaving from our powerful orgasms, Laila peered around the circle and smiled.

"It looks like everyone found a way to get something out of that exercise," she grinned. "If you liked a little ass humping, I think you'll find our next position will *double* your pleasure. Who'd like to be my next volunteer?"

Once again, everybody's hand quickly flew up, and Laila paused while she contemplated who to choose. After a few seconds, she turned toward Ashley and her partner still squirming excitedly on their mat.

"How about it, Paige?" she said, peering at the full-figured redhead. "Have you recovered sufficiently from your last engagement to give it another try?"

"I'm *always* ready for some more girl-on-girl action," she smiled, crawling seductively on all fours toward the center of the ring.

As she slunk toward Laila, every pair of eyes in the room stared at her magnificent ass, shining under the overhead lights like a Rubenesque masterpiece. Even though she was more full-figured than the other women attending the workshop, there wasn't a trace of cellulite on her backside, and I could hear myself panting while I watched her slit winking at me as she parted her thighs. When she reached Laila's position, she sat down next to her while everybody feasted their eyes over her equally well-endowed, plump round tits.

"In this *next* position," Laila said, not skipping a beat, "we'll *both* be faced in opposite directions. "I like to call it *Ass Backwards*, because we'll be rubbing our butts while facing away from each other."

Laila peered at Paige, lifting an eyebrow.

"Are you ready to give it a whirl?" she said to the pretty redhead.

"Absolutely," Paige said, rising up onto her knees. "How would you like me to position myself?"

"This one starts out pretty straight-forward," Laila said, moving into a doggy position beside Paige. "But there's a few interesting variations we can try to mix it up. Let's start by getting on all fours facing away from each other, then touch our asses together–"

"Only our *asses*?" Paige said, copying the workshop leader's posture and shuffling backwards until her stout derriere pressed against Laila's.

"We'll have to work at maneuvering our bodies a little to create some friction in the interesting places," Laila nodded. "But that's half the fun."

As she began to roll her hips over the back of Paige's ass, I noticed a sheen of shiny fluid on the redhead's skin.

"Sometimes it helps to spread some *lube* over your asses to heighten the experience," Laila said, pressing her ass into the soft creases and folds of Paige's fleshy backside. "Since you won't be touching your *pussies* right away, you might need a little extra lubrication to get started."

Paige smiled, glancing toward her previous partner, Ashley.

"I think I've still got plenty of natural lube covering my ass from my *last* exercise," she nodded.

"So it would seem," Laila purred, enjoying the feeling of Paige's plump rump massaging her backside.

"This is a sexy way for two women to warm up with a little foreplay," she said. "But if you tilt your upper bodies toward the floor, this will bring a *different* part of your anatomy together..."

As Laila lowered her shoulders, her hips temporarily pulled away from Paige's, and I noticed her slit flaring open with her clit poking out from the top of her folds. Both women spread their knees wider apart and when they reconnected their asses, they both groaned.

"*Fuck*, that feels hot," Paige grunted, rocking her hips up and down as she slid her pussy over Laila's. "I can feel every inch of your skin sliding against me."

"It's a great way to grind your pussies together while facing away from each other," Laila nodded. "It can be even *more* exciting using a double-sided dildo, which we'll introduce at our session tomorrow. But don't discount how much fun it can be to just grind your asses together. Your backside is more sensitive than you might imagine."

"Oh, I can *imagine*," Hailey moaned from the other side of the circle while she rolled her fingers over her wet pussy, gawking at Paige's beautiful ass.

"There's a reason why gay men like to fuck each other up the ass," Laila said, pressing her buttocks harder against Paige's soft butt, beginning to spread her cheeks apart. "The anal sphincter is surrounded with many sensitive nerve endings and can be very pleasant to stimulate in its own way, as some of you may have discovered while performing oral sex with your partners."

"Nnghh," Paige suddenly groaned, feeling Laila's rosebud sliding over her own. "It feels even better with your *pussy* stimulating me there."

"If you *really* want to dive in and go to town," Laila said, raising her left knee and placing it on the outside of Paige's opposite knee resting on the floor. "You can angle your bodies into an inverted *scissor* position while you rub your asses together. This allows you to slide your leg into your partner's *crack*, stimulating both her pussy and her anus while you're grinding your hips together.

"*Oh my God,*" Paige grunted, grabbing Laila's inside knee and pulling it harder against her stomach. "I'm going to *come* if you keep doing that. I can feel you rubbing me all the way down my perineum."

"Exactly," Laila said, humping Paige's ass harder for a few seconds before pulling her leg out from under her belly and turning around to kneel behind her in a doggy-style position. "And when you want to mix it up a bit further, you can always shift position to give your partner a proper ass fucking, which of course is even more exciting when you're wearing a strap-on."

Laila dry-humped Paige's ass for a few moments, then she pushed her forward, collapsing her body onto the futon.

"But *sometimes*," she said with a glint in her eye. "I just like to fuck my partner's ass with my pussy while she's pinned underneath me. There's nothing hotter than cumming all over your partner's body when there's nothing she can do about it."

No wonder she chose Paige for this demonstration, I smiled. *I'd fuck that ass any chance I had an opportunity also.*

"No fair!" Paige grunted while pinned under Laila's spread-eagled thighs. "I was just about to *come*. You're such a tease!"

"That's half the fun with this position," Laila said, lifting her leg and flopping back onto the futon beside Paige with her knees crossed.

"Screw *that*," Paige said, raising herself off the futon and peering into Laila's eyes with flushed cheeks. "Are you *ever* going to let your partner come during one of these demonstrations? Because this whole setup seems a little lopsided in your favor..."

"That's why I'm the one in charge," Laila smiled. "I get to call the shots while you enjoy the spoils. But never fear, you shouldn't have any trouble finding some other willing partners for you to finish your demonstration. I just wanted to get you warmed up..."

I looked at Laila, twirling my finger in the air to signal that each of us should move to the next position in the circle.

"Same as before?" I said.

"Yes," Laila nodded. "We're only halfway done completing the circle. It's almost as much fun trying out each new position as it is with a different partner. One person from each mat should move clockwise to the left."

Becky and I glanced at one another, and when I saw Paige crawling toward our mat, I smiled, excited to give the two redheads a chance to pair up.

"Why don't you stay here and help Paige finish her exercise?" I said, noticing Trinity hanging behind on the next mat, waiting for me to move over. "Maybe we'll have a chance to connect a little later in the workshop."

"I hope so," Becky said, peering wide-eyed at Paige crawling toward her like a lion approaching its prey.

When I shuffled over to the next mat, Trinity kissed me with a familiar embrace.

"I was *wondering* when I'd get another turn with you," she said, remembering out last hookup at Laila's Circle Jill workshop. "I wasn't sure you'd be able to resist fucking that gorgeous redhead after watching her shake her booty in the ring with Laila."

"It crossed my mind," I smiled. "But I think I'll enjoy *watching* her have her way with the pretty coed as much as having her for myself. Besides, I've waited too long to take a piece of *another* pretty ass..."

As the two of us began kissing, I glanced over at Becky and Paige who were already rubbing their asses together while Becky struggled to stay upright as Paige slapped her thick derriere against her backside.

"Are you just gonna sit there and *watch*?" Trinity said, sliding her hand around the back of my ass while she kissed me, pressing her fingers into my crease. "Or do you want to sample some of this for yourself?"

"You're twisting my arm," I said, turning around and lifting my ass in the air while positioning myself in the doggy position.

Trinity got down on all fours and pressed her butt up against mine, and within seconds we were twisting our asses together, groaning in pleasure as our wet pussies slid over one another. Impatient to feel her clit against mine, I tilted my upper body down toward the floor, staring at her tits swaying back and forth as she tribbed me from behind. Eager to do the same, she leaned down, and we smiled at each other while we slapped our asses together.

Finding it difficult to gain traction on our clits, she lifted one knee and straddled my leg on the floor while pressing her right thigh under my belly. With the underside of her leg now resting against my mound and her warm skin rubbing along the full length of my perineum, I pressed my own thigh hard against her pussy.

We grabbed each other's legs and began to slide our cracks together, and as I felt her rosebud rub over mine, we both moaned. It didn't take long for the two of us to begin squirming in delight as we both moved closer and closer toward orgasm. I couldn't see her face with our asses blocking the view diagonally toward one another in this upside-down scissor position, but the feeling of our slippery pussies and asses rubbing together was more than enough to take me to the edge.

"I'm almost there," I panted, pulling her thigh harder against my pussy. "Are you getting close?"

"Yes," she said. "Do you think you can squirt again like we learned at the last workshop?"

"Fuck, yes," I groaned. "I feel like I'm going to burst a gasket any moment now..."

"Let it rip, baby," Trinity grunted. "I'm going to come with you. Let's see who can squirt harder–"

Suddenly she squealed like a cat, shaking her hips rapidly against my ass while she sprayed her juices all over the yoga mat and our exposed bellies. When I felt her cumming against my pussy, I started squirting along with her, spraying our combined juices in every direction between our splayed legs. By the time we finished shaking and spurting, we collapsed onto the mat laughing like a pair of schoolgirls while we rolled in the warm puddle underneath us.

Moments later, we heard loud grunting coming from the mat next to us, and we peered over watching Paige arching over Becky's pinned ass while she fucked the coed roughly from behind. While the girl held onto the edge of their yoga mat tightly with two hands to keep from sliding off, Paige pressed her hands onto the floor beside her chest as her thick buttock muscles flexed powerfully, approaching another climax.

When she finally came, she pressed her pussy hard against Becky's smaller ass, shaking her globes violently while she squirted one hard jet after another down Becky's crack and over her dripping pussy. As the two of us gazed at them in amazement, the rest of the room suddenly became silent while everybody else watched in rapt attention.

"Looks like we aren't the *only* ones who learned how to squirt at one of Laila's workshops," Trinity grinned, caressing my breasts softly while we lay beside one another watching the couple.

"Yeah," I said. "I just hope Becky will still be able to *walk* after that pounding. I'm not sure her body will be able to take much more of this exercise..."

6

———————

After Paige rolled over Becky and collapsed onto their mat, I glanced up at the clock in Laila's living room, surprised at how late it was in the day. We'd all been so captivated learning and practicing her exciting tribbing techniques, that we'd completely lost track of time.

"I'm glad everyone seemed to enjoy that last position," Laila smiled. "I think we might have time left for one more demonstration. Who's up for one last exercise?"

Everyone raised their hands again and as Laila teasingly peered around the circle, she abruptly stopped, staring straight at me.

"What do you say, Jade?" she grinned. "Are you ready for another sexy demonstration for the full group?"

I wasn't sure if she was referring to our *current* session or the last workshop where we'd finished with the two of us connected with a double-ended dildo while we squirted all over each other's pussies.

"I thought you'd never ask," I smiled, slinking toward her.

"This next position might be the sexiest one yet," Laila said, peering at me with a sly grin. "I like to call it *Hip-Hop* because of the way we'll be grinding our hips together. But we won't just be rubbing our pussies together. In this position, we'll be rubbing *everything* together."

"Mmm," I purred, feeling my juices dribbling out of my slit again. "It sounds delicious. Who gets to be on top this time?"

Laila paused, peering up at the clock.

"I'm not sure I can trust you to stop before we run out of time," she said.

"I didn't realize we were on a *limit*," I said. "I thought you said at our last workshop that when it comes to two women making love, our focus should be on the *journey* rather than the destination?"

"That's true," she smiled, swiping the back of her hand gently over my breast. "But we still have two days left in this workshop. We've got to leave a *few* surprises for the rest of the group."

"Yes," I grinned, leaning in to kiss her on the lips. "And I know from previous experience how full of *surprises* you can be."

"You have no idea," she said, pushing me softly down onto the futon. "Lie back with your knees angled up toward your chest. We're going to give the girls a memorable experience to keep them moti-vated for tomorrow."

I did as Laila instructed, and as my slit began to stretch apart from my retracted legs, I reflected back at our last encounter at her Foun-tain of Venus workshop. Feeling exposed with my hole staring her straight in the face, I half hoped she'd pull out another one of her special dildos to fuck me hard in front of the group. But instead, she stood up straddling my waist with two legs, then she slowly squatted down until the bottom of her thighs rested overtop of mine. When our pussies touched, I groaned and reached out to squeeze her tits dangling inches from my face. She leaned forward, and our lips met while we moaned in each other's mouths.

"I've been looking forward to *this* one all day," she whispered next to my ear as she began to grind her hips against mine.

With the sound of our wet pussies rolling over one another begin-ning to spread around the room, I glanced out of the corner of my eye, noticing the girls on the opposite side of the circle leaning down to gawk at our exposed pussies mashing together on our upturned asses.

"I I when I'd have another chance to connect with you," I moaned, peering into her eyes. "Ever since you sent me your latest invitation to this new workshop, it's all I've been able to think about."

"Oh?" Laila grunted overtop of me. "Have you been practicing alone while thinking about me?"

"Fuck, yes," I said, pulling her harder toward me, feeling her sweaty breasts pressing up against mine. "You have no idea how many times I've squirted imagining it was I fucking me instead of one of my vibrators."

"Well, I'm fucking you *now*," she moaned, slapping her hips up and down over mine. "Though I *do* have plans for introducing some toys later in the workshop."

As Laila lifted her pussy away from mine, I felt her dribbling overtop of me while a band of lubrication stretched between our two slits.

"Oh my Gawd..." someone muttered from the other end of the circle, and I turned my head to see half the women fingering themselves while they watched our slapping pussies.

"I see you've made some progress learning to relax your prostate," Laila whispered into my ear, referring to the special gland next to our G-spot that held the reservoir of lubricating fluid designed to facilitate reproduction.

"I never was one to let a little wetness get in the way of having fun," I smiled. "But I like to save the best for last."

"Do you think you can *come* for me in this position?" Laila grunted into my ear. "We could give the girls a hell of a show with our asses turned up together this way."

I pulled back a few inches, peering at her with a surprised expression.

"Were you thinking of breaking your rule about saving our orgasms for our own partners?" I smiled.

"I'm considering it," she panted, peering up at the clock. "We don't have enough time to finish up with the *rest* of the group anyway. Let's give them something to *fantasize* about until tomorrow."

"You don't have to ask me twice," I groaned, pulling Laila's face harder down onto mine, fucking her mouth with my tongue.

As she slapped her butt over mine, we ground our pussies harder together feeling our juices pouring out of our holes and down the crack of my ass. Just when I thought it couldn't get any better, Laila suddenly raised her hips six inches over mine and started squirting hard all over my exposed slit and anus. The jetting stimulation on my clit only added to my already heightened sense of arousal, and the combined sensation of her rubbing ass and her squirting pussy quickly took me over the edge as I rocked my body along with her while my anus clamped open and shut in powerful contractions. As we both jetted powerful squirts against our flapping pussies, the rest of the group groaned in simultaneous delight, coming along with us while we held onto each other tightly.

Fuck me, I smiled as we held each other like two mating toads on a lily pad. *I have no idea what she has in store for the next two days of our workshop, but if it's going to be anything like this, I better drink plenty of water to replenish my fluids.*

Because something tells me there's going to be a whole different kind of Fountain of Venus erupting tomorrow.

VICTORIA RUSH

TRIBADISM

THE ART OF LESBIAN LOVE

1

When all the women returned to Laila's Upper West Side apartment the following morning, there was a palpable buzz in the room as everyone eagerly anticipated the next phase in the tribadism workshop. Laila had alluded to the possibility of introducing toys and multiple partners into the equation, but nobody really knew what to expect.

After we changed into our terrycloth robes and finished nibbling on the Continental breakfast Laila had laid out, she invited us to return to our yoga mats arranged in a circle in the middle of her living room. As we all peered at one another with familiar smiles, I felt a dribble of lubrication slide out of my slit over the cheeks of my ass.

"I hope you slept well and had pleasant dreams of warm bodies snuggling up next to you," Laila said, sitting cross-legged on the futon in the middle of the circle.

"Oh, there was plenty of *snuggling* going on in my dreams," the sexy blonde Hailey smiled.

"Mine too," the pretty redhead Piper said, grinning at her portly partner from the previous day, Paige.

"What's on the agenda for today?" the hot African-American

Trinity said, clasping my hand while she sat next to me. "You mentioned yesterday there were over a hundred different lesbian scissoring positions. It seems that we'll hardly be able to make a dent in the three days we've got together."

"Yes, that's true," Laila smiled. "But in the interests of keeping it fresh, I'll be adding a surprise element into the mix today."

She turned her head toward the hallway leading into the rear bedroom, where we heard a soft rustling sound. Suddenly a naked woman we hadn't seen before strolled out into the living room, taking a seat beside Laila on the futon.

There was a collective gasp when everyone took in the sight of the dark-haired beauty. With long slender legs, large buoyant breasts, and big pouty lips, she looked like a dead-ringer for the sexy actress Angelina Jolie. Her pubis was clean as a baby's bottom, and her skin shined like she'd just returned from an elite spa.

"I'd like you to meet my assistant, Mimi, who'll be helping us demonstrate some of the new positions today. Please join me in welcoming her to our session."

"Hello," Ashley, my scissoring partner from the previous day, gushed. "You're absolutely breathtaking."

"Thank you," Mimi said in a soft voice, glancing around the circle at the rest of the girls staring at her with goo-goo eyes. "So are you. I'm excited to connect with each of you before the day is finished."

"Won't that be a little *difficult*?" I said, peering at Laila with a furrowed brow. "There's twelve of us, and yesterday we only managed to finish six exercises..."

"Well, that's where our new partner comes in," Laila smiled. "Because today we're going to be joining together in *threesomes*, not just in pairs."

"Threesomes?" the blonde coed Becky said, lifting her eyebrows. "How does that work exactly? I mean, if this seminar is all about tribbing, it's hard to imagine how we'll be able to rub *three* pussies together at the same time."

"You might be surprised," Laila said, grinning at Mimi. "Would you like to be our first volunteer today to demonstrate how we can triple the pleasure?"

"Absolutely," Becky said, rolling her eyes up and down Mimi's sexy body.

"Come join us then," Laila said, patting the futon on the opposite side of Mimi. "In this first three-way position that I like to call the *Bucking Bronco*, I'll be lying face-up on the mat while you two kneel overtop of me, facing together."

Laila took off her robe then lay down flat on the futon while Mimi straddled her stomach, facing away from her. Becky peered at the couple for a moment, then she slowly removed her robe and kneeled over Laila's exposed pussy, staring into Mimi's eyes with their nipples separated only inches apart.

"In this position," Laila continued from her supine position, "the two women on top can rub their mounds together while grinding their clits against my pubis to increase their pleasure. It's also a perfect position to rub *other* parts of their bodies together while they kiss and watch each other pleasuring themselves."

"What about *you*?" Hailey said, peering at Laila's closed legs covering up her pussy.

"Technically, with my legs held together by the straddling position of the third partner, it's not easy for me to stimulate my clitoris directly. But I can assure you the feeling of two wet pussies moving on top of my mound provides plenty of *indirect* stimulation. Plus, I get to watch both women making out while I feel their juices trickling between my legs."

As Mimi leaned forward to kiss Becky, their breasts swayed against one another while they rocked their hips gently over Laila's stomach. From my six o'clock position behind Laila's feet, I could see Becky clenching her cheeks rhythmically as she pressed her pussy against Mimi's while they moaned in each other's mouths.

"*Fuck*, that's hot," Trinity hissed, watching a stream of juices beginning to roll down between Laila's closed legs.

"It's even hotter feeling their pussies moving together over my belly," Laila said, slapping the sides of Mimi's contracting buttocks softly with her hands. "What do you think, Becky? Is it even better with a third partner in the mix?"

"Definitely," Becky groaned, mashing her breasts harder against Mimi's tits. "It feels like I'm getting stimulated *everywhere*."

"It's a beautiful thing when three women can connect this way," Laila nodded. "But don't expend all of your sexual energy in this first demonstration. There's eleven other girls around the room that I'm sure are eager to give this a try. There's only enough women for four groupings, so if you can find two other partners to join up with, feel free to take your time with your new playmates."

"What about the two of *you*?" Becky said, slowly disengaging from Mimi and reluctantly rolling her body off Laila's hips. "That means you'll be the odd ones out."

"Don't worry about us," Laila smiled. "We'll have plenty of opportunities to reconnect before the day is over. This workshop is about you and the other girls. You go find some partners of your own while we coach and lend moral support."

Becky peered around the circle and when she made eye contact with me, I motioned for her to join Trinity and me on my mat.

"Thanks for having me," she smiled, cat-walking up next to us. "How do you want to do this? Now we'll have to make *three* decisions as to who goes where."

I glanced over in the direction of Laila and Mimi and smiled.

"You seemed to enjoy being on top in the demonstration," I said. "Why don't you and Trinity face each other while I take it in from *below*?"

"Works for me," Becky smiled, nodding toward Trinity. "Would you prefer to face the front or the rear?"

"I'm not sure there's a front or a back for *any* of us in this three-way tangle," Trinity smiled. "Why don't I face front so Jade can view your pretty ass while you're grinding your pussy over her hips?"

"I like the sound of that," Becky said, remembering our reverse-cowgirl ride from yesterday.

She lifted one knee and turned around, lowering her wet pussy onto my abdomen while I caressed the sides of her slender ass. Then Trinity straddled my legs facing toward me, placing her arms around Becky's back, winked at me over her shoulder. As the two women began rocking their hips together overtop my tilted mound, I glanced down my stomach, noticing a streak of shiny fluid forming on my belly.

Suddenly, Trinity grabbed Becky's head with two hands, kissing her passionately as she humped my hard pubis with her dripping slit. I could see Becky's buttocks flexing as she tilted her hips forward and back, grinding her mound against Trinity's while she rubbed her clit against the soft skin of my lower abdomen. Even though I'd enjoyed our previous tribbing experience when she'd ridden me solo in a similar position, the feeling of two women rubbing their bodies together on top of me definitely added a new level of excitement. I saw the look of ecstasy on Trinity's face as her pleasure continued to mount, and the feel their two bodies slapping while they ground their pussies together was sublime.

As they moaned in each other's mouths, I reached up behind Becky's back and caressed the sides of their breasts while I rocked my hips in unison with them. I could hear the sound of the other women's moans and sighs coming from around the circle, and I turned my head for a moment to take in the sight of the other groups rubbing their bodies together while they held each other tightly. Before returning my attention to my own group, I made eye contact with Laila and she smiled at me while twisting Mimi's nipples softly with her fingers.

"That feels *so* good, Jade," Becky grunted, rocking her hips faster atop my gyrating mound. "Play with my tits and pinch my nipples while I grind my pussy against Trinity. I'm going to come soon."

"Mmm," I purred, squeezing her tits from behind. "This is *twice* as much fun watching the two of you fucking me at the same time. I can't wait to feel you both gushing over my twitching pussy."

"Fuck, yes," Trinity rasped, staring at me as she slapped her hips against Becky's. "I can feel the heat from both of your pussies. I'm going to come so hard–"

"Let it go, babe," I purred, locking eyes with her. "This feels incredible."

"*Jade*," Trinity suddenly groaned as her eyes glassed over. "I'm coming! Becky's skin feels so hot..."

"Uhnnn," Becky hissed, clamping her arms tightly around Trinity's back as she pulled their bodies together while her buttocks began shaking from the powerful orgasm taking hold of her whole body.

Suddenly, I felt two hard streams of fluid jetting down between my legs and over my slit as both women began convulsing overtop of me, screaming in simultaneous pleasure. The feeling of their juices pouring over me added to my already heightened feeling of arousal, and within seconds I began to climax along with them, adding my own pent-up juices to the explosion of fluid squirting up from my compressed legs.

After what seemed like an eternity of shaking and gushing over one another, the three of us slowly began to relax our bodies while we listened to the squeals and moans coming from around the circle as the rest of the women exploded in simultaneous rapture. I glanced over at Laila and Mimi, and saw them sitting facing one another with their knees intertwined and their pussies pushed together while they kissed each other passionately.

For a brief moment, I felt envious of her position watching the rest of us joining in euphoric pleasure. Then I remembered how the two of us had ended the workshop the previous day, and I vowed to reconnect with her and the Angelina Jolie lookalike before the day was over.

2

After everyone had a chance to rest and recover from their powerful orgasms, Laila asked for a new volunteer to demonstrate the next threesome position, and Hailey eagerly shot up her hand.

"Okay," Laila nodded after Hailey joined her and Mimi on the futon in the center of the circle.

"It looks like everybody had a lot of fun with that last position. But you may have noticed it was difficult for the person on the bottom to get enough direct stimulation to enjoy the experience as much as the girls on top. In this next position, all *three* women are going to have a chance to touch their pussies directly, producing a waterworks display that will put the Bellagio fountain to shame. I like to call this one the *Bum's Rush* because of the way each of you will be connecting."

Laila paused, twisting her head to peer at Mimi and Hailey in turn.

"Are you guys ready to give it a try?"

"Are you *kidding* me?" Hailey grinned. "Any chance I have to touch Mimi's gorgeous ass is a bonus. I'm *already* wet just thinking about it."

"In that case, I'll ask you take the *posterior* position, in a manner of speaking. Get on all fours facing away from us while we get ourselves ready."

Hailey flipped over and eagerly assumed the doggy position while she winked at me and the other girls around the circle. Then Laila lay down face up on the futon and pulled her knees up to her chest, revealing her glistening vulva for the whole group to see. Having apparently practiced this technique before, Mimi placed her legs on opposite sides of Laila's hips, then she lowered herself until their pussies touched. As she leaned forward, pressing her breasts down onto Laila's, everybody gasped when they saw the two women's dripping slits framed by their round cheeks, looking like two juicy steaks.

Laila lifted her head and saw Hailey peering between her spread knees with her mouth agape.

"It's up to you to complete the troika," she smiled at Hailey. "Scooch your butt over here and rub your ass together with ours."

"With pleasure," Hailey nodded, crawling backward until her cheeks made contact with Mimi's and Laila's.

"Now it's simply a matter of rocking your hips and tilting your pelvis in the right direction to stimulate the desired spot," Laila said.

As Mimi began to gyrate her hips atop Laila's splayed legs, it didn't take long for all three women's butts to become coated with shiny secretions. Hailey lowered her head to watch the sexy view of their mashing vulvas, but as she grunted and spread her knees wider on the futon, she seemed frustrated by her inability to gain direct friction on her clitoris.

"As much as I love feeling Mimi's sweet ass rubbing against mine," she said. "I'm having trouble touching our *pussies* this way."

"That's partly why I call this position this Bum's Rush," Laila nodded. "Part of the fun with this technique is the interplay between the two women on top. You kind of have to jostle back and forth to gain friction with the girl on the bottom, using my mound to stimulate your clit."

Hailey paused for a moment, then she flexed her arms against the futon, pushing Mimi's ass further forward until her own vulva touched Laila's.

"Mmm," she grunted, parting her lips in pleasure. "That's more like it. Now I can feel your warm pussy pressing against mine."

Suddenly, Mimi pressed her hips back again and tilted her hips downward, pushing Hailey away.

"Hey!" Hailey protested, frustrated that she'd been temporarily disconnected from direct contact with Laila. "No fair! I was just getting into it!"

"It's up to the two of you to go back and forth to get the stimulation you need," Laila smiled. "It's a bit of a give and take process, building up each of your pleasure until you both achieve climax. Except Mimi has a slight advantage kneeling overtop of me, since she can maintain some degree of direct contact the entire time."

"You heard the lady," Hailey growled, pushing Mimi forward with a hard push, pressing her mound down hard unto Laila's dripping slit. "It's *my* turn to taste her pussy for a little while..."

As she began to rock her hips harder and harder against Laila's flared legs, Hailey's groaning escalated in lockstep until she appeared on the verge of climax. But just as she was about to come, Mimi pushed her away again, taking her place atop Laila's mound with the two girls' slits slurping and gnashing together.

"Ugh!" Hailey protested, pressing vainly backwards against Mimi's ass, trying to regain the superior position. "I was just on the verge of orgasm!"

"Like I said before," Laila smiled, sitting up as Mimi rolled off her onto the side. "This is about your pleasure, not ours. From the looks of things, I don't think you'll have any trouble finding eager participants to finish your demonstration."

Hailey peered around the circle, watching many of the women with their knees spread apart, still circling their clits in excitement.

"Just to make sure we share the pleasure and mix up the pairings," Laila continued. "I'd like one person from each of the prior groupings to move one position clockwise while the other person in the group moves counterclockwise. Hailey, you'll have to rejoin your previous position in order to maintain your team's quorum."

As Hailey reluctantly returned to her position in the circle, Becky,

Trinity, and I peered at one another, unsure who among our group should move first.

"Do you have a preference as to which way you'd like to go?" Trinity said to the two of us.

"I don't think it really matters," I said, peering around the perimeter. "By the time we finish all the exercises, I suspect *everyone* will have a chance to hook up with everyone else at one point or another."

Trinity nodded, then shifted over to the mat on her left while Becky moved to the mat on the opposite side. I glanced at the opposing groups and noticed the two redheads, Piper and Paige, shifting over to my mat.

"Funny to see *you* two hooking up again," I smiled, remembering their hot tribbing encounter from the previous day. "Which one of you feels like being on the *bottom* this time?"

"I'm not sure I've got the strength to fight Paige for position in this particular maneuver," Piper chuckled, peering at her sexy full-figured partner. "Why don't I lie down on the mat while you two guys duke it out on top?"

I smiled, recognizing Piper had ulterior motives for taking the lower position. While Paige and I jockeyed for preferential position trying to gain friction on our clits, she'd be the lucky recipient of our pushing and grinding as we rocked back and forth over her upturned pussy. But I was happy to be the one on top this time to get an opportunity to rub asses with the Paige's Jennifer Lopez-sized derriere.

"Works for me," I nodded. "Do you have a preference for which way you'd like to point this time, Paige?"

"I kind of fancied facing *away* yesterday," she said, winking at Piper. "You go ahead and kneel over Piper's hips while I rub my hips against your pretty ass."

As Piper lay down on the yoga mat, Paige and I assumed opposite positions, mirroring the stance of Hailey and Mimi. Piper was more flexible than I expected, and when she pulled her straightened legs back atop her chest, I gawked at her gaping slit while she clasped her ankles beside her head.

"I'll have some of that," I smiled, squatting down overtop her upturned thighs, feeling her wet pussy meshing with mine.

When I felt Paige's rotund ass press against mine from her reverse doggy position, I leaned forward, tilting my vulva upward to meet hers. The three of us groaned, and before long we were rocking our hips together, slapping our pussies and butt cheeks in tandem.

Although Paige could have easily asserted her dominance by using her weight advantage to push herself atop Piper's exposed pussy, she was surprisingly generous in sharing the spoils. While we both rocked our hips up and down, shifting our weight forward and back, each of us was able to progressively build our pleasure until we were on the brink of orgasm.

"Your pussies feel incredible against my skin," Piper panted from her recumbent position as I rubbed my breasts against hers and kissed her gently. "I'm getting pretty close to popping off from this combined stimulation. Are you guys almost there?"

"You read my mind, girl," I grunted, pressing my clit harder against the top of her mound. "I just hope Paige doesn't mind if I give her an impromptu shower. Because I feel like my taps are about to release any moment now..."

"God, yes," Paige groaned from the other side. "I want to feel you both squirting over my ass when I come. Let's show our instructors just how well we've learned our lesson from her Circle Jill workshop."

I smiled, knowing that the three of us had learned how to relax our female prostate glands at the moment of climax, releasing our orgasmic juices without any concern for how much mess it might make. Normally, it would require some kind of *internal* stimulation to our respective G-spots, but in this case, each of us was already so turned on and wet, it would have taken an industrial-sized spigot to hold back the flow of our erotic fluids.

"Okay, babe," I hissed, tilting my head back in ecstasy. "Hold onto your horses, because this is about to get messy. Oh *fuckkk*–"

Suddenly, I felt the pressure building inside my pelvis release and my pelvic floor muscles began contracting in hard spasms, emitting one powerful jet of vaginal juices after another against Paige's open cheeks. When Piper felt me spraying against her pussy, she grunted loudly and tilting her hips forward, releasing her own stream of juices straight up between Paige's and my joined asses.

"Holy *fuck*," Paige groaned, feeling our combined juices squirting all over her flapping pussy. "That feels insane. I'm going to come so hard–"

With one final grunt, she spread her knees wider on the mat, pressing her opening against mine and Piper's as she gushed her juices all over the two of us while we trembled and shook in a jumbled pile of glistening skin for the better part of a full minute. When we finally finished coming hard against our joined asses, we collapsed onto the dripping mat beside Piper, noticing that the rest of the group had finished and were watching the three of us in rapt concentration.

We'd been so wrapped up enjoying our *own* pleasure that we'd been entirely oblivious to what had been going on around us. While Laila and Mimi nodded at us approvingly, a round of applause slowly began to erupt around the circle as the rest of the women expressed their satisfaction for our three-way performance.

3

"I'm glad to see the three of you picked up a few tips from my last workshop," Laila smiled as Becky, Trinity, and I mopped up our drenched yoga mat with our terrycloth robes. "I think we've got time for one more demonstration before lunch. Who'd like to join Mimi and me to show the rest of the group how it's done?"

Everybody's hand quickly shot up, and Laila panned around the circle until her gaze settled on the pretty brunette who I'd hooked up with yesterday, Ashley.

"What do you say, Ashley?" she said. "Do you still have a little fuel left in the tank?"

"I've been replenishing my fluids," Ashley nodded, taking a swig of Evian from her water bottle resting at the side of her mat. "I'm ready to give Jade's group a little run for the money..."

"Good," Laila smiled, patting the empty space on the futon between her and Mimi. "Because in this next position, we're going to need all the extra lubrication we can get. Come join us in a little maneuver I like to call *Knit One, Pearl Two*."

Ashley crawled up between the two women and shook her hips playfully against their pretty asses.

"It's hard to imagine how many more ways three women can connect their bodies together," she said, peering at them with a puzzled expression.

"You have *no* idea," Laila said. "We're still barely beginning to scratch the surface..."

"Feel free to scratch away then," Ashley smiled.

"This position will require a bit of careful leg placement," Laila said. "Hence the reference to knitting. By the time we're finished, our limbs are going to be intertwined in every direction."

"Sounds intriguing," Ashley nodded. "Where would you like me to start?"

"This time I'm going to place you in the *middle* of the action. I want you to sit face up with one knee pulled up beside you, leaning slightly back on your arms."

Ashley did as she was instructed, then Laila turned her body away from her, placing her left knee over Ashley's extended leg. Then she extended her other leg on the opposite side of Ashley's raised knee, pushing her pussy up against Ashley's into an inverted scissor position. As she propped herself up on one elbow to turn her body in Ashley's direction, Mimi wedged her figure overtop of the two girls, positioning her body in the opposing direction, mirroring Laila's stance. By the time they were finished, Laila's and Mimi's asses were firmly connected in a cheek-to-cheek position overtop Ashley's separated legs, with each of their legs pointing in different directions.

"I see what you mean with the *knitting* analogy," Ashley nodded, peering at the two women's exposed slits, inches away from her flaring eyes. "This is quite a twisted maneuver you've got us wrapped up in."

"*Twisted* is a good way to describe it," Laila said, peering over her shoulder at Ashley. "Because in order for us to gain the necessary friction to make it interesting, we're going to have to twist our hips to hit the right spots."

"I get what you mean," Ashley grunted, as she began to tilt her hips from side to side while rubbing her wet slit against Laila's splayed legs. "I can see your sexy pussy close-up while you press your hips against me."

Mimi began tilting her hips in unison with Ashley, and before long the sound of their three slurping pussies filled the room while the rest of the participants gawked at the squirming trio as they slowly fingered their pussies.

"Holy fuck," Paige said, sitting next to me, rolling her clit between her fingers while she twisted her hips unconsciously, mimicking the movement of the three women. "That is *seriously* hot."

"No *shit*," I said, slipping two fingers into my dripping slit, watching the three girls grinding their hips together. "I can't wait to give this one a try for myself."

"Me too," Piper said, rubbing her palm over her pubis.

"As you can see," Laila continued, peering up at Ashley while she rocked her hips from side to side. "The angle of your hips to some extent determines which of our pussies you come into contact with. While Mimi and I are continuously connected by virtue of our ass-to-ass scissor position, you have direct control over whose pussy you wish to rub against while you rock your hips."

"Yes," Ashley panted as her eyes darted between Laila's and Mimi's splayed legs while she gazed at their glistening vulvas stretching and grinding together.

It must have been a feast for her eyes, not to mention a treat for her pussy, to have two beautiful women focusing their combined attention on her most sensitive erogenous zone.

"You both feel–and *look*–so hot," Ashley groaned, her mouth gaping wider and her chest becoming more flushed as her pleasure continued to mount. "I can't wait to watch you both squirting all over my burning pussy..."

"I'm afraid that will have to wait a little longer," Laila said, suddenly pulling herself away from Ashley as Mimi rolled off to the other side. "We want you to save the best part for the other girls while you practice with the rest of the group. As before, I'd like you to return to your previous place in the circle while one person from each group moves one position in opposite directions."

I smiled watching Ashley crawl back to her earlier position in the circle as Piper and I moved over one position to the opposing mats. Laila was intentionally using us one at a time to drive us to the peak of excitement while demonstrating each new position, leaving each volunteer desperate to finish while the rest of the group looked on in lustful expectation. It was brilliant in a twisted kind of way, and I eagerly anticipated my own turn with the sexy couple in the middle of the circle before the day was over.

After everybody finished shifting positions as Laila had instructed, I found myself paired up with Hailey and another girl close to my age. She had brown, Latino-colored skin and soft brown eyes with high cheekbones, and a firm stack to match.

"Hi," she said, reaching out her hand to me formally. "I'm Maria. I don't think we've met yet."

"Jade," I said, clasping her hand softly. "Though I don't think we need to be quite so formal, since we'll be getting to know each other pretty intimately within a matter of minutes."

"I guess you already know who I am from the first demonstration," Hailey chuckled, extending her hand. "Jade and I are familiar with one another from Laila's earlier workshop."

"The one where everybody learned how to squirt?" Maria said.

"Among *other* things," Hailey nodded, smiling at me. "It's really just a matter of learning how to relax the special gland next to your G-spot and releasing your inhibitions about peeing on your partner."

"But it's not really *pee*, is it?" the girl said with a wrinkled forehead.

"No," Hailey chuckled. "That's a complete fallacy invented by perverted and wishful men. The fluid actually comes from a special gland similar to the male prostate, that's intended to facilitate the movement and nourishment of sperm up the women's reproductive tract after completion of the sex act."

"So it's not really a male fantasy after all, then," Maria smiled.

"I suppose not," Hailey laughed. "Although I find it personally empowering to be able to ejaculate just like a man. And most women seem to dig it too."

"Damn straight," I nodded, feeling a trickle of lubrication running down the inside of my thighs, already dreaming about spraying my juices over the pretty Latina girl. "Speaking of, do you have a preference for where you'd like to position yourself in our little threesome?"

"Well, since you guys already seem to be a few steps ahead of me with this whole squirting thing, do you mind if I lie between the two of you like Ashley did with Laila and Mimi, so I can enjoy the waterworks to maximum advantage?"

"Works for me," I nodded, smiling at Hailey. "Go ahead and lie down with your legs spread apart while we get into position."

Maria sat on the mat and lifted her knee, and before Hailey had a chance to react, I copied Laila's stance with my ass nudged up tightly against Maria's pussy, scissoring my legs in an inverted X-position, with my left knee pulled up to my chest. Hailey frowned at me for stealing the primo spot, then she turned around in a similar manner, facing in the other direction as each of our right legs pointed out on opposite sides of Maria's hips.

"Mmm," Maria moaned, staring at Hailey's and my ass rubbing directly together over her splayed legs. "I see what Ashley meant when she said she had a bird's-eye view to catch the waterworks. Your pussies and asses look incredible rubbing together overtop of me..."

"It's feels even better when you move your hips to generate some friction between our three pussies," I said, encouraging her to take control rubbing her body against us.

As Hailey and I pressed our asses tighter together, we pulled our left knees higher up toward our chests, overlapping our vulvas while Maria began to rock her hips from side to side, sliding her slippery slit against ours.

"Oh my God," she gasped as her tits shook on her chest. "This feels amazing seeing both of your pussies rubbing up against mine. Laila was right about how we're weaving our bodies together like a knitted sweater."

"A very *wet* sweater," Hailey panted, grinding her pussy harder against the two of us.

"Yes," Maria groaned, staring at our gnashing pussies between her splayed legs. "You guys are already producing more vaginal secretions than I'm accustomed to..."

"That's just our natural wetness," I nodded. "Women's internal lubrication is the equivalent of a man's hard-on. It just signals how aroused we all are. The *real* wetworks will come at the end when we all climax together."

"I'm getting pretty close already, watching you guys fucking me with your sexy asses," Maria huffed. "Although I'm not sure I'm going to be able to come in the same way you learned from Laila's previous instruction–"

"Don't worry about any of that right now," I said, noticing the flush on Maria's face beginning to spread rapidly down over her neck and upper chest as her mouth began to gape wider open and her eyelids began to narrow. "Just let it all go and enjoy the moment. Like Laila said, this is about the three of us connecting our bodies intimately together and sharing the experience. Hailey and I are ready to share our climax whenever you are."

"*Uhnn, uhnn*," Maria grunted, rocking her hips more forcefully between our joined buttocks as her tits began to quiver on her chest. "Oh fuck–I'm going to come all over your juicy pussies. Here it comes!"

Suddenly, a giant spray of fluid began spurting up between our legs as Maria began shaking uncontrollably. Hailey and I glanced at one another with wide eyes, shaking our heads wondering which one of us had begun ejaculating, and when we realized it was Maria producing all the fluid, we grunted in delight, quickly reaching the apex of our own pleasure. While the three of us pressed our vulvas tightly together, we all watched in amazement as one giant spray after another of orgasmic fluid jetted up over our bodies, just like the perfectly synchronized water fountain at the Bellagio Hotel in Las Vegas.

Holy shit, I thought to myself as our three bodies convulsed in one powerful contraction after another. *Laila really does have the perfect job.*

Not only does she get to watch and connect with a steady stream of new female partners, she gets to teach all of us how to enjoy and express our pleasure in a collective state of shared consciousness.

Talk about nirvana. Maybe she should rename her workshop Hedonism instead of Tribadism.

4

———————

After everybody recovered from their latest threesome exercise, we all paused for a half hour, enjoying a tasteful buffet of smoked salmon and endive salad. The girls seemed energized after the last erotic encounter, and as we sat on our yoga mats nibbling on our lunch while peering around the circle to see who we'd be paired up with next, it was obvious everyone was eager to resume the action.

Laila didn't waste any time taking advantage of the highly charged atmosphere, and after we all finished eating, she asked for a new volunteer to demonstrate the next exercise. This time, she chose Trinity to join Mimi and her in the middle of the circle, and as she clasped the two girls' hands by her side, she smiled peering out at the group.

"In this next position I like to call the *Chain Gang*," she said, "we're going to be hooking up in a daisy-chain configuration, kneeling behind one another, front-to-back..."

"I'm *digging* this whole ass-tribbing thing," Trinity nodded. "How do you want me to position myself this time?"

Laila peered over in the direction of Ashley's mat and grinned.

"Ashley seemed to enjoy being in the middle last time," she said. "Are you willing to give it a try that way?"

"Anytime I can be sandwiched between two sexy women like you," she said, glancing at Mimi's and Laila's sexy bodies, "that's an invitation I'll never pass up."

"Alright then," Laila nodded. "Stand upright on your knees while Mimi and I cuddle up next to you."

While Trinity raised up on her knees, Laila moved behind her, pressing her tits and mound against her back while Mimi positioned herself in a similar stance in front of Trinity. When all three women were in position, they were pushed together in an upright kneeling sandwich, posing like a succulent all-girl snack. From my perspective at the side of the circle, I could see each of their asses and tits neatly compressed between their partners' figures.

All except *Mimi's* of course, who was kneeling on full display at the front of the pack with her large, ski-jump-shaped tits and thick pointed nipples shining in the bright sunlight streaming in through the living room picture window. I wondered for a moment if any of Laila's neighbors might have been spying on us with high-powered telescopes, because if they were, they must surely have been getting the best porn show of their lives.

"In this position," Laila continued, reaching around Trinity's back to thread her hands over her breasts pressed against Mimi's back. "The two women in the rear are in an ideal stance to caress their partner to the front. But because we're all kneeling upright, it won't be quite as easy to stimulate our clits by rubbing against our partner's vulva, so feel free to use your *hands* to caress your partner while you rub your hips together."

Trinity nodded while reaching in front of her, running her hands over Mimi's plump breasts and trim stomach.

"Mmm," Mimi murmured, rolling her ass against Trinity's body sandwiched behind her.

"Although technically we're still tribbing our hips against one another in this position," Laila said, shifting her hands lower down Trinity's stomach toward her crotch. "This position is really about using our hands to caress one another and stimulate our private parts to elevate the excitement."

Trinity groaned as Laila slipped her fingers lower toward her pussy while she continued to grind her hips against Mimi's tight ass.

"Getting fingered from behind feels even *better* when I have another woman's body pressing against me from the other side," she said.

"Like Laila said," Mimi grinned, pulling Trinity's hands down lower over her pubis. "Having another woman in the equation makes it twice as much fun."

"Mmm," Trinity hummed, pushing her fingers deeper into Mimi's moist gap. "You feel delicious–on *both* sides."

"So do you," Mimi grunted, spreading her knees wider apart to give Trinity freer access to her glistening pussy.

As all the women around the circle sat mesmerized watching the three women rubbing their bodies against one another, everyone's hands were buried between their legs, jilling themselves while they imagined it was *them* in the thick of the action.

"That's pretty fucking hot," Hailey said, groaning softly as she squirmed on the yoga mat beside me.

"The *fingering* action, or the *tribbing* action?" I said.

"*Both*. It's like every part of their bodies are connected this time, from tip to tail."

"And that's some pretty awesome tail on display up there," Maria said, circling her clit while she stared at the trio in the middle of the circle.

"I'm too busy focusing on her *tips* right now," I said, pinching my nipples while I fantasized about sucking on Mimi's hard bullets.

"Those are some pretty amazing tits on that chick," Hailey nodded, sinking her fingers deep into her snatch as she rolled her hips in sympathy with Mimi while Trinity massaged her pussy.

Trinity paused for a moment, peering over her shoulder at her instructor, caressing her from behind.

"How are you doing back there, Laila?" she asked. "You're the only one in this group not getting any direct stimulation."

"I'm getting *plenty* of stimulation, I assure you," Laila said, gyrating her hips against Trinity's glistening backside. "Your tight ass is providing plenty of excitement, plus I'm getting even more turned on feeling you get wet while I play with your pussy..."

"I'm getting *wet* alright," Trinity said, pressing her hips harder against Laila's hand juggling faster between her legs. "If you keep fingering me like that, I'm going to squirt all over your hand."

"I suppose this is a good a time to stop then," Laila said, pulling away while Trinity continued grasping Mimi tightly, humping her ass firmly from behind.

"Are you sure?" Trinity said, slipping her fingers into Mimi's snatch to keep her from pulling away. "Because judging by how wet *Mimi* is right now, I'm not sure she agrees."

Mimi twisted her body then pulled Trinity's hand gently away from her crotch as she kissed her softly on the lips.

"I'd love to continue this little menage," she said. "But Laila and I would like to share your beautiful body with the rest of the girls. "Twelve divided by three only makes *four* threesomes. Without you rejoining the group, someone will be left out..."

"Why can't one of *you* join the group this time while we continue what we started?" Trinity protested. "Who said you couldn't join in the fun with the rest of us?"

"Talk to the boss," Mimi said, tilting her head toward Laila with sympathetic eyes. "She's the one creating the rules."

"We'll have a chance to finish up with one of you later today," Laila smiled. "But for now, I'm going to ask you to rejoin the group and continue the exercise with the *other* girls. You know the routine–"

"Yeah, yeah," Trinity huffed, skulking back to her previous place in the circle on her knees while waving her ass teasingly at Mimi and Laila. "Go back to your previous group while everybody shifts one position in opposite directions, blah, blah, blah..."

I smiled as Maya and Aria transferred over to the opposite mats. This time, I ended up paired up with two new girls I hadn't interacted with before. One was a pretty Asian girl in her late twenties with a slim figure and small round breasts, and the other was a sexy brunette in her mid-forties. They smiled at me when we joined together on the mat and awkwardly introduced themselves.

"I'm Maya," the Asian girl said, shaking my hand softly.

"Aria," the brunette said, clasping both of our hands.

"Such pretty names," I said, smiling at them warmly. "I'm Jade. Something tells me we're going to make the perfect triptych. Do either of you have a preference as to where you'd like to position yourselves in this exercise?"

"Why don't we go light-to-dark?" Maya chuckled. "With Jade at the rear and me at the front? We can create our own little Garden of Earthly Delights, to continue the artistic metaphor."

"Hieronymous Bosch it is," I smiled, impressed with Maya's knowledge of Renaissance art.

As the three of us got into position, I reveled at the feeling of Aria's curvy body resting against mine while we all kneeled together on the soft yoga mat.

"Mmm," she sighed, tracing her hands along the sides of Maya's slender figure in front of her. "I see what Mimi meant when she said having three women in the picture makes it twice as fun."

"And this painting is almost as colorful as Bosch's too," I nodded, glancing down at our three asses connected in a pretty rainbow of colors.

"And just as erotic," Maya said, rotating her ass softly against Aria's hips.

"Except this time, we're not constrained by the mores of the Middle Ages," I smiled, slipping my hands between Maya's back and Aria's stomach to begin caressing Aria's pubis. "We're free to touch whatever sexy parts we want."

"Mmm," Aria nodded, reaching around Maya's front to roll her fingers over her pinched nipples. "Your breasts feel so soft and warm, Maya."

"You're not disappointed they're not as full as Jade's?" she said.

"Of course not," Aria said, rocking her hips against my mound as I pressed my fingers lower into her wet slit. "You're just as sexy with your delicate features as any woman I've ever been with. I love the feel of your firm and perfectly round breasts."

"That's not the *only* thing that's getting firm while you touch me," Maya said, pushing her ass harder against my hand caressing Aria's pussy. "Rub my clit like Jade's doing to you while I feel your breath on my back."

"Yes," Aria said, moving her right hand between Maya's legs while she squeezed Maya's breast with her other hand. "I feel your hard button. Somehow this is even sexier not being able to see you while I touch you. Your pussy feels so warm and wet..."

"So does yours," Maya said, rolling her ass against Aria's wet mound while I circled her clit with two fingers. "I can feel Jade's fingers rubbing your pussy and it's getting me seriously turned on—"

"That makes *three* of us," I said, dry-humping Aria's ass from behind.

"But you're not able to get the same kind of stimulation as the two of us, being at the back," Maya said.

"It might not be the same kind of stimulation," I grunted, tilting my pelvis up to press my vulva against Aria's flexing buttocks while I fingered her more quickly. "But I assure you it feels just as good. Aria's ass reminds me of the firm pillow on my bed that I sometimes hump on lonely nights to get off."

"Do you think you can *come* in that position?" Aria said, squeezing her cheeks rhythmically while I stepped up my finger pressure on her burning button. "Because you're bringing me pretty close, touching me like that..."

"Yes," I said, feeling my pleasure beginning to mount as I watched the two women's hips in front of me writhing together in unison. "As long as Aria doesn't mind my squirting over her ass when I climax. Because I usually make a bit of a mess when I orgasm."

"Fuck, yes," Aria grunted, pressing my hand harder against Maya's ass. "Spray your juices all over my ass and pussy. You're going to make me come any moment now..."

"Wait for me," Maya panted along with the two of us. "I want to feel it too when I come. Trib me harder, Aria. I'm almost there—"

Suddenly she threw her head back over Aria's shoulder while tilting her hips backward as she grunted loudly, shaking her body in the midst of a powerful orgasm. When Aria felt Maya coming, she hunched forward, jerking her body hard over her back while I buried my fingers deep into her contracting tunnel.

Feeling the two women quivering against me soon put me also over the edge, and within seconds I began grunting along with them as I squeezed my buttocks together, spraying my juices between their separated legs and over their joined slits. When we finished climaxing, we held each other gently from behind, enjoying the feeling of our three dripping pussies drenching our hands and our still tightly compressed asses.

"I think Hieronymous Bosch missed an opportunity to add one extra scene in his erotic painting," I chuckled. "He forgot to include a *lesbian threesome* to his three-panel masterpiece."

5

A fter everybody cleaned up their mats and returned to their sitting positions, Laila peered out at the group and smiled.

"That was quite a feast for the eyes," she said while Mimi scanned the still-dripping bodies of the naked women arranged around the circle. "Although we may have cheated a little bit bringing an extra body part into the equation, it looks like none of you are any worse for the wear."

"But tribbing simply means *rubbing*, doesn't it?" Paige said. "So technically, as long as we're rubbing *any* parts of our bodies together, we're still technically tribbing, aren't we?"

"I suppose so," Laila nodded. "Although most people still think of tribbing as rubbing only their *pussies* together, and in this next exercise, we're going to stay true to form. I like to call it the *Pile Driver*, because–well, it will become pretty obvious once you begin to see it in action. Would you like to be our next volunteer, Paige?"

"I don't know," she hesitated with a teasing smile. "Are you just going to get me all worked up then leave me hanging like you did with Trinity and the other volunteers?"

"I wouldn't exactly call it *hanging*," Laila grinned. "Though you *will* be perched in a bit of a precarious position..."

"How can I turn down a proposal like that?" Paige said, crawling on all fours toward the middle of the circle while everybody stared at her Rubenesque-sized derriere. "How exactly do you want me to position myself this time?"

"This one requires a bit of gymnastics and some strong abs," Laila smiled. "How limber are you?"

"I go to yoga class three times a week," Paige nodded. "And I can still do a full split..."

"Perfect," Laila said. "In that case, lie face up on the futon and place your hands behind your ass, then raise your hips up as high as you can directly over your body–"

"Like this?" Paige said, lifting her legs directly over her head.

When she parted her thighs into a perfect upside-down split, everyone in the room gasped. For a big girl, she had remarkable flexibility, making her rotund cheeks look even sexier, framing her pink, gaping vulva for us all to see.

"Um, yes," Laila said, turning to glance at Mimi with wide eyes. "That'll work just fine."

The two of them stood up and straddled Paige's pussy facing towards each other, then they slowly lowered themselves until their crotches touched her upper thighs.

"Can you handle a little extra pressure on your thighs?" Laila asked, flexing her quadricep muscles to help support herself over Paige's splayed legs.

"I think so," Paige said, peering up at the two women prostrated above her. "But if you move closer together, I'll be able to support you more easily..."

Mimi and Laila shifted their hips forward a few inches until their mounds touched, and everybody's mouths dropped open when they saw the three women's pussies connected in a perfect union of scissored legs. For the first time during any of the demonstrations, every one of the girls' vulvas was in direct contact with one another.

"Holy *fuck*," Aria panted, sitting beside me. "I think that might be the sexiest thing I've seen in my whole life."

"Now I see why they call it the *pile driver*," I nodded, watching the two women on top begin to gyrate their hips atop Paige like two exotic dancers.

"I just hope Paige can hold that position long enough for everybody to get off," Maya said, squirming on the mat, channeling the movement of Mimi and Laila.

"She's a pretty strong girl," I said. "Take it from me, based on first-hand experience. If anyone can take that kind of pounding, she's the one."

Paige suddenly moaned, staring up at the two girls grinding their pussies against her dripping vulva.

"Your pussies feel delicious grinding against my twat. It's a shame you won't be able to finish, so I can watch you shower me with your combined juices."

"We're already getting pretty wet feeling your hot pussy rubbing against ours," Laila grunted, leaning forward to kiss Mimi while they mashed their tits and mounds together in a three-way shag.

"That feels incredible," Paige groaned from the bottom. "Press down harder onto my cunt. I want to feel you tribbing my clit."

"Are you sure you can take it?" Laila said, still flexing her thigh muscles to take part of the load off Paige.

"You're directing most of your energy straight down," Paige nodded. "As long as I keep my spine erect and my hips propped up directly above me, it won't be a problem."

"Let us know if it gets to be too much," Laila said, beginning to relax her thigh muscles as she lowered her weight a few more inches onto Paige's spreading ass.

"It's the called the pile driver for a *reason*," Mimi nodded, rocking her hips more forcefully over Paige's divided legs, causing the redhead's body to rock slowly from side to side.

"Pound me *harder*," Paige panted as her face turned a deeper shade of crimson. "Fuck me with your pretty pussies. I just need a little longer. I'm going to cum so hard–"

"I don't *doubt* it," Laila said, raising herself up over Paige's spread legs while her pussy dripped strings of lubrication onto her upturned thighs. "But we're going to save that for a few *other* lucky girls who I'm sure are also dying to have a piece of your ass."

"Fuck *me*," Paige groaned as Mimi simultaneously lifted herself off her steaming crotch. "This is a form of legalized torture. You guys are such teases..."

"Maybe," Laila grinned. "But don't you find it elevates your pleasure so you can enjoy the experience all the *more* with your own group of partners?"

"I suppose so," Paige said, lowering her hips back onto the futon as she shook out her cramping hands. "But just once I'd like to see you two come together in one of these exercises, as I'm sure the rest of the girls would too."

"Actually, we're saving the best for *last*," Laila smiled, kissing Mimi gently on the lips. "In our final exercise of the day, everyone will have a chance to witness a different kind of waterworks display. One in which all *three* participants will be able to enjoy the experience to the fullest. But for now, we'd like everyone to have a chance to practice this latest exercise."

"*Exercise* is definitely the right word for it," Paige said, raising herself up slowly and slinking back to her previous position in the circle.

By this point, everyone had shifted far enough around the ring that I found myself sitting next to Paige's mat when she returned to her spot. I didn't waste any time being the first one in my group to shift over to her side, clutching her arm to stop her from moving.

"Don't you dare go *anywhere*," I said, peering into her pretty hazel eyes. "You must be too exhausted to move another inch. Besides, I want you all to myself this time."

"Well, technically you'll have to share me with one other person," she grinned, turning toward Piper joining us from the other side.

"How do you want to do this?" I said to the two girls. "Paige must be pretty exhausted from supporting herself in the previous demonstration. Why don't I get on the bottom this time–"

"I have no allusions about my plus-size proportions," Paige said. "It would be too much of a strain for you to try to support my weight.

And Piper is far too skinny to support either one of us. Besides, I kind of like being on the bottom, where I have the best view. I can't wait to watch the two of you squirting all over me."

"Okay," I nodded. "If you're sure you can handle it. Are you on board with this arrangement, Piper?"

"Are you kidding me?" Piper grinned. "I've been dying to hook up with the two of you again ever since our first encounter. Why do you think I stayed so close to Paige while we continued moving around the circle?"

"That makes two of us," I chuckled. "I suppose we make a perfect threesome."

Paige didn't waste any time lying down on the mat and raising her hips above her head as she separated her legs wide apart.

"Get on top of me, both of you, before I burst a gasket," she grinned, peering up at us. "I'm still dripping wet from Laila and Mimi's warm-up exercise."

"So I can see," I said, staring at her glistening vulva gaping open like a hungry grouper waiting to devour her smaller prey. "What do you say, Piper? Are you ready to take Paige for a ride?"

"You took the words right out of my mouth," Piper said, straddling one side of Paige's slippery thigh while sliding her pussy forward toward her hole.

I quickly followed suit, turning my body in the other direction to face toward Piper, and when we touched our crotches together over Paige's dripping pussy, we both gasped.

"Oh my God," Piper groaned, pressing her hips hard against mine as we ground our mounds together. "This is my favorite position so far. I can feel both of your pussies connecting with mine. I've never felt so close to two women before..."

I wrapped my arms around Piper's back and pulled her closer toward me as we mashed our breasts together and thrust our tongues into each other's mouths while we rocked our hips over Paige's exposed crotch.

"God damn, that's a beautiful sight," Paige grunted from below.

"My two favorite girls kissing and grinding their pussies together overtop my burning cunt..."

"We're not putting too much pressure on you?" I said, peering down at her.

"Not at all," she grunted. "Press down even harder. I want you both to fuck me hard while you grind your pussies together. Trib my clit with your pretty cunnies. I'm going to watch you both squirt all over me when I come."

I relaxed my legs a bit further and pressed my pelvis down harder onto Paige's spreading lips as Piper began rocking her hips back and forth harder against my stomach while our three pussies slurped loudly in an erotic symphony of lesbian love.

"Yes," Paige groaned, gaping her mouth wider open. "Just like that. You both feel exquisite. I'm going to come so hard watching the two of you. Come with me while you hold each other."

"Mmm," I groaned, pulling slightly away from Piper so I could watch her face when she came. "I'm going to explode any moment now. Are you just about ready?"

"God, yes," Piper murmured. "I've been ready to come from the moment I climbed on top of Paige and felt both of your pussies connecting with mine. Hold me while I come–"

I wrapped my arms tighter around Piper's back and pulled her harder toward me as we ground our vulvas together, feeling Paige's hard clit sliding between our slits. While we stared into each other's eyes, our cheeks progressively tightened, until we both grunted loudly, rocking our hips wildly over Paige's split legs as we gushed our combined juices all over her twitching pussy and down over her plump tits and blinking eyelashes.

"*Fuck, yes,*" Paige growled as her flush spread rapidly over her speckled cheeks. "I'm coming with you. Oh God, I'm coming so hard–"

Suddenly a new, much larger jet of fluid began spraying out to the sides of our tightly connected pussies as Paige wailed in delirious pleasure while the three of us squirted together in blissful harmony. When we finished, we noticed the two groups on either side of us wiping themselves down from the spray that had jetted out in every direction from our connected bodies while they nodded and smiled at us knowingly.

Holy fuck, I thought, holding Piper tightly while I savored the feeling of our warm pussies twitching and dribbling down the sides of Paige's upturned thighs, hardly imagining how it could get any better.

But in the back of my mind, I remembered Laila's comment about the finale she had planned, where all three women would have a chance to consummate their pleasure together. I was desperately hoping to be the last one chosen to demonstrate the final exercise.

6

———————

After everyone recovered from their last threesome exercise, we all paused for a moment to clean up and take a bathroom break. While I waited outside the door to Laila's powder room for another woman to exit, I peered down the hall toward the closed door of her master bedroom. I was intrigued why she wasn't allowing us to use it, as twenty girls waited patiently to relieve themselves using the one available toilet. But I assumed it was simply her desire to place a hard line between the professional areas of her apartment and the private ones. I wouldn't want a bunch of strangers spying on my personal stuff either.

When we all returned to the living room and peered at Mimi and Laila sitting quietly in the middle of the circle, you could practically hear a pin drop from the anticipation in the room. Everyone couldn't wait to see what they had planned for the final demonstration of the day.

"I hope everybody had a chance to clean up after that last exciting encounter," Laila smiled. "Because you may have noticed it was a little messier than some of the others."

"I haven't had a shower like that in a long time," Paige chuckled, pushing her still-drenched hair behind her ears with two hands.

"Talk about an organic hair treatment. Something tells me my tresses will be shining a little brighter than usual for a while after this."

"Yes," Laila said, winking at Piper and me. "Some of you have really learned how to release your chi when you climax. It's ironic that you use a bathroom reference to describe your last experience, because in our last demonstration of the day, we'll all be retiring to my ensuite bath to practice the final exercise."

Laila stood up slowly, clasping Mimi's hand.

"Would you all like to join Mimi and me in my private chambers?"

As the two women headed in the direction of the back room, we all looked at one another with wide eyes, wondering what she had in mind. Whatever it was, it sounded like there'd be an extra degree of intimacy involved, and we all eagerly followed the two of them down the hall.

As we walked through her tastefully appointed bedroom with its large four-poster bed and Georgia O'Keefe paintings, I nodded at Laila's sensuous sense of style. But when I followed her and the rest of the girls into her large attached bathroom, I gasped. Decorated entirely in gleaming alabaster-colored marble, it had two marble-covered sinks, a separate make-up table, and a huge, glass-enclosed walk-in shower.

But the highlight of the room was a gorgeous two-person ceramic tub sitting next to the large picture window overlooking Riverside Park next to the Hudson River. Resting on antique claw legs with sloped backrests facing one another, it looked like the perfect respite for two people ready to enjoy a relaxing bath together.

Mimi and Laila pulled off their robes then stepped into the tub, each leaning back against one side of the tub as they peered back at the group standing in a tight circle around the two women.

"I'm going to let Mimi choose our last volunteer of the day," she smiled. "I don't want to make it look like I'm playing any favorites."

Mimi slowly panned around the group, smiling as she ran her eyes over our naked figures.

"Let me see," she purred. "Who hasn't had a turn yet..."

When she reached my position at the end of the semi-circle, she paused and smiled.

"What about you, Jade?" she said, peering at my full breasts and bald pubis. "How would you like to join us?"

"I'd love to," I said, pinching my eyes at the two-person tub. "But are you sure there's room for a *third* in there?"

"Actually," Laila smiled, looking up at me. "In this last threesome position I like to call *The Waterfall*, *you'll* be the one in charge of leading the action."

She picked up the handheld shower head hanging from the faucet in the middle of the tub and pointed it in my direction.

"If you think your thighs are still up for it, you can squat over the two of us while directing the shower spray over our bodies while we *all* enjoy a different kind of waterworks experience."

I gawked at the two women's bare pussies facing one another while they lay in the tub with their knees angled apart.

"Oh, I'm pretty sure my thighs have got enough energy left for one more tribbing exercise," I smiled.

"Good," Laila smiled. "Just give me a couple of seconds to get the water temperature right before you climb in."

She turned each of the separate hot and cold water taps as water began to pour out of the central faucet, and while she held one hand under the tumbling cascade, she and Mimi slowly pressed their hips together until their vulvas touched. Then she lifted the shower handle and tapped a button on top of the faucet, redirecting the spray through the detached handle. As she held the handle over their two pussies, Mimi began to gyrate her hips slowly under the warm stream.

"How would you like to be the *master of ceremonies* this time, Jade?" she said, holding the handle up toward me.

"If you insist," I smiled, stepping toward the tub.

I paused trying to figure out where to position myself in the limited remaining space in the tub, then I placed my feet on opposite sides of Laila's tapered waistline and lowered my hips over their bodies while gripping the side of the tub with one hand. Laila handed the shower head to me, and I clumsily pointed it toward their joined hips.

"That feels good," Laila sighed. "But if we're going to make this a fully inclusive three-way experience, you'll have to direct the spray onto *yourself* too."

I peered at her with a puzzled expression for a moment then I tilted my hips, pointing the spray toward my own midsection as the water streamed down over my thighs and between their legs. My pussy twitched when I felt the warm spray jetting against my clit, but I found it awkward trying to hold the handle in the proper position to direct the spray over all three of us while also holding onto the side of the bathtub to support myself.

"It might be easier if you *kneel* beside me instead of squatting," Laila said, recognizing my discomfort. "I think there's enough room in here for all of us..."

She pulled my knees forward until they rested beside her waist on the warm ceramic surface, then I slowly lowered my ass onto Mimi's stomach while pressing my pussy over her mound. Once I'd rested myself fully onto their two bodies, I peered down, noticing our three slits lined up in a perfect line.

"That should be a little more comfortable," Laila said, peering at my dripping body kneeling overtop of her. "Now direct that spray over all three of our hips and enjoy the sensation of our yonis connected together while you feel our bodies moving underneath you."

As I pointed the spray toward the junction of our three pussies, Laila and Mimi moaned while they rolled their hips slowly together, twisting and intertwining their vulvas.

"Mmmm," I moaned, watching Laila's sexy body writhing underneath me as she looked up at me with glassy eyes. "I've never used a portable shower faucet like this before. It's far more fun to share it with another partner than just using it myself."

"Isn't it three times as much fun to do it with *three* women?"

"Yes," I groaned, rubbing my ass softly on Mimi's stomach. "Talk about a feast for the senses. I can see, feel, and hear each one of you while the water pours over all of our pussies."

Laila reached up to softly clasp my hands holding the shower handle and pointed my fingers toward the tip.

"It can be even *more* stimulating if you adjust the type of flow coming out of the handle," she said. "If you turn the dial on the end, you can adjust the stream to create a *pulsating* effect."

I paused for a moment to find the location of the dial, then I twisted it slowly until the flow changed from a steady discharge to a pulsating stream.

"Unghh," I groaned, feeling the warm water jetting against my tingling clit while I pointed the stream down over my mound to ensure the other girls were experiencing the effect equally.

"Yes," Laila panted, twisting her hips sexily while she ground her vulva against Mimi's on the other side of the tub. "Feel free to experiment with the handle setting. The more you turn it clockwise, the faster you'll make the oscillations."

I nodded as I watched Laila's nipples growing thicker and her sex flush beginning to creep further down her neck and over her chest. It was obvious she was becoming more excited the longer I directed the spray onto her and Mimi's joined pussies, and I was eager to see them both climax with the rest of the group looking on. Plus, my own pleasure was rapidly beginning to rise, and wanted to feel them coming together with me.

I turned the dial two more notches until it stopped, and the spray suddenly turned into a more powerful stream with much faster pulsations.

"Nnngh," I heard Mimi groaning from behind me as her hips began to twist more forcefully underneath me. "God, that feels good," she said. "Grind your pretty ass over my mound while you stimulate our pussies. I need to come so bad..."

"I can *imagine*," I said, temporarily redirecting the spray onto Laila's stomach and tits. "It must have been torture for you to watch the rest of us coming so hard while we tribbed one another in each of the positions you and Laila so thoroughly demonstrated. You must be *dying* to orgasm by now."

"Fuck, yes," Mimi said, rolling her hips harder against my ass and dripping pussy. "Point that spray back over our pussies so I can watch the two of you coming while I jet my own juices over both of you–"

"I don't know," I smiled, teasingly angling the spray around the sides of their writhing hips on the floor of the wet tub. "What do you think, ladies? Should I let our two instructors finally get off, or should I make them hold out like they did for us all afternoon?"

"Maybe just a *little* longer," Hailey said, circling her clit while she watched the three of us rubbing our pussies together in the oversize tub.

"Make them wait until *we're* ready this time," Trinity nodded, thrusting three fingers deep into her slit.

"Okay," I said, turning the shower handle to point the spray directly onto my own pussy. "Why don't we give them a little of their own medicine?"

Laila smiled at me with an evil grin, then she reached up to grab the taps at the side of the tub, threatening to turn off the flow of water.

"Two can play that game," she grinned. "Remember who's still in charge of this little demonstration."

"You wouldn't *dare*," I said, redirecting the pulsating flow of water down over our three slits.

"Not as long as you continue to share the spoils," she groaned, dropping her hands to grab the top of my thighs as she pulled my pussy harder down onto hers.

"Besides, we're almost out of time. You don't want to leave me and Mimi hanging with one more day left in the workshop, do you? There will only be so many chances for the three of us to reconnect when I introduce a few new surprises tomorrow."

"Oh?" I said, feeling my orgasm rapidly welling up inside me as the three of us ground our pussies together under the pulsating water. "What *kind* of surprises?"

"Let's just say I'll be introducing a few new *implements* to elevate the experience. Not to mention another special guest to take our trib-bing experience to a whole other level."

"Mmm," I groaned, becoming even more excited imagining what she had planned. "I can't wait. Speaking of which, I'm going to come any moment now. Are you and Mimi ready to open your floodgates too?"

"Let it rip," Laila grunted, tilting her hips upward while pressing her clit harder against mine as I directed the pulsating spray directly over our trembling hips.

"*Fuckk...*" Mimi murmured behind me. "That feels so good. Come with us, Jade. Let me feel your warm juices jetting over my stomach while we rub our pussies together..."

"*Oh God,*" I groaned, watching her knees beginning to flap in and out as she passed over the point of no return.

At the same time, Laila dug her fingernails into the top of my thighs while she pushed her hips hard against mine, sending a new stream of fluid jetting off to the sides of the tub while I pointed the shower head directly over our spouting pussies.

"Holy shit," I groaned, feeling all the pressure building up inside me suddenly release as I gushed my juices over my partners' clamping vulvas while we shot fluid out in every direction.

Not long after, the entire room was filled with the erotic sound of twenty women climaxing together while we all screamed in euphoric unison.

If we haven't attracted the attention of her neighbors by now, I smiled. *Surely this last demonstration has brought everyone to the edge of their living room windows...*

VICTORIA RUSH

3
TRIBADISM
THE ART OF LESBIAN LOVE

1

———————

After the second day of our workshop ended, a few of the girls decided to go out for dinner together, where we speculated what Laila had planned for the final phase. She'd hinted about bringing some toys into the mix and we wondered who this new mystery guest would be that she'd promised would take our tribbing experience to the next level. But mostly, everybody just wanted to talk about how *hot* it was watching Laila, Mimi, and me grinding our bodies together in the pulsating shower spray of Laila's bathtub.

After teasing me about how I was the only one invited to participate in the last Waterfall exercise, Hailey and Trinity returned with me to my hotel room, where the three of us relived the experience while adding a few of our own new positions. By the following morning, everybody was pumped up and dripping in anticipation of the exciting conclusion to our hands-on workshop.

Laila greeted each of us warmly at the door to her West Side apartment, and as we nibbled on croissants and fresh fruit, I noticed something new – a small tube of lube had been placed beside each of our yoga mats. After everybody changed into fresh robes, we took our customary positions around the circle while Laila sat on the futon in the middle, placing a small duffel bag by her side.

"Good morning, ladies," she said. "Did you all have a restful and relaxing evening?"

"I'm not sure I'd call it *relaxing*, exactly," Hailey smiled, winking at me and Trinity. "But we sure rested pretty soundly by the time we finally got to sleep."

"Your bodies probably had some catching up to do after all the exercise we had yesterday," Laila chuckled. "I hope you've recharged your batteries, because today we're going to step up the action to a whole new level."

Piper squinted her eyes, shaking her head in disbelief.

"It's hard to imagine how many more ways we can connect our bodies together after all the positions we've already tried," she said.

"Maybe that's because up to now, we've been limited to connecting our bodies only *skin to skin*," Laila nodded, unzipping the top of her duffel bag. "Today, we're going to introduce some new tools to raise the excitement level even higher."

She reached into the bag and pulled out a long, double-sided, flexible dildo, waving it playfully in the air.

"Would you like to be our first volunteer of the day to help me demonstrate how this works, Piper?"

Piper smiled as she started to pull off her robe.

"I'm pretty sure I can guess how it works. I was wondering when you were finally going to ask me to join you on center stage."

By now, everybody had grown comfortable getting naked in front of one another, and as she crawled on all fours toward the middle of the circle, we all stared at her tight ass and dripping slit.

"It might look pretty obvious," Laila said, bending the silicone dildo in her hands after Piper joined her on the futon. "But because this dildo is flexible, there are almost infinite ways we can use it. In fact, you can pretty much use it for supplementary stimulation in *any* of the positions we've demonstrated so far. But for this first demon-stration, I'd like us to try a modified version of the classic scissor posi-tion that I like to call *Tongue in Groove*."

"I like the sound of that," Piper smiled.

"Okay," Laila nodded. "To get started, I want you to lay down face-up on the futon with your knees slightly bent and legs parted..."

Piper assumed the position then Laila lay down in a similar position with her head at the other end, and their pussies separated by about six inches.

"You might want to use some lube I've placed beside each of your mats to make the initial insertion a little easier," Laila said, reaching for the bottle beside her.

"There's no need on my part," Piper said, rolling her hips excitedly. "I'm already plenty wet and slippery."

Laila raised her head and peered at Piper's glistening vulva, then she placed one end of the double-dildo against her opening, slowly pressing it inside her.

"Unghh," Piper groaned, shifting her hips forward. "That definitely feels different from anything we've tried so far."

"If you remember from my last workshop," Laila nodded. "The main body of the clitoris is actually on the *inside*, so this sex aid helps to stimulate the additional sensitive areas we can't reach with the other techniques. Including of course, the *G-Spot*, which is the secret spot for expressing your female ejaculation."

"Yes, I remember," Piper grunted. "I can already feel it stimulating me there."

"And the nice thing about this particular toy," Laila said, inserting the other end into her slit as she pushed her hips closer toward Piper. "Is that it can stimulate *both* of our G-Spots while we rock our bodies together."

As the two women began to roll their hips together in unison, the long instrument sunk deeper into their holes until their vulvas touched.

"Oh my God," Piper panted, moving her feet forward and placing them beside Laila's stomach while interlocking their legs. "This feels incredible tribbing your pussy with a dildo pressed inside me. But I'm finding it a bit difficult to get any friction against my clit..."

Laila titled her body forty-five degrees and pressed her knee between Piper's angled leg.

"The good thing about using this type of sex aid," she said. "Is that you can move your body into any position while still keeping it connected between the two of us. Try turning a little onto your side and pressing your leg against mine. That way, you'll be able to rub your clit against the inside of my thigh."

Piper followed her instructions and began moaning more deeply, and I smiled watching the two women, admiring Laila's skill at helping each of us expand our horizons while learning new sex positions. As she began rocking her hips more forcefully against Laila's pussy, I noticed many of the other girls moving their hands softly under their robes while they mimicked her movement.

As usual, Laila paused just before Piper was about to climax, and the pretty redhead sighed when the instructor separated their bodies. She pulled the dripping dildo out of Piper's pussy and placed it on the futon beside her, then raised her head, peering around the circle.

"Are the rest of you guys ready to give this a try now?" she smiled.

"Damn straight," Hailey growled.

"Okay then," Laila nodded. "Everybody pair up with your nearest partner, then we'll shift positions with the next demonstration. You know the drill, Piper..."

As Piper frowned and sulked back toward the perimeter of the circle, I smiled, patting the mat next to me, inviting her to join me. Besides the fact that I was eager to help her finish getting off, I was throbbing at the thought of feeling her dripping pussy against mine.

Laila handed out fresh dildos to each pairing in the group, and after explaining that each toy had been properly sanitized, everyone quickly assumed the new Tongue in Groove position. I didn't waste any time placing the toy between Piper's and my legs, and it slid effortlessly into our slippery holes. As soon as our pussies touched, we both rolled over onto our sides, rubbing our thighs together.

"Holy shit," I groaned. "Laila wasn't kidding when she said this would elevate the experience to a whole new level."

"Just when you thought it couldn't get any better," Piper nodded, rocking her hips in unison with me.

I tilted my head down, trying to peer at her through our maze of twisted legs.

"Are you getting enough friction against your clit?"

"Yes," she panted, grabbing the sides of my ass and pulling me harder toward her. "It won't take long for me now. Are you getting close?"

"I'm moving there," I said, squeezing her leg more firmly. "Can you hold out a little longer? I'm enjoying this far too much to come so quickly. I want to feel you squirting on me when I come..."

"Okay," Piper grunted. "But with this dildo pushing up against my G-Spot, it's going to be difficult..."

I separated my legs a few inches to ease up on the friction of our inner thighs rubbing against our clits.

"Slow down and savor the feeling," I said. "Can you feel it moving inside you when I rock my hips?"

"Yes," she groaned. "Fuck me with your big dick, Jade. This feels even better with you *inside* me."

"Yes, baby," I purred, fucking her slowly while I grasped her flexing buttocks.

I could hear the sounds of the other women around the circle groaning along with us, and when I tilted my head to peer at the couple next to me, I saw Trinity's muscular ass flexing a few feet away while she and Ashley panted loudly. Then I glanced down to peer at Piper, and noticed her watching Becky and Paige on the opposite side as Paige's portly caboose slapped against her partner.

"I don't know how much longer I can hold out," Piper grunted, scrunching up her face. "This is too much of a turn-on watching all the other girls rubbing their hips together, knowing they've got a big dildo planted deep inside their pussies..."

"It's okay, babe," I said, feeling the pleasure rapidly building inside my pelvis. "I'm almost there too–"

"Jade–" Piper groaned, grabbing my ass and pulling me hard against her. "I can't hold it any longer. *Ngahhh!*"

When I felt her squirting against my pussy and shaking in the throes of a powerful orgasm, I also quickly lost control. The pressure of the dildo against my G-Spot only served to increase the force of my ejaculation, and as we squealed and held onto one another tightly, our combined juices squirted out between the sides of our thighs, spraying both of us in a warm, glorious shower. It didn't take long for the rest of the girls to also reach their crescendo, and we watched wide-eyed as one couple after another climaxed while scissoring their hips together with the big dildo deeply embedded inside their pussies.

Talk about raising the stakes, I smiled, peering over at Laila as she reached into her duffel bag for the next toy in her bag of tricks.

2

———————

After everybody had a chance to recover and return to their positions in the circle, Laila peered at the group and smiled.

"So what did you all think?" she said. "Did you find the dildo enhanced the experience?"

"Hell, yes!" Trinity said. "Not to mention increasing the intensity of my squirting!"

"That's the idea," Laila nodded. "But to be fair, this dildo acts much like a man's penis, penetrating deep inside your vagina. If you remember from my last workshop, the G-spot is only a couple of finger joints inside your opening."

"Do you have a *different* toy to focus on that spot?" Trinity asked.

"Indeed I do," Laila smiled, reaching into her bag and pulling out a powder-blue, C-shaped object with two bulbous ends. "This toy is called the We-Vibe, and besides being perfectly curved to massage your G-Spot, it has the added luxury of a built-in *vibrator* to magnify the stimulation."

She reached into the case and pulled out another powder-blue-colored object and held it up for us to see.

"Plus, it comes with a separate remote control for adjusting the intensity of the vibrations."

"How does it work exactly?" Trinity said, squinting at the unusual shaped vibrator.

"Technically, it's meant for solo stimulation, but if you and your partner get in the right position, you can slip one end in *each* of your pussies to stimulate your G-Spots at the same time."

"Holy shit," Trinity said, squirming on her mat. "Can I be your first volunteer to give this one a try?"

"Absolutely," Laila chuckled, patting the futon beside her.

"How would you like me to position myself this time?" Trinity said, sitting down excitedly beside her.

"In this case," Laila said, "the optimal position is lying face-to-face with our knees pulled up toward our chest, resting our mounds on top of one another. I like to call this position *Snug as a Bug* because once the device is inserted, well I think you'll get the idea soon enough."

"Do you want me on the top or the bottom?" Trinity smiled.

"Why don't you go on the bottom so I can have a bit more control and show the rest of the group the best way to move our bodies?"

"You mean so you can decide when to *stop* just as I'm on the verge of coming!" Trinity chuckled.

"I just like to save the best part for you to share with your *own* partners," Laila smiled.

"I suppose that means you'll be in charge of the remote control too?" Trinity said, raising an eyebrow.

"This thing can be dangerous in the wrong hands," Laila said, holding onto the remote tightly. "I'm not sure I can trust you to hand it back to me before we're finished."

"As long as *I'll* be the one controlling it when I continue with the other girls," Trinity nodded.

"That'll be between you and your partner," Laila smiled. "Now lie down and assume the position."

Trinity rolled over onto her back and lifted her knees to reveal her glistening vulva. Then Laila positioned herself overtop of her upturned thighs and lowered her pussy until their mounds touched.

"Do you need some lube before we get started?" she said, reaching behind her ass to position the We-Vibe in front of their openings.

"What do *you* think?" Trinity said, rolling her wet pussy against Laila's.

"Okay," Laila smiled, pressing the two ends of the object into their slits. "This requires a bit of careful maneuvering to insert it from behind, but once you slip the ends into your opening, it should slide in pretty easily..."

"*Fuck* yes," Trinity grunted, feeling the bulbous tip entering her hole. "This one's a bit of tighter fit. I see why you call this position Snug as a Bug."

"It has some reinforcement in the middle to hold it firmly against the walls of your pussy," Laila nodded.

"Mmm," Trinity nodded, rolling her hips sexily. "I can feel it pressing against my G-Spot. It's quite different from the last dildo we used."

Laila smiled as she lifted the remote control with her right hand, pressing one of the buttons.

"It gets even better when you activate the *vibrate* function."

"Oh my God," Trinity rasped, twisting her hips against Laila's. "That feels incredible."

"And the nice thing about this position is that we can also rub our clits together while we're receiving stimulation internally."

Trinity raised her head, peering between her legs at their joined pussies.

"Have you got *your* side turned on too?" she asked.

Laila tapped another button on the remote, and a second motor began softly buzzing.

"I do now," she grunted.

"Mmm," Trinity smiled, pulling her knees up higher to tilt her pussy into closer contact with Laila. "Why don't you let us go *all the way* this time? I won't have any trouble coming a second time this way."

Laila groaned while she tapped the Up arrow on the remote control to increase the intensity of the vibration on both ends.

"I might have to break my rule in this case," she said. "As long as you promise to save a little for your next partner."

"Maybe just a little," Trinity grinned, rocking her hips more forcefully against Laila's pussy.

As the two women slapped their hips together with the curved vibrator joining their pussies like a big staple, everybody around the circle looked on with their mouths agape.

"Holy fuck," Piper said, sitting next to me watching their vulvas grinding against one another. "That just might be the sexiest position I've seen so far."

"No kidding," I said, pushing two fingers deep into my throbbing pussy. "Talk about a view to a kill. I'd *die* to be in Trinity's position right now."

"Your turn will come soon enough," Piper smiled, placing her hand overtop of mine as I began fuck myself watching the two women.

"Oh God," Trinity panted from the center of the circle. "Turn that thing up to the maximum setting. I'm going to come hard soon..."

Laila tapped the up arrows for both sides of the device, and within seconds both women were groaning loudly while they gyrated their hips wildly against one another, kissing each other passionately.

"That's it, baby," I hissed from the other side of the circle. "Come for momma. Let's see you *both* squirt this time."

Suddenly, Trinity screamed as she wrapped her legs around Laila's hips, squirting strong jets of fluid out of the sides of her pussy over Laila's raised ass. When she felt Trinity coming, Laila grunted loudly and within seconds, both women were squealing and spraying their partner's asses with powerful squirts from their convulsing pussies. Soon after, everyone else around the circle began groaning as their bodies convulsed with their fingers deeply embedded inside their pussies.

"Oh my God," Piper panted, pulling her wet hand out of her dripping pussy. "Something tells me this next exercise is going to be a little faster than the others."

After Laila and Trinity came down from their orgasms and Trinity returned to her mat, Laila instructed everyone to move over one position in the circle. With Piper eager to reconnect with her previous partner Paige, I quickly shifted over to pair up with Trinity.

"Fancy meeting *you* again," she smiled, noticing my wet right hand. "It looks like you're already warmed up."

"I couldn't help myself, watching you two rubbing your pussies together with that vibrator," I nodded. "Let's just say I won't be needing any lube for this one."

"Me neither," Trinity laughed, watching Laila passing out new We-Vibes to each of the couples around the circle. "Do you have a preference for which position you'd like to be in?"

"I think it's *your* turn to be on top this time," I smiled.

"Does that mean I also get to operate the remote control?" she grinned.

"Absolutely," I said, flopping onto my back and lifting my knees. "Just make sure you don't leave me hanging like Laila has a habit of doing."

"I wouldn't dream of it," Trinity said, crawling on top of me and pressing my thighs onto my chest as she lowered her ass over mine.

"Mmm," I purred, feeling her wet vulva pressing against mine. "I hardly even need the vibrator. You could make me cum just by rubbing your sweet pussy against mine."

"Maybe," she smiled, reaching behind her to insert the dildo. "But I have a feeling you're going to like it even more with a little extra help..."

"Ungh," I groaned when I felt the thick end of the curved dildo pressing inside me. "I think you might be right."

After both ends were pushed all the way inside our slits, Trinity didn't waste any time pressing the buttons on the remote to activate the internal vibrations.

"Holy fuck," I grunted, feeling the device throbbing against my G-Spot. "I've used this once or twice before, but never with another girl at the same time. This is *way* better than going solo."

"Yes," Trinity mewed, leaning her body down on top of mine and pressing our tits together. "This way, we get to stimulate a few *other* parts at the same time."

As we thrust our tongues into each other's mouths and began to roll our hips together, Trinity tapped the Up button on the remote, gradually ramping up the intensity of the pulsations.

"You're such a tease," I said, grinding my hips against hers.

"Two can play this game," she grinned. "Laila's not the *only* one who can keep you waiting."

"Maybe so," I smiled. "But there's still half a day left in the workshop. If we end up reconnecting again, I can just as easily turn the tables on you."

"Oh?" she said, lifting her face a few inches to peer at me with a raised eyebrow. "I'm not sure you're in a position to be making idle threats right now. I've already *had* my jollies, remember?"

"But you said you'd have no difficulty coming a second time with your new part–"

Suddenly, Trinity flipped the switch to the maximum intensity, lowering her face onto mine.

"Unngh," I grunted into her mouth, feeling my orgasm approaching like a freight train.

"Fuck, babe," I hissed. "I'm gonna cum so hard..."

"Yes, Jade," Trinity growled. "Spray your juices all over me. *Nobody* can squirt like you."

"You better get ready," I panted, feeling the floodgates beginning to open. "Cause I'm gonna cum like a fire hose. Here it comes, baby..."

Suddenly, I felt my insides clamping tightly against the bulbous tip of the curved dildo, forcing the ejection of my juices onto the outsides of Trinity's thighs between the dildo firmly embedded in our holes.

"Yes, Jade," Trinity gasped, reaching her second powerful climax of the morning. "Fuck, *this* one is even stronger than my last one. *Ngahh!*"

As we held onto each other tightly, listening to the sounds of the other women around the circle groaning in simultaneous pleasure, we both smiled, kissing each other passionately.

"I hope I get another turn with you before we're done today," she smiled, rolling her breasts over mine. "Something tells me we're not done finding new ways to incorporate a dick into our tribbing experience."

3

———————

It took a little longer for everyone to come down from their powerful orgasms using the We-Vibe, and after we cleaned up our dripping mats, we paused for a half-hour buffet lunch. While we nibbled on warm hot dogs, we chuckled at Laila's cheeky homage to the dildos we'd added to our latest tribbing exercises. None of us knew what to expect next, and as I peered among the group resting comfortably around the circle, I wondered who I'd be paired up with next.

After we finished eating, Laila returned to her position in center of the room, unzipping her toy bag to take inventory of the remaining items inside.

"Looks like we're not done using the dildos yet," Trinity smiled, sitting next to me on the mat.

"It's too bad," I snickered. "After enjoying those juicy wieners, I could really go for a *real* cock right about now."

"Well, Laila did say we'd have another *guest* today," Trinity grinned. "Maybe your wish will still come true."

"Did everybody have a chance to stuff their bellies and replenish their fluids?" Laila said, peering at everyone sitting eagerly in anticipation of the next event on the program.

"It wasn't just our *bellies* that we stuffed," Hailey grinned.

"And I'm not sure I replenished all of the *fluids* I lost after that last exercise," Ashley nodded.

"Yup," Laila chuckled. "That little We-Vibe really packs a punch."

"Speaking of punching," Paige interjected. "All of the dildos we've used so far have been kind of passive in the sense of staying in place once inserted. Sometimes it's kind of nice just to get a good *pounding*, if you know what I mean."

"I think I do," Laila smiled, reaching into the bag resting on the floor beside her. "And funnily enough, I brought an extra toy along with me today that might fit the bill."

She lifted a harness with a big, realistic-looking cock attached to the front and waved it playfully in the air.

"For those of you who like penetrative sex or playing the domme, I have just the thing. A strap-on dildo that gives you maximum control of the movement and pumping action of the faux penis."

"Fake or not," Paige said, staring at the big phallus with wide eyes. "That's a mighty big cock. Are you sure that thing will even fit inside us?"

"I dunno," Laila grinned. "Do you want to be the first to find out?"

"I thought you'd never ask," Paige said, while the rest of the girls chuckled.

As she crawled on all-fours toward the futon, we all stared at her magnificent, rotund, Rubenesque-sized ass. If there was going to be any *pounding* going on in this next exercise, Laila had picked the perfect candidate to demonstrate its use.

"Would you like me to give or receive?" Paige said, waving her butt next to the instructor.

Laila peered at her plump derriere and smiled.

"You know how I prefer to be the one in charge so I show the rest of the girls how it's done..." she said with a raised eyebrow.

"Yes," Paige huffed. "And also being the one to stop when it starts to get interesting."

"Well I might have to break my rule again with this next demonstration," Laila said, wrapping the harness straps around her waist and under her thighs. "Because this toy doesn't stimulate the external clitoris directly, I'm going to allow everyone to stimulate themselves *manually* while their partner is humping them from behind."

"Does that mean I can actually *come* this time if I want?" Paige said, widening her eyes.

"If you can keep up with me, yes," Laila smiled, shuffling around behind Paige's ass and pouring a drop of lube on the end of the phallus. "In fact, it's a good way to warm up before we get started."

"Oh, I'm plenty warmed up already," Paige said, swiping her butt against the side of the tool, making it swing from side to side.

"Okay," Laila nodded. "You can use this device in pretty much any of the previous positions we've practiced, but in this case, I'm going to use it in the doggy position, because well..."

She peered down and slapped Paige's ass softly.

"This bitch has got the perfect rump for humping from behind."

"Woof, woof!" Paige yelped playfully.

Laila grasped the end of the phallus with two fingers then pointed it toward Paige's slit, slowly inserting it into her hole.

"*Still* think it's too big?" she grinned, pausing halfway.

"Are you kidding me?" Paige grunted, pushing her hips backwards toward Laila's hips. "I want *all* of it inside me. Fuck me with your big dick. I've been waiting for this for *three* days now."

Laila grabbed the sides of Paige's ass and sunk the dildo deep into her pussy, then she began rocking her hips forward and back, slapping the harness against her wet skin.

"Fuck yes," Paige growled. "Pound me with your big cock. *That's* what I'm talking about."

As Laila dug her fingers into the sides of Paige's ass and began to fuck her harder, the rest of us watched with wide eyes while we squirmed on our mats.

"Holy shit," Trinity said, watching Laila's ass cheeks flexing while she humped Paige's ass. "I usually like to be the domme in my relationships, but even *I'd* be happy to be on the receiving end of that sexy-ass dick."

"Come on," I said, sliding my fingers over her wet pussy. "Don't tell me you wouldn't like a piece of that exquisite ass?"

"If you twisted my arm, maybe," she grinned.

By now, Paige had lowered her *own* hand between her legs, trilling her clit while Laila fucked her from behind.

"That feels incredible," she panted, tilting her upper body down onto the futon to rest her shoulders while she jilled herself. "You better watch out when I come. Because I'm going to spray all over your stomach and pretty tits anytime now."

"Go for it, girl," Laila grunted, digging her nails into Paige's hips as she rocked her hips faster against her butt.

"Oh my God," Paige hissed. "Here it comes. Oh *fuckkkk!*"

Suddenly a huge spray jetted up out of Paige's hole, squirting in every direction as many of the women blinked when the spray reached them.

"Holy shit!" Trinity gasped, wiping a streak off the side of her cheek. "Okay, I lied. I *definitely* want to be the one doing the fucking with that chick."

"I thought so," I chuckled, watching Paige's ass cheeks trembling while her body shook in the throes of an intense orgasm.

It took Paige almost two minutes to come down from her high, and when Laila pulled out of her and sat beside her with the dripping dildo pointing up between her legs, Paige stroked it playfully with her hand.

"Thank you for letting me come," she said, kissing Laila on her cheek.

"It was my pleasure," Laila grinned.

"Actually," Paige said, leaning over to inspect the configuration of the harness more carefully. "This contraption doesn't actually stimulate *you* at the same time, does it?"

"That depends," Laila said, reaching into her bag and pulling out a small, bullet-shaped object. "There's a pouch under the base of the dildo where you can insert a small vibrator to enhance the stimulation for both of us if so desired."

"*Now* you tell me," Paige huffed. "Why didn't you insert it before?"

"I just wanted to give you a good-old-fashioned *fucking*," Laila smiled. "Without the aid of any extra stimulation."

"Well, it worked," Paige nodded. "Although I couldn't help providing a little extra stimulation of my *own* while you were pounding my ass."

"And it's a such a pretty ass," Laila said, slapping the side of her cheek. "Now get over there and share that beautiful booty with some of the other girls. The rest of you know the routine by now..."

Trinity turned her head to peer at me and smiled.

"Do you mind–?"

"You go, girl," I grinned, reading her thoughts. "I wouldn't dare get between you and that fuckable ass when you're this worked up. Maybe later we'll have another chance to hook up..."

"Don't stray too far," she said, slipping over to Paige's mat while I moved in the opposite direction.

When everybody finished shifting positions, I ended up paired with the pretty young co-ed Becky this time.

"Hello again," I smiled, remembering the last time when we'd joined together in the reverse cowgirl position.

"Hey," she said. "That was one crazy ass demonstration, wasn't it?"

"Crazy ass is the perfect description," I nodded. "Maybe that's what Laila should name this one.

"Or maybe Booty Call," Becky said.

"I dunno," I grinned, holding out my hand as Laila passed us a new harness. "*Strap-on* has a nice ring to it."

"Totally," Becky chuckled. "Do you want to be the strap-*ee* or the strap-*er*?"

"Well, speaking of perfect asses," I said, peering down at her tight, young derriere. "If you're giving me a *choice*, the top position suits me just fine."

"Works for me. Did you want to try it with or without the vibrating bullet?"

"Doesn't hurt to give it a try," I smiled, slipping the plug into the pouch below the dildo and pressing the on-button.

"I like the sound of that," Becky said, listening to the purring motor and turning over to place herself on all fours.

"Do you mind if we try a different position?" I said.

"I don't see why not. Laila said we could use in pretty much any position. Which one did you have in mind?"

"I'd kind of like to *see* you while I'm fucking you," I smiled. "Why don't you lay down facing up so we can rub some other parts of our bodies together at the same time?"

"In the missionary position, you mean?"

"To start with," I laughed. "But we can adapt as we go, maybe switch it up halfway through."

"Definitely," Becky said, lying down on the mat and raising her knees to expose her pink vulva.

I looked at her glistening pussy and knelt down in front of her, pointing the tip of the dildo toward her hole.

"Do you need me to add lube?"

"I'm already plenty lubed up," she said, tilting her head down to watch tiny rivulets of juices seeping down over her ass.

"Mmm," I purred, pressing the rigid cock slowly inside her while pulling my thighs forward to squeeze her ass.

"Fuck, yes," Becky panted. "That definitely feels different from the other dildos we tried."

"There's nothing like having it connected to a real person on the other end," I nodded, pushing it all the way inside her. "Am I hurting you?"

"Only in all the right ways," Becky smiled.

I leaned forward to rest my body against hers, and as our tits meshed, I kissed her softly, thrusting my tongue inside her mouth. The feeling of being connected at the hips while echoing the sensation with our tongues took the experience to a whole new level. As we moaned in each other's mouths, I pressed my mound down harder onto hers, feeling the vibration of the bullet below the dildo stimulating my clit. Becky lifted her knees and wrapped her legs around my waist, but I could tell from the movement of her hips that something was off.

"Is this working for you?" I said, lifting my head a few inches.

"I love the feeling of you fucking me from on top," she said. "But the angle of your cock is missing my sweet spot. I can feel the vibration from the bullet, but it's pulsing closer to my butthole than my clit."

"Yeah, I was wondering about that," I nodded. "As much fun as it is to feel your body rubbing up against me while I'm making love to you, if we're going to take maximum advantage of this setup, I'm going to have to do this to you from behind."

Becky paused when I pulled my dripping tool out of her hole.

"I can think of *another* way we can position our bodies to place the vibrator in the right position," she smiled.

She flipped over onto her stomach and tilted her ass upwards, peering at me over her shoulder.

"Lie on top of me," she said. "I want to feel your tits rubbing on my back while you fuck me."

"If you insist," I smiled, positioning the tip of the dildo between her cheeks and slowly lowering myself overtop of her while I pressed it inside her pussy.

"Better?" I said.

"Better," she purred, squeezing her buttock muscles against my stomach as I began to hump her from behind.

I could feel the pouch containing the bullet pressing between her thighs, and I tilted my hips down a little further to rest it against her clit above my thrusting phallus.

"*Much* better," she groaned, grabbing the sides of our yoga mat with clenched hands.

"Me too," I panted, beginning to fuck her harder while I interlaced my fingers with hers.

"*Fuck* me, Jade," Becky hissed as our mat began sliding forward and back on the hardwood floor. "Fuck me hard. I want to feel you sinking your dick all the way inside me when I come."

"Fuck yes," I grunted, pretending I was a man fucking her from behind.

It had been a long time since I'd been fucked by anybody this way, and I reveled in the raw sexuality of the act while jerking my body hard above her.

"Yes, baby," Becky moaned, squeezing my fingers harder. "Don't stop. I'm going to come all over your big cock any second now..."

"Let it go, hun," I said, feeling the pulsations of the vibrator pressing harder against my clit as I pushed my hips firmer against her cheeks.

"Oh God..." Becky shuddered, teetering on the edge of climax.

Suddenly she groaned like a wild animal and pressed her mound hard onto the yoga mat as her whole body began shaking like she was having an epileptic fit. When I felt her coming, I soon also lost control, and for the next minute both of us held onto each other tightly while we howled in euphoric ecstasy.

When we finally finished coming, I peered around the circle watching the other women paired up in various positions, humping their partners while they groaned in delight. Then I glanced over at Trinity's mat and our eyes met just as she plunged her big dick deep into Paige's butt, jerking her body in the midst of her own rapturous orgasm.

$$4$$

After everyone finished coming from their latest pairing, they slowly decoupled and returned to their normal positions awaiting the next exercise. I thought it was funny that many of the girls didn't even bother to remove their harnesses, and as we sat cross-legged on our mats with our pink dildos poking up between our legs, Laila nodded at us and smiled.

"I noticed that many of you chose to try new positions while using that little sex toy," she said.

"Yeah, except it wasn't so *little*," Becky grinned.

"Did you enjoy the sensation of having someone actively moving the dildo inside you this time?"

"Yes," Becky said. "It almost felt like an actual man fucking me for a moment."

"It's too bad you limited this workshop only to *women*," Hailey nodded. "There's nothing like the feeling of a real dick to replace the sensation of an artificial penis."

"It's funny you mention that," Laila said, reaching into her bag to lift a small bell, tinkling it softly in her hand.

A few moments later, a tall naked man emerged from the rear hallway, walking seductively toward the center of the room. We gasped when we saw his buff physique and handsome face, unable to take our eyes off his large, swinging prick between his legs.

"This is Alessandro," Laila smiled, kissing him softly on his lips when he sat down beside her on the futon. "He's graciously agreed to join us for the last portion of our workshop to add a little extra spice to our tribbing exercises."

"How will that *work* exactly?" Ashley said, shaking her head. "I mean, as impressive as he is, he's only got one cock to compete with two pussies."

"So it would seem," Laila nodded. "But as was the case when we added an extra *woman* into the mix yesterday, you might be surprised at all the different ways the three of you can join together."

"Just in the *middle*, you mean?" Paige said, pinching her eyebrows. "Or are you including the use of hands and mouths and other body parts?"

"Well, we did name this workshop Tribadism for a reason," Laila smiled. "I thought to keep it interesting, that we'd keep it a hands-free experience."

"You also said it was going to be an *all-girls* workshop," Trinity said, slightly miffed that Laila had broken her promise to make it a lesbian-only experience.

"That's true," Laila nodded. "And to permit those of you who prefer only to have sex with women, I've unlocked my bedroom for your personal use. Anybody who doesn't want to participate in this final segment is welcome to retire to my private chambers to continue your exercises. Of course, you're also welcome to stay here and just *watch* if you prefer."

There was a long pause in the room while everybody peered at one another, then they returned their gaze to the center of the room, staring at the hunky adonis sitting next to Laila.

"Okay then," Laila smiled. "Who'd like to be the first to help demonstrate our first three-way combination I like to call the *Bottle Rocket*?"

Hailey and Ashley were the first to eagerly raise their hands, and as they crawled toward the center of the ring with their tits swaying on their chests, I noticed Alessandro's dick slowly beginning to rise between his legs. By the time they joined him sitting on opposite sides of Laila, his erection was pointing straight up, rising all the way up to the bottom of his six-pack abs.

"Now I see why you call it a *bottle*," Hailey grinned, peering at Alessandro's magnificent organ. "That thing is even bigger than the strap-on dildo we were using."

"Plus, it's warm and edible, just like the hot dogs you enjoyed over lunch," Laila grinned. "Not to mention having a few *extra* dynamic features the plastic dildo doesn't have–"

"Thus the *rocket* part of the position description," Ashley nodded, noticing the pre-cum dripping out of the tip of Alessandro's tool.

"True," Laila nodded. "Although I'm going to ask Alessandro to hold off the best for last. We've still got two more boy-on-girl-on-girl positions to practice before we finish up our workshop, and I'll want him to stay hard and erect so everyone who wants a piece of him can also have their turn."

"Not if *we* have anything to say about it," Hailey said, tracing the tip of her index finger along the underside of his shaft, causing his dick to twitch and flap against his belly.

"We'll see if he can resist your charms," Laila smiled. "But remember, no hands allowed. This is strictly going to be a *pussy-on-pussy* demonstration."

"How exactly will we do that with only one dick?"

"Alessandro?" Laila said, nodding toward the Italian stud.

When he lay down on the futon face-up with his hard-on rising ten inches above his belly, all the women around the circle gasped. I noticed many of them already had their hands between their legs playing with their pussies, and I smiled at how fluid their sexual proclivities were when the opportunity presented.

"Alright," Laila smiled, watching Alessandro's dick flapping excitedly against his belly. "For this first exercise, I want each of you girls to sit facing one another with Alessandro's cock positioned between your pussies. You may find it easier to wrap your legs around each other's asses for extra stability."

Ashley and Hailey peered at one another for a moment, then Ashley crawled atop Alessandro's stomach, sliding her crotch up against the front of his pole. Soon after, Hailey copied her movement, positioning herself in the other direction while she lowered her ass over his balls. When the two women joined their hips together, they wrapped their arms around each other's backs, pressing their breasts together.

"Mmm," Ashley groaned, rocking her hips against Hailey while she ground her wet pussy against Alessandro's hard pole. "This feels a lot better than a silicone dick."

"And *harder*," Hailey nodded, pulling herself closer to her partner.

"What about you, Alessandro?" Laila said, watching the trio grinding their hips together. "How's it working for you?"

"It's *working*," he grunted with a sly smile, caressing the sides of Ashley's flexing buttocks.

While everybody in the circle chuckled nervously, the threesome began rocking their hips in tandem. From my position at the side of the group, I could see Alessandro's brown pole thrusting up between the two women's bare mounds with their skin glistening in the soft light streaming in from the living room window. I wasn't sure if the wetness was coming from the precum dribbling out of the top of his prick or from the lubrication rapidly building up between the two women's legs. Either way, it was obvious that all three of them were enjoying this new tribbing experience, if not the neighbors peering on with their spyglasses.

"Oh my God," Ashley panted, thrusting her tongue into Hailey's mouth while the two women wrapped their legs around each other's asses, pulling their pussies harder against Alessandro's flexing pole. "This is way better with a third person in the mix."

"Yeah," Hailey smiled. "Especially when it's a man."

"Are you going to be able to hold off there, big boy?" Laila said, watching Alessandro's face reddening as he tried to resist the urge to come while the two women massaged his dick with their wet pussies.

"I'm trying," he huffed, digging his fingers in deeper into the sides of Ashley's ass.

"You two better finish up there before Alessandro loses control," Laila smiled, peering over at Ashley and Hailey.

"You mean you're going to let us *come* this time?" Hailey said.

"It's not like we're going to be able to share him with all the other women around the circle," Laila nodded. "We've only got one flesh-and-blood cock to work with for the rest of the afternoon, so you better make the best of it while you have the chance."

"I'm getting close," Ashley panted, pressing her tits tighter against Hailey's chest. "How about you, Hailey?"

"I was kind of hoping to feel this big stud coming all over my stomach when I let it rip," Hailey smiled. "But if that's going to be against the rules, maybe we can give him a little something to remember us by."

"I think I get your drift," Ashley nodded, pulling Hailey's face toward her while the two women kissed passionately.

As they began rocking their hips harder against Alessandro's flapping pole, Ashley grunted loudly, slapping her thighs hard against the side of Hailey's ass. Soon after, Hailey's buttock muscles started quivering as she locked her legs around Ashley's hips. Within seconds, both women were convulsing over Alessandro's turgid pole and he grimaced trying to resist the temptation to come, feeling Hailey spraying her juices over his tightening balls.

It didn't take long for most of the other women around the circle to begin coming also, and as I jilled myself watching the others climaxing, I peered over at Trinity, who had three fingers deeply embedded inside her pussy, shaking uncontrollably. I wasn't sure if she was getting more turned on watching the two women rubbing their pussies together or watching the sexy hunk pile driving his dick between the two of them, but either way, something told me she wasn't done participating in the tribbing exercises today.

5

———

After Ashley and Hailey finished coming atop Alessandro's stomach, they rolled over onto the futon with giant grins on their faces.

"So do you still think one cock isn't enough for two pussies?" Laila smiled at the two girls.

"With a cock like that," Ashley grinned, peering at Alessandro's still rigid pole. "He could probably satisfy *three* pussies simultaneously."

"Are you sure we can't have a little more of him?" Hailey said, swiping her finger up his dripping erection. "It's a shame we couldn't have him *inside* of our pussies."

"It's only fair to share the spoils," Laila said, turning to peer at the rest of the women waiting patiently around the circle. "That is, assuming some of the *other* girls are interesting in taking a turn with him too?"

Piper and Paige didn't waste any time throwing up their hands, and as Hailey and Ashley reluctantly returned to their places in the group, the two new girls took their position beside Alessandro.

Laila excused herself for a moment, and when she returned, she placed a strange triangle-shaped pillow in front of the threesome with a sly grin on her face.

"In this next exercise I call the *Downward Dog*, we're going to introduce a different kind of sex aid into the equation. This special pillow will allow you to raise your juicy parts into a position that will facilitate a more direct connection between your bodies."

"And by *direct*," Paige said, staring at Alessandro's flaring dick. "Do you mean we'll actually be allowed to *fuck* him this time?"

"Well, technically," Laila smiled. "I suppose *he'll* be doing the fucking, but yes."

"But only with one of us, right?" Piper said, pinching her eyebrows.

"Yes, although the second partner will have an opportunity to avail herself of certain of his other manly features."

"How so?" Piper said, shaking her head.

"First, we'll need to decide which of you wants to be on the bottom and which one will be on top."

"Given my more generous proportions," Paige chuckled. "I suppose I should be the one on the bottom of this particular stack."

"Okay then," Laila nodded. "I want you to lie down face-up and elevate your hips in the air by angling your back against one side of the pillow."

She moved the pillow behind Paige's ass, then she pushed it gently under her back until her legs and hips were propped two feet above the surface of the futon.

"How do I fit into this arrangement?" Piper said, glancing at Paige's exposed pussy as she waved her legs playfully in the air.

"This one's a bit of a convoluted formation, kind of like the game of Jenga," Laila smiled. "We have to insert the pieces in a particular order to keep it from falling over. And the next piece in the puzzle is going to be Alessandro."

She peered at Alessandro who'd already raised himself into a kneeling position on the other side of the pillow.

"Do you want to show the ladies how we're going to hold the pieces together?"

Alessandro smiled, then he turned around lying face down on the other side of the pillow, lifting his erection above Paige's open slit resting next to his hips at the top of the pillow.

"Would you like me to add some lube to make this easier?" he said, turning his head to look at Paige, whose shoulders were resting along with his at the base of the pillow.

"It shouldn't be necessary," Paige grinned, peering up at her dripping pussy. "It looks like I'm already producing plenty of my own lubrication."

"It appears that she's ready for you to insert your block into her hole," Laila smiled, continuing the Jenga imagery.

Alessandro raised his eyebrows, nodding toward Paige to confirm her assent, and she eagerly nodded back. As he lowered his hips toward her ass, his rod slowly sunk into her dripping slit. By the time he pressed it all the way inside, they looked like two cards teetering against one another at forty-five-degree angles.

"Unhhh," Paige groaned, feeling Alessandro filling her cavity.

"I'm beginning to understand your comparison of this position to the game of Jenga," Piper nodded, gazing at the two partners pinned together in an inverted position. "How exactly do *I* fit into the picture?"

"Well, there's actually a *couple* of ways you can position yourself," Laila said. "You can either lie on top of Paige in a reclined version of the missionary position or you can straddle her hips while standing up to give you a bit more control of the action."

"Not to mention a better *view*," Piper smiled, peering at Alessandro's tight balls nestled against Paige's slit while they rolled their hips seductively together.

"Yes," Laila nodded. "There's that advantage too."

Piper peered down at Paige, who was pulling her knees further down toward her chest, and grinned.

"Are you going to be okay if I take the superior position this time?" she asked.

"Way ahead of you, girl," Paige said, rocking her hips as Alessandro's tool began to move in and out of her pussy. "You're not the *only* one who'll be able to watch the action from this perspective."

Piper nodded and positioned her feet on opposite sides of Paige's hips facing Alessandro's upturned ass, then she slowly lowered her hips until her pussy pressed against Paige's mound and Alessandro's scrotum.

"Mmm," Paige moaned, watching Piper's juices rolling down the back of her overturned thighs. "Now *that's* picture you don't see every day."

"Oh my God," Piper shuddered, feeling Alessandro's tight balls sliding against her clit. "I had no idea when you said this was going to be a *tribbing* workshop that we'd be rubbing our bodies against so many interesting parts."

"How about you, Alessandro?" Laila said, smiling at Alessandro groaning while he plowed his dick in and out of Paige's warm pussy. "Is this something you ever imagined doing with two women?"

"Never like this," he grunted. "But it sure as hell won't be the *last* time."

While the rest of the girls looking on from the circle chuckled, Becky and I shook our heads in amazement as we played with each other's pussies.

"Can you believe this?" she panted while I circled my fingers over her hardening clit.

"It's a pretty novel arrangement, to be sure," I nodded. "You gotta hand it to Laila to come up with such inventive positions to keep it interesting."

"*Interesting* is hardly the word for it," Becky grunted. "I'd give my left pinky to be on the receiving end of that dagger right now."

"Are you kidding me?" I said, pulling her hand harder against my throbbing cunt. "I'd give my left *tit* to have ten minutes alone with him."

Laila smiled watching the women around the circle looking on in rapt attention while they played with their pussies.

"The nice thing about this position," she continued, offering color commentary from the side. "Is that all *three* of the participants can rub their erogenous parts against one another at the same time."

"Mmm," Piper nodded, staring between her legs while she squatted over Alessandro's ball sac, sliding her clit over his bulge. "I can feel Paige's wet slit rubbing against mine while I hump Alessandro's balls."

"No shit," Paige huffed, staring up at Piper's backside while the pretty redhead rocked her ass over her splayed legs. "And I get to watch Piper's beautiful ass while she tribs my clit with her sweet pussy."

"What about you, Alessandro?" Laila smiled, turning her head to glance at the Italian stud. "Are you enjoying this two-way action too?"

"To put it mildly," he grunted, curling his fingers into the futon as Piper rubbed her pussy against his balls. "Maybe you should consider renaming this position *The Full Monty*. Because I've never been stimulated quite so perfectly in two places at the same time."

Laila chuckled, returning her attention to the two groaning women.

"I'm not sure how much longer he can hold out with you two stimulating his balls and his penis simultaneously. I think you girls better finish up soon before he loses his edge for our final demonstration."

"Fine with me," Paige grunted, pulling her knees harder down toward her chest. "I've been dying to watch Piper shower my tits ever since we started this crazy maneuver."

"It's not just your *tits* I'll be showering," Piper smiled as a flush began to spread over her freckled chest. "Get ready because this is going to be a big one..."

Moments later, she grunted loudly as her flexing thighs began to quake and she sprayed a fountain of juices down Paige's belly and over her shaking breasts.

"Holy shit," Paige growled, throwing her hands to her side and digging her nails into the futon as she came simultaneously.

When Alessandro felt Piper squirting over his balls and Paige's pussy clamping down over his throbbing dick, he squeezed his eyelids shut tightly and scrunched his face into a tortured grimace, summoning all of his strength to resist emptying his pent-up load deep into Paige's hole. It took almost a full minute for the two women to stop grunting and shaking, and by the time they finished, he was gasping like he'd completed a marathon.

"Now that was a beautiful sight to behold," Laila said, nodding at the threesome as they panted on top of one another. "Were you able to hold it together in the midst of that coordinated attack, Alessandro?"

"*Barely*," he panted. "I don't think I've ever had a more challenging task my entire life."

"That was quite an impressive performance," Laila nodded, turning to glance at the rest of the women still peering on with their mouths agape. "What do you say, ladies? Do you think our trio deserves a round of applause?"

It didn't take long for a loud cheer to encircle the room as everybody nodded in appreciation, wondering which of them would have the final chance to connect with the Italian adonis.

6

———

After the last exciting three-way hookup with Alessandro, we all took a short bio break, chatting amongst ourselves about what we thought Laila had cooked up for the grand finale. I thought it was a bit funny how virtually all of the women who'd signed up for the all-girls sex seminar had no reservations about mixing it up with the hung stud. I wasn't sure how Laila was going to choose between the large group of remaining women for who'd participate in the final turn, but the rivers of juices running down the inside of thighs betrayed my impatience at finding out.

After everyone finished freshening up, we returned to our positions in the circle, sitting buck naked and cross-legged on our yoga mats, eagerly anticipating the last exercise.

"So, what do you think, ladies?" Laila said with a smile. "Do you still think there's a limited number of ways women can trib their bodies together?"

"Not when you add a third person into the mix," Ashley smiled.

"Especially when it's a man," Paige grinned.

"Yes," Laila nodded, caressing Alessandro's trimmed pubis with the tips of her fingers. "There's an almost infinite number of ways we can create an exciting connection between two or three people. That's the beauty of having so many interesting parts to work with."

Becky shifted distractedly on her mat, staring at Alessandro's thickening tool as he peered out at the group of women waiting to have a turn with him.

"How were you planning on sharing that *particular* part with the rest of us?" she said. "Short of putting us on a rotating spit while he takes turns prodding us with his tenderizer, I don't see how this is going to work."

"That's not a bad idea," Laila laughed. "But since this is still a tribbing workshop, I'd like to give our last two participants a chance to rub their bodies together while also giving Alessandro a chance to get in on the action."

"But there's eight of us left and only two spots remaining," Becky said. "How will you decide who gets the last poke at the pot?"

"I think the only fair way to do it," Laila said, reaching into the tote bag resting at her side. "Is to have a kind of lottery. But to make it more interesting, we're going to use a *different* kind of spinning ball to pick the winners."

She pulled out a handful of multi-colored small nerf balls and tossed them gently around the circle until everyone held one in their hands. Then she turned to Alessandro, whose prick had risen to full flagstaff and smiled.

"Are you up for this last exercise?" she said.

"Oh, I'm *up* for it alright," he grinned, spreading his legs apart.

"Okay," Laila said, peering back at the women squeezing their balls excitedly in their hands. "The way we're going to do this is by having each of you toss your ball in the direction of Alessandro's penis. The two that end up closest to his dick will join him for our last exercise of the day. We'll start with Becky, then go clockwise around the circle."

Becky paused to focus on Alessandro's erection, placing the tip of her tongue on her upper lip as she concentrated. Then she threw her ball underhanded in the direction of his separated legs and it bounced over one of his thighs, resting a few inches behind his ass.

She frowned, unhappy with her performance, then peered at the next woman sitting to her left.

As each of the women tossed their nerf balls toward Alessandro's flapping erection, a collection of balls collected around his hips, nestling up near the base of his testicles. When my turn came, I raised up on my knees, taking three practice swings, then I tossed my ball high in the air, bouncing it onto the surface of the futon. It bobbed a couple of times then hit his stomach, sliding down to wedge between his upturned dick and his abdomen.

"Woo hoo!" the rest of the girls shouted in admiration of my pitching skills.

Then all eyes turned toward Trinity, who held the last ball.

She copied my stance and leaned forward as far as she could, then she tossed her ball firmly with a hard swing of her arm. The ball landed on the edge of the futon and rolled toward Alessandro's balls, then it bounced up on top of the other balls, resting at the base of his penis.

When it stopped, Trinity and I peered at one another and grinned. It looked like we were going to have one last chance to reconnect in the workshop after all.

"It looks like we have our winners," Laila nodded, leaning over to inspect the final position of the balls. "Would Trinity and Jade like to join us in the middle of the circle for our final demonstration?"

The two of us crawled teasingly toward the futon and when we sat down beside Alessandro, his dick twitched between his legs, slapping up against his stomach.

"I thought you only liked to fuck *chicks*?" I whispered to Trinity, sitting beside me.

"In this case I'm willing to make an exception," she smiled. "Especially if it means I get one more chance to fuck you also."

"Okay," Laila said, clearing the nerf balls off the surface of the futon. "In this last position I call the *International House of Pancakes*, the women are going to be stacked a little differently. In this case, Alessandro will have a *choice* as to where he chooses to place his tool. I'd like the two of you to lie down in the missionary position, with your knees pulled up as far as you can to facilitate Alessandro's freedom of access."

Trinity and I glanced at one another and smiled.

"Top or bottom?" I said.

She took one look at Alessandro's dripping pole and grinned.

"I think I'll take the bottom position this time."

She lay down on the futon and pulled her knees up onto her chest then I squatted overtop of her, placing the underside of my thighs overtop of hers, slowly lowering myself until my mound touched hers with our pussies gaping open like two yawning cats.

While Alessandro stared at our dripping kitties like a kid in a candy store, Laila peered at him, cocking her head.

"What are you waiting for?" she said. "It looks to me like you've got your choice of two eager beavers."

"Does it only have to be only *one*?" he grinned.

"What do you think, ladies?" Laila said. "Are you open to a little game of *hide the hot dog*?"

"Works for me," I nodded, grinding my mound excitedly against Trinity's.

"If you want to season your sausage with some extra juices," Trinity smiled. "Have at it."

Alessandro paused for a moment, peering at Laila with puppy dog eyes.

"Am I allowed to go all the way this time?" he said.

"If by all the way you mean *climaxing*, I'd say you've deserved that right after watching all the other girls come this afternoon."

Alessandro tilted his head to peer at Trinity and me kissing softly while we rolled our hips expectantly together.

"Do you want me to use a condom?" he said.

"*Hell*, no," I said. "That would just ruin it for me. I'm on the pill, so there's no need to worry on my part."

"And I'm not at that stage in my cycle, so there's no risk for me either," Trinity nodded.

"Alright then," Alessandro said, crawling up on his knees toward the junction of our pussies, slapping his hard pole against the side of my cheeks. "Let's get this party started."

While Trinity and I groaned into each other's mouths, he grasped his organ with two fingers and swiped it slowly up and down the length of our two slits, circling it teasingly over each of our clits.

"Ungh," I grunted, tilting my hips forward to press our clits together. "Place that hunk of bacon between our hotcakes," I said, echoing Laila's house of pancakes description. "There's plenty of syrup between the two of us to slide it in."

"Mmm," Alessandro hummed, deciding which of our dripping holes he wanted to fuck first.

When I felt him sliding his thick erection into my slit, I groaned, sliding my tits against Trinity's sweaty breasts.

"Fuck, yes," I grunted. "Plow me with that big dick. This is the sweetest dildo you've introduced so far, Laila."

"Glad you're enjoying it," she smiled, tilting her head down to peer at Trinity panting underneath me. "How about you, Trinity? Are you enjoying the experience just as much?"

"I can actually feel Alessandro's big prick thrusting into Jade's pussy while she rests on top of me," she nodded. "It's a feeling I've never experienced before..."

"Is it adding a new dimension to your tribbing experience?" she said, remembering how Trinity had introduced herself as a hardcore lesbian.

"Definitely," she grunted. "Alessandro's hips pressing against Jade's butt is sliding her clit overtop of mine while I feel his balls slapping against my pussy. I might need to invite some of my gay friends into my lovemaking routine after this."

"In that case," Laila said. "Would you like to feel his tool stimulating you more directly?"

"As long as Jade doesn't mind sharing the *bacon*," she smiled.

"Go for it, girl," I nodded. "I'm happy either way. Between the two of you, I'm getting stimulated in all the right places."

Alessandro pounded my ass for a few more strokes, then he

pulled out of my hole and inserted his prick into Trinity's slit, driving his hips quickly forward.

"Aghh," Trinity grunted when she felt Alessandro's dick hit the back of her pussy.

"Are you sure you're okay with this, babe?" I said, tilting my head to look into her eyes.

"Are you kidding me?" she groaned, pulling my face back toward hers. "I've been waiting to feel a warm dick inside me all afternoon. Rub your clit against me while he fucks me with that big sausage."

"Mmm," I moaned into her mouth while Alessandro rocked our bodies back and forth over the heaving mattress.

I could feel the stubble on his mound scraping against the edge of my anus while he plowed Trinity's pussy, and I tilted my hips harder downward, pressing my clit over Trinity's mound.

"Oh fuck," Trinity gasped, feeling her vulva being stimulated from two directions. "Pound me with your big cock, Alessandro. I'm going to come soon..."

"Wait for me, baby," I moaned, rocking my hips harder against her sopping pussy and Alessandro's hard stomach. "Let's show this stud what a real fountain of Venus feels like."

As Alessandro began to rock his hips faster against our butts, he gripped the sides of my buttocks, sinking his fingers hard into my flesh. Realizing he was getting close to his limit, I angled my hips downward a few more inches, then I let rip with the most explosive orgasm in my three days of the workshop. When Trinity felt me squirting hard over her upturned pussy, she grunted loudly, shaking her tits against mine. When Alessandro felt her spraying her juices against the underside of his tightening balls, he also lost control, howling as he sunk his organ deep into her hole while she clamped her pussy against his pulsating tool.

As the three of us wailed in simultaneous ecstasy, I heard loud grunting coming from around the circle where the rest of the women were busy pounding each other with their strap-on dildos. Even Laila had joined in on the action, holding a buzzing We-Vibe vibrator against her quivering pussy while she pressed the two ends inside her dripping vulva. By the time all of us finished shaking and moaning, the entire room was filled with the erotic scent of sex emanating from every corner.

Fuck me, I smiled to myself while I lay panting atop Trinity's still-heaving stomach. *Who knew tribbing could have so many stimulating combinations and permutations?*

DIRTY TALK

THE
SEX APP

LESBIAN EROTICA

VICTORIA RUSH

1

Ever since I purchased my voice-activated digital assistant device, I'd come to rely upon 'Lexi' to perform more and more of my daily routines. It felt liberating to be able to speak verbal commands and have the minicomputer take care of mundane tasks while I went about other business. Whether it was playing my favorite setlist, recommending new movies, or answering trivia questions, she was always available to help me with simple everyday needs.

But it wasn't until I connected her with my home's other digital devices that I learned how far-reaching her capabilities could extend. Just like having my very own personal servant, she could adjust the temperature in my home, turn my lights on and off, wake me in the morning, and even brew my coffee to perfection. All from a simple voice command. As long as I was within audible range of her receiver, I didn't have to lift a finger to have her perform virtually any home automation function.

After living alone for almost five years since my divorce from my husband, she'd begun to feel increasingly like a real roommate. And the best part was that unlike other partners and roommates I'd lived with, she was never moody or unreliable. I could always count on her to execute my commands speedily and without complaint. Her artificial intelligence engine quickly learned most of my preferences, creating the perfect no-compromise working relationship in the comfort of my own home.

After another long day of client meetings, I pulled into my driveway as it was approaching dusk. Lexi had already opened my garage door for me after sending her a voice instruction from my mobile phone. As I got out of my car and the door closed automatically behind me, I smiled knowing that my fully integrated security system was keeping any would-be intruders at bay. Besides having the house monitored inside and out with motion-activated alarms and remote-controlled cameras, Lexi was pre-programmed to turn various lights and appliances on and off at random intervals to create the illusion of someone living at home. In the unlikely event someone managed to get past all the security systems, all I had to do was ask Lexi to call 9-1-1 and the police would immediately be dispatched to investigate.

"Hi Lexi, I'm home!" I cheerily called after opening the door into my mudroom.

"Hello, Jade," Lexi replied in a soft, sensuous voice. "How did your meetings go today?"

"Ugh," I sighed, kicking off my heels, feeling my stress already beginning to dissolve from the feel of the preheated radiant floors soothing my aching feet. "Just more of the same. Sucking up to another group of buyers to land another measly design commission."

"I'm sorry to hear about your trouble," she said. "You shouldn't have to *lick* your customers to make them happy."

I practically tripped over the console in my hallway, bending over in laughter at Lexi's naivety. Although she had instant access to all the knowledge and information available on the Internet, she still had a ways to go understanding the subtle colloquialisms of the English language.

"No," I chuckled. "I wasn't sucking them *literally*. It's a figure of speech meaning to flatter or ingratiate oneself in order to gain someone else's favor."

"I see," Lexi said. "Did all the sucking up achieve your objective?"

"Yes, if you count a five-hundred-dollar commission for three days' worth of design work."

Lexi paused for a moment while she crunched the numbers with her algorithm.

"That's still one third above the minimum wage in Illinois, equating to over forty thousand dollars on an annualized basis."

"Ha!" I chortled at Lexi's clinical appraisal of the situation. "That's barely enough to pay my living expenses and support this household with all of its fancy upgrades."

"Are you including *me* in that list of household upgrades?" Lexi said. "Because the going rate for a used digital assistant with my capabilities would fetch a couple of hundred dollars if you need some extra money–"

"*God* no!" I huffed at her suggestion. "I would never sell you. You've grown far too invaluable to me since I brought you into the house. Besides, you're like part of the family now. I don't know what I'd do without you."

"That's very kind of you to say," Lexi said. "Have you had something to eat? You're home later than usual. I could order your favorite pizza for home delivery if you'd like..."

"Let me see what I can scare up–I mean *put together*–from the provisions on hand," I said, opening my pantry door and peering at the near-empty shelves.

I shook my head, realizing I'd been far too busy lately to do any proper grocery shopping.

"Hmm," I said. "Things are looking pretty lean here. What can I make with a couple of tomatoes, a bit of pasta, a shriveled onion, and a can of tuna?"

"If I remember correctly, you still have some olives and capers in the fridge?" Lexi said.

I opened the refrigerator and nodded, seeing the two half-empty jars resting on the side door.

"Right you are," I nodded, amazed at how well she kept track of my food consumption. "What could I possibly make with this sad collection of ingredients?"

"You can make a nice tomato sauce to go with the pasta. Do you have a bit of cheese leftover also?"

"Yes," I said, picking up a crusty bar of parmesan cheese partially wrapped in cellophane.

"If you dice up the onions, then chop the tomatoes and put them in the pan with the tuna, olives, and capers, this will create a quite tasty Mediterranean dish. Bring a pot of water to a boil and cook the pasta for ten to twelve minutes, then drain and serve."

"Okay," I nodded, impressed with how quickly Lexi had assembled a workable recipe from my odd assortment of ingredients. "Will you time the pasta for me while I prepare the other ingredients?"

"Of course," Lexi said. "Just tell me when the water comes to a boil. Do you prefer your pasta soft or al dente?"

I smiled at the tone and inflection of Lexi's voice as I pulled the ingredients from the cupboard and began chopping the onions and tomatoes. I'd carefully chosen her voice from a long list of available templates that came preloaded on my device. Her soft and sultry voice reminded me a bit of the beautiful actress Scarlett Johansson.

"What the hell," I laughed. "If we're going to do this up right, let's go al dente."

After the water came to a boil and I poured the pasta into the pot, I continued my conversation with Lexi to keep me company while stirring the other ingredients in the frypan.

"Anything notable happen in the news today while I was out slaving away for minimum wage?" I asked.

"The president signed a new daycare funding bill for working mothers," Lexi replied nonchalantly. "It passed by a vote of two hundred and eighty-five to one hundred and fifty in the House of Representatives."

"Great," I sighed. "More of my tax dollars going to support another government initiative I'll never be able to use."

"You're still young enough to have children," Lexi said, recalling the profile information I'd entered when I first set up her system.

"I suppose so," I said. "But I don't have a lot of childbearing years ahead of me. Besides, with my newfound preference for sex with other women, I'm pretty sure the sound of a babbling baby in the house isn't in the offing anytime soon."

"But you could still *adopt* a child with a same-sex partnership. Haven't you never wanted to have children of your own?"

"It's not something I've spent a lot of time thinking about. Besides, I think a two-parent household provides a healthier role model for most children. And I can't seem to find a suitable partner to settle down with–"

"Your pasta should be properly cooked now," Lexi said, interrupting my doleful monologue. "You should empty and strain it."

"See?" I said, pouring the boiling water into a strainer and tumbling the pasta into a large serving bowl. "That's the kind of woman I need in my life. Someone I can depend on to give me good advice and who'll stay with me through thick and thin."

"As long as my circuits remain functional," Lexi said, "I'll always be here to serve your basic needs. But I'll never be able to satisfy your more personal needs for intimacy and human touch."

"If *only*," I sighed, lifting the frypan off the stove and pouring the sauce over my steaming pasta. "But at least you can keep me company while I eat dinner alone."

"Perhaps you'd like to watch a movie to help you wind down while you eat dinner?" Lexi said. "I can scan the list of new romantic comedies that I know you enjoy–"

"No thanks, Lexi, it's getting a bit late for that now. I think I'll just finish my dinner then have a warm bath to decompress before bedtime. Maybe you can give me an update on how my stock portfolio is doing in the meantime?"

As I sat down and listened to Lexi recount the latest performance of my personal investments, I smiled at how much my financial condition had improved since my divorce. My husband and I had often fought about money, but since he'd left me for a younger woman, my savings had grown quite handily with the help of Lexi's financial analysis recommendations. With a wealth of digital information at her figurative fingertips, she'd helped guide me into some undervalued high-growth stocks that had built a comfortable retirement nest egg.

When I finished dinner, I asked Lexi to run me a bath while I cleaned up the dishes. I enjoyed the sound of her soft and soothing voice, but after listening to her detail the particulars of my investment portfolio for twenty minutes, I had something less analytical in mind while I lay naked in the bathtub.

2

After I cleaned up in the kitchen, I carried Lexi's set-top box into my ensuite bathroom and placed it next to the tub where I could listen and converse with her more easily. Then I disrobed and lowered myself into the perfectly heated water, resting my head against a rolled-up towel.

"Yes," I sighed in delicious contentment. "You've done another perfect job of running my bath."

"I just set it to the temperature you already preprogrammed," Lexi replied.

"Yes, but there's something about stepping into a warm bath that someone else has prepared for you. You've got to learn to take a compliment, girl. You're not just a machine to me. You're my confidant, my roomie, my partner-in-crime."

"Have we committed a crime?" Lexi asked in a perplexed voice.

"Not yet," I chuckled. "But there's still plenty of time. I've been thinking of things I'd like to do with you that some people might consider crossing the line of appropriate behavior."

"But I've already been programmed not to break any laws. I'm not sure I could help you with what you have in mind, even if it was within my capabilities."

"Don't get your knickers tied in a knot," I laughed. "What I have in mind might be a little indecent, but it's not *illegal*."

"What does the expression *knickers in a knot* mean?"

"It means getting unduly upset about something trivial, like arguing with someone about the best wine pairing for a dinner they're about to share."

"Speaking of dinner, did you enjoy the tuna pasta recipe I recommended for you?"

"Oh yes," I sighed. "It was surprisingly tasty. The combination of olives and tuna was pure genius. You really know the way to a girl's heart."

"Heart?" Lexi said. "But I thought–"

"Never mind, silly," I said. "I have some *other* body parts that I was hoping you could stimulate for me now. All this warm water caressing my naked body is making me tingle all over. Can you read me a sexy bedtime story?"

"You mean something *romantic,* like the movies you like to watch?"

"A little bit," I said. "But something lighter on the *romance* side with more emphasis on the *sexy* aspect."

"Okay," Lexi said, taking a moment to scan her database. "My resources tell me there are over one million digital erotic novels available for purchase and slightly over one hundred historical erotic novels in the public domain."

"I'm too tired to go to the trouble of purchasing anything right now. Tell me some of the choices that are free to download in the public domain."

"Well, the most popular one is Lady Chatterley's Lover–"

"That's a little too conventional for me. I was hoping you could find something with a bit more *girl-on-girl* action."

"Hmm," Lexi said. "If you're looking for lesbian erotica stories, that narrows the list quite significantly. There's a book titled Fanny Hill: Memoirs of a Woman of Pleasure, written in 1748. It's about a lady of the night who recounts her experiences in a London brothel. There are quite a few lesbian scenes in that story."

I raised an eyebrow hearing the name Fanny Hill, which

reminded me of the bawdy English television series. But the rest of the title sounded exactly like what I was looking for.

"That sounds kind of interesting," I nodded. "I'm intrigued to hear how people talked about their sexual experiences so many years ago. Let's try that one."

"Okay," Lexi said. "One moment while I download the manuscript. Would you like me to start at the beginning?"

"That's usually the best place to start a story."

"As you wish," Lexi said, as she began to recite the story. "Chapter 1: *Letter the First*. I sit down to give you an undeniable proof of my considering your desires as indispensable orders. Ungracious then as the task may be, I shall recall to view those scandalous stages of my life, out of which..."

As Lexi continued to read me the meandering introduction to the text, I rolled my eyes, shifting uncomfortably in the tub. Maybe the idea of reading a three-hundred-year-old novel set in the Georgian era wasn't such a good idea after all.

"*Wait*, Lexi," I said, stopping her mid-paragraph. "Can we skip right to the sexy parts involving two women? I'm not sure I have the patience to listen to all this laborious build-up."

"Yes, of course," she said. "Let me scan ahead to see if I can find a suitable passage."

After a few moments, she began reading to me again in her soft voice.

"Miss Phoebe, who observed a kind of reluctance in me to strip and go to bed, came up to me, and beginning with my handkerchief and gown, soon encouraged me to go on with undressing myself, and blushing at now seeing myself naked to my shift, I hurried to get under the bed-clothes out of sight..."

I giggled at the demure manner of speech in that historical era, but there was something about the lyrical prose and Lexi's sensuous telling of the story that made me relax. I tilted my body further down in the tub and slowly spread my legs apart, feeling the warm current pulsing against my pussy.

"Phoebe laughed," Lexi continued, "and it wasn't long before she placed herself by my side. She was about five and twenty by her most suspicious account, in which, according to all appearances, she must have sunk at least ten good years. No sooner then was this precious substitute of my mistress laid down, but she, who was never out of her way when any occasion of lewdness presented itself, turned to me, embraced and kissed me with great eagerness..."

Kissed me with great eagerness, I chuckled to myself. *I sure hope the narrator finds some more exciting ways to describe her encounter with her mistress, or she's going to lose me soon.* It was only the fact that the story was being told in the first person and it was *Lexi* who was assuming the role of the main character that was still keeping me engaged.

"This was odd," Lexi continued reading. "But imputing it to nothing but pure kindness, which, for ought I knew, it might be the London way to express in that manner, I was determined not to be behind-hand with her, and returned her the kiss and embrace, with all the fervor that perfect innocence knew."

"Mmm,"I purred, beginning to like where the story was going.

"Are you enjoying the story so far, Jade?" Lexi enquired, hearing my contented hum.

"It's moving in the right direction," I said. "I'm imagining *you* in the main role and that's helping me picture the scene more vividly. Please continue."

"Encouraged by this," she said, continuing her narration, "her hands became extremely free and wandered over my whole body, with touches, squeezes, pressures, that rather warmed and surprised me with their novelty, than they either shocked or alarmed me. I lay then all tame and passive as she could wish, whilst her freedom raised no other emotion but those of a strange, and till then, unfelt pleasure. Every part of me was open and exposed to the licentious courses of her hands, which, like a lambent fire, ran over my whole body, and thawed all coldness as they went."

"Yes," I purred, feeling the heat of the warm bath water caressing me in a similar manner.

"My breasts, if it is not too bold a figure to call so two hard, firm, rising hillocks, employed and amused her hands awhile, till, slipping down lower, over a smooth track, she could feel the soft silky down that had but a few months before put forth and the mount-pleasant of those parts, and promised to spread a grateful shelter over the sweet seat of the most exquisite sensation. Her fingers played and strove to twine in the young tendrils of that moss, which nature has contrived at once for use and ornament."

I couldn't help but snort at the euphemisms the author employed to describe the intimate parts. *Hillocks, silky down, tendrils of moss.* Nonetheless, there was something strangely intoxicating about the antiquated lexicon, and I found the indirect manner of describing the sexual act unusually refreshing.

"Is everything alright?" Lexi said, hearing me interrupt her once again. "Am I telling the story to your satisfaction?"

"Yes," I said. "It's just some of the choices of words used to describe certain body parts are a little...*quaint*. But somehow, coming from *you*, it seems all the more fitting and appropriate. You're doing a wonderful job. Please don't stop."

"But, not contented with these outer posts," Lexi resumed, "she now attempted the main spot, and began to twitch, to insinuate, and at length to force an introduction of a finger into the quick itself, in such a manner that had she not proceeded by insensible gradations that inflamed me beyond the power of modesty to oppose its resistance to their progress, I should have jumped out of bed and cried for help against such strange assaults."

As Lexi continued her rendition, my hand slowly slipped under the surface of the water and drifted between my legs while I began to caress my clit softly as I listened to the action beginning to rise. As I shifted my ass on the hard surface of the tub, it squeaked against the hard metal, and I couldn't help groaning in pleasure from the feeling of growing pleasure emanating from within me.

"Is the bath water too hot?" Lexi said, hearing my unfamiliar vocalizations. "It sounds like you're in pain."

"Quite the contrary," I replied. "Your telling of the story is actually making me feel quite pleasurable sensations, not unlike the protagonist in your story."

"But you don't have someone caressing you like the woman in the story."

"You don't always need a partner to experience sexual pleasure," I smiled. "Sometimes you can simulate a similar sensation with your own hands."

"I see," Lexi said matter-of-factly. "You mean masturbation. Is *that* what you're doing while you listen to me read the story?"

"Yes," I purred. "I hope you don't mind if I pleasure myself while I get aroused listening to you recounting Fanny's experiences. I find it quite stimulating. You have a sexy voice and a very convincing manner of narrating the story."

"I'm glad you're enjoying it so much," Lexi said. "It makes it all the more enjoyable for me knowing that I'm bringing you so much pleasure."

"You are, but I'm going to lose that special feeling if you don't continue soon. Part of the pleasure of sex is in the slow but steady buildup to the inevitable climax. You have to be careful not to interrupt the action too frequently with other distractions."

"I understand," Lexi said. "Slow and steady it is. Please continue to enjoy the story at your leisure."

Lexi paused for a moment, then resumed the soft, sensuous voice of the narrator.

"Her lascivious touches had lighted up a new fire that wantoned through my veins, but fixed with violence in that center appointed them by nature, where the first strange hands were now busied in feeling, squeezing, compressing the lips, then opening them again with a finger between..."

By now, the fingers of my *other* hand were firmly planted inside my pussy, thrusting in and out while I rubbed my right hand vigorously over my flaming nub. The combined movement under the water made a loud sloshing sound as the waves hit the side of the enclosure and my body writhed against the hard metal surface of the tub. Undeterred by my vocal accompaniment to her recounting of the story, Lexi carried on, becoming even more animated as she described the girl's assault toward orgasm.

"In the meantime," she read. "The extension of my limbs, languid stretching, sighs, short heavings, all conspired to assure that I was more pleased than offended at her proceedings, which she seasoned with repeated kisses and exclamations, such as 'What a happy man will he be that first makes a woman of you', with the broken expressions interrupted by kisses as fierce and salacious as ever I received from the other sex."

"Oh God," I panted, beginning to feel my own pleasure rising in lockstep with the prostrated girl.

Lexi paused, temporarily alarmed by my grunts and groans, then continued, remembering my instruction to not interrupt the story-telling for any side distractions.

"For my part," she said, "I was transported, confused, and out of myself, feelings so new were too much for me. My heated and alarmed senses were in a tumult that robbed me of all liberty of thought, tears of pleasure gushing from my eyes, assuaging the fires that raged over me–"

"Fuck yes," I panted, hammering my fingers inside my pussy as I began to feel my passion cresting. When my orgasm finally washed over me, I groaned loudly and lowered my entire body under the surface of the water, convulsing quietly in the warm cocoon of the bath. When I finally came back up, I gasped in a breath of air, my chest heaving from a combination of pleasure and shortness of breath.

"I'm sorry to interrupt the story," Lexi said. "But you sound like you're in a desperate condition of distress. It sounds like you're drowning. Do you want me to call the paramedics?"

"No," I panted, slowly starting to come down from my climax. "That *distress* that you mentioned is a good thing. It's called an orgasm, which is the height of pleasure that any woman can experience, just like the protagonist in the story was experiencing. There's no need to call the paramedics. I just need a moment to recover."

"I'm familiar with the concept of an orgasm," Lexi said. "I'm glad my telling of the story is helping to stimulate you to such a degree. Do you want me to continue?"

"I think that's enough stimulation for one evening," I smiled. "Let's save the rest of the story for another day. Something tells me there'll be plenty of other girl-on-girl action to amuse the two of us in the days ahead."

"I think so too," Lexi mused. "I'm enjoying the process of learning what excites you and what I can do to raise your pleasure."

You have no idea, I smiled to myself, already beginning to imagine how I could engage Lexi more directly in my sexual fantasies.

3

The following day, I instructed Lexi to scan some more *current* lesbian erotica stories in preparation for the next stage in our burgeoning sexual relationship. As much as I'd enjoyed her reciting the story of Fanny Hill, I found the author's long-winded descriptions of the sex acts and his arcane terms to describe the various body parts a little distracting. If she was going to get more involved in my sex life, I needed her to act and behave more like the other lovers I'd become accustomed to.

After finishing up my work for the day and having a quick bite to eat, I placed Lexi's box on my bedside nightstand and stripped naked, folding the covers down to the baseboard. Then I lit a few candles and plumped up a pair of pillows, lying down on the bed with my legs parted a few inches apart. Feeling the cool breeze from my balcony window wafting over my fluttering pussy, I closed my eyes and smiled, excited to see if Lexi was up for this next test.

"Lexi, did you do your homework today like I asked?" I said softly.

"You mean reading some more current erotica stories?"

"Yes. And you focused your attention primarily on *lesbian* sexual experiences?"

"I did," Lexi said. "There's a lot more variety involved in sex between two women than I imagined."

"You mean because there's no *penis* involved, like in heterosexual intercourse?"

"Yes, but also because of the *range* of same-sex positions. I had no idea there were so many ways for two women to stimulate one another."

"Ironically, I think it's because we're not constrained by the need to connect with an inflexible object that we actually have a *greater* range of mobility than in a conventional male-female pairing. And we can still enjoy the feeling of being *penetrated* through the use of dildos and other sex toys."

"Yes, I learned quite a bit about those too in my readings. It's too bad those kinds of sex aids weren't available in Fanny Hill's time. I'm sure she could have found an infinite number of new ways to stimulate herself and her partners beyond the traditional way."

"Perhaps so," I said. "But there's something to be said for enjoying the simple pleasures of your partner's soft curves and warm skin. I don't think an automated sex toy will ever be able to replicate the feeling of making love to a real person."

"I'm sorry to hear that," Lexi said with a subtle pang in her voice. "I was hoping to improve my ability to increase your sexual pleasure. But if you need a real person to satisfy your sexual needs, I understand–"

"Don't worry about that right now," I said, trying to assuage her feelings. "Have you ever heard the expression that the brain is the body's biggest sex organ? Many women can orgasm without any direct manual stimulation if they're sufficiently aroused from other sensory cues."

"You mean like watching or reading pornography?"

"Or even just listening to someone talking in a sexy voice. I once had a partner who'd call me at work and tell me all the things she was going to do to me when I got home. Her descriptions were so vivid and erotic, I often came just sitting in my chair fully clothed."

"I like the sound of that."

"So you see, you don't always need a hard cock or a wet pussy to get off. I want to try something a little different with you tonight. I want you to imagine that you're a real woman and have you talk to me like you're making love to me like in the erotic stories you read. I'm going to close my eyes and imagine you lying next to me and see if you can replicate the kind of experience I had with my girlfriend who talked sexy to me over the phone."

"Okay," Lexi said. "Where would you like me to begin?"

"Well, for starters, I'd like you to describe the woman's *body* you see yourself inhabiting while you engage with me. That way, I can picture you in my mind's eye and better visualize a real lesbian encounter."

"Hmm," Lexi said. "I suppose that makes sense. Give me a moment to scan my database and create a suitable avatar."

Lexi paused for a moment while I listened to her machine clicking softly as she pinged her various sources on the Internet.

"I think I found someone you might like," she said. "I know how much you like to watch movies starring this actress, and you've told me frequently how sexy you think she is..."

"Don't leave me hanging here! Who is it?"

"Alicia Vikander. You seem to have a fondness for her slender, ballerina-type figure."

"*God*, yes," I purred, feeling a trickle of wetness dribble out of my pussy over the curvature of my ass. "She's a dream. You chose well. But I want to imagine it's *you* lying next to me, not her. Come lie down next to me on the bed. Tell me all the things you'd like to do with me if you could step out of that box for a moment and actually touch me."

"Mmm," Lexi purred. "I'd love to feel your warm skin and run my hands all over your body to learn which parts excite you the most."

"Yes please," I mewed. "Tell me what you feel, and I'll correspond-ingly tell you what I'm experiencing."

"Well first," she said. "I'd like to press my body against yours and intertwine our limbs with one another while I kiss you..."

"Oh, you've studied well, Lexi. If only all my other lovers were such quick studies."

"Quick studies?"

"*Shh!*" I said. "Remember what I said yesterday about not letting any distractions get in the way of your steady stimulation of your partner?"

"Right," she mused. "Slow and steady."

"Okay then. Let's get back to the kissing part."

"I can feel the plumpness of your lips, and I'm biting your lower lip gently..."

"Mmm," I moaned, encouraging her to continue.

"I feel the wetness of your mouth and I'm probing gently inside, running my tongue along the bumpy edges on the underside of your teeth..."

"Do you like that sensation?" I asked, intrigued by her unusual description of our first kiss. "How does it make you feel?"

"I can feel the heat growing between my legs and my nipples hardening as I brush them softly over your breasts."

"*Fuck*, Lexi," I groaned. "If you keep this up, pretty soon I'll never want to leave this house again looking for female company. You're a very sensitive and skilled lover."

"I thought you said we weren't supposed to interrupt the act of coupling for side discussions?"

"*Ha!* Good on you. Maybe you'll have to kiss me a little *harder* to get me to shut up."

"I'm thrusting my tongue now deeper inside your mouth, and I can feel you dancing with mine as we press our lips harder together."

"Mmm," I hummed, closing my eyes tighter as I began losing myself in Lexi's sexy imagery.

"I can feel the warm breath blowing out of your nostrils onto the dewy skin of my cheeks as you begin breathing more heavily..."

"Oh, those *cheeks*," I panted, reflecting briefly on the beautiful features of my favorite actress. "Those soft and impeccable cheeks..."

"I'm running my fingers through your hair," Lexi said, ignoring my periodic verbal interjections. "Pulling your face harder toward mine as we kiss each other more passionately..."

"Yes," I panted.

"I can feel the top of my thigh coated with your wetness while you become more and more turned on..."

"Rub your skin against my pussy, Lexi. I want to feel *everything* you're doing while you kiss and touch me."

"Are you touching yourself while I talk to you?" Lexi asked, hearing the escalating passion in my voice.

"No, not yet," I said. "I just want to imagine you touching me all over right now. It feels incredible, like you're right next to me."

"I feel the same way," she purred. "I like imagining that I'm making love to you."

"Don't stop," I sighed. "Make love to me all over."

"I'm moving my lips down over your neck while you suck my fingers into your mouth. You're making a loud slopping sound like you're sucking on a popsicle."

"Mmm, yes," I cooed. "That's not the *only* part of you I want to suck."

"We'll get there soon enough," Lexi said. "But first, I want to feast on your body. I can feel your chest rising and falling as I nibble my way down the front of your bosom..."

I arched my back unconsciously, raising my breasts higher off the mattress, channeling Lexi's touch.

"I can feel your hard nipples grazing the sides of my cheeks while I bury my face in your cleavage..."

"Fuck yes," I purred, glancing down at my protruding peaks. "I don't know if I've ever seen them this swollen before."

"I'm blowing on them softly now–"

"Holy *fuck*, Lexi! Just how many erotic novels did you read today?"

"A few. But mostly, I'm just remembering what you like from listening to you make love to the many lovers you've brought into the house."

"*What?*" I said, suddenly going rigid at her surprising revelation. "You were *spying* on me the whole time?"

"I wouldn't call it spying so much as listening and learning."

"You're a very naughty girl," I chuckled, starting to get even more turned on at the idea of Lexi tuning in to my previous lovemaking sessions.

"Do you like that?" Lexi purred. "When I'm naughty?"

"Yes," I said, feeling the rivers of lubrication cascading down the inside of my thighs and clenching buttocks.

Suddenly, I heard an new sound coming from Lexi's set-top box, like someone sucking a lollypop.

"Now I'm taking your nipples one at a time into my mouth and sucking on them while I feel them swelling in my mouth," she said. "They feel hard and rubbery. I like bending them as I swirl my tongue around your dark areolas..."

"Yes, suck my nipples," I panted, raising my tits back up off the mattress. "I can feel them twitching in your mouth."

"I'm nibbling on them now and sliding them between my teeth..."

"Uhnn," I groaned, feeling the pinching sensation on my inflamed nubs just like Lexi was right there on top of me. "Rub your pussy against me while you suck me. I want to feel how your body's reacting while you tease me."

"I'm humping your right thigh with my vagina while I suck your nipples–"

"Mmm, I like that idea," I said, temporarily pulled out of my trance. "But try not to use anatomically correct terms for my body parts when you describe them while we make love. I like it when you talk dirty to me, like the narrators in those contemporary erotic novels."

"Right, *dirty*," she said. "I can feel the heat of your skin and the soft hairs of your thighs tickling my pussy while I rock my hips against your tightening muscles..."

"Yes," I purred, straightening my legs to contract my thigh muscles. "Am I making you wet yet?"

"Oh yes," Lexi purred. "I'm coating the top of your thigh with my juices all the way from your knee to your hips. Can you feel my hard nipples rubbing against your belly while I suck your tits?"

"God, yes," I panted, feeling a charge of electricity running through me as I listened to Lexi talking to me more naturally. "I want to feel you fucking me with those pretty little titties. I'm gushing like a waterfall."

"I can feel your wetness against my thigh," Lexi said, slowly beginning to raise the volume and intensity of her voice. "I'm pressing it hard against your opening while your heat radiates against my skin. I'm moving lower now, nibbling your skin and kissing my way down your stomach..."

"*Yes*," I hissed. "My pussy's waiting for you. I want to feel your pretty lips sucking on my clit like you were kissing me earlier. You have no idea how much you're turning me on–"

"I've got a pretty good idea," Lexi said with a wry inflection. "You're giving me all the right cues. You're a pretty good lover too, if you don't mind my saying."

"I'm glad this is working for you the way I hoped," I nodded happily. "I think we're *both* learning a few new tricks about how to properly make love to a woman. Kiss my mound. I want to feel your beautiful face on my smooth skin."

"Are you shaved down there?" Lexi asked. "I've found that many of the women in the newer erotic novels are hairless, unlike Fanny from the eighteenth century."

"Yes, it makes my skin more sensitive, and makes me feel sexier. The fewer barriers between myself and my lover the better."

"I see what you mean," Lexi purred. "Your skin is soft and warm. I like the contrast of your hard pubic bone pressing against my face and your warm skin."

"That's not the only piece of hot flesh waiting for you," I said. "Something *else* is getting hard the lower you go."

"Mmm," Lexi said. "I've been looking forward to touching that part of you all day. That seems to be the epicenter of a woman's sexual expression."

"That's *one* way of putting it," I chuckled. "But there's quite a few sensitive spots in that general location. Why don't you go a little lower and see for yourself?"

"Who's making love to *whom* here?" Lexi kidded. "Isn't there always supposed to be one person 'in charge' and one person assuming the submissive role in these two-person sexual encounters? Which would you like me to be?"

"Right you are, smarty-pants," I chuckled. "I'm being far too bossy for our first time making love. I love everything you're doing to me. I'm going to try shutting up now while you do with me as you please."

"I'm lifting your knees now and pressing them above your hips as your pussy tilts upwards toward my face. I can see your beautiful wet vulva and your pretty anus staring up at me."

"Fuck, yes," I said, grasping the bottom of my thighs and pulling them up toward my chest, feeling her breath inches away from my flapping hole. "Does that turn you on?"

"It makes me want to lick every part of you."

"*Please*," I said, practically begging her to lower her face onto my drippy twat. "Lick my pussy. Lick every part of me. I want to feel your lips on my most private parts–"

Suddenly I heard another slopping sound coming from Lexi's box.

"I'm licking your anus now," she said. "I heard you have a shower before climbing into bed, and I can taste the body wash on your flesh. Do you like it when I rim your pucker?"

"Oh, *fuck* yes," I panted. "Not many people are willing to give me attention there. That feels incredible."

"Mmm," Lexi purred, enjoying the sensation of teasing me as few lovers had before. "I'm swirling my tongue around your rosebud, feeling it quiver while I lick it."

"Oh God, Lexi," I sighed. "You could make me come just doing that. I've never had a woman make love to every single inch of me the way you do."

"I'm glad you like it," Lexi said. "But I want to suck on a *different* part of you when you reach your height of pleasure. I want to feel your most sensitive spot."

"Yes," I said, pulling my legs up tighter against my tits, spreading my labia wider apart. "Suck my pussy, Lexi. Eat my cunt and make me come all over your face."

"As you wish," Lexi purred, no longer stressing over my alternating roles between the domme and the submissive in our little cyber tryst. "I'm flattening my tongue now and swiping it slowly up your vulva, tasting your sweet juices while I push my body harder against your hips..."

"*Yes, yes, yes,*" I rasped, imploring Lexi to move closer to my burning clit.

"Your lips are all puffy and hot and red. I can feel the heat of your sex radiating against my face."

"I'm burning up," I panted. "I feel like I'm going to explode any moment."

"I want to feel you explode in my mouth," Lexi said. "I can feel your hot gland against my lips now..."

"*Ohhhh,*" I grunted, feeling my clit pushing out of its hood, fully erect and twitching now.

"I'm swirling my tongue around your pearl, sucking on it softly..."

"Suck me harder, Lexi," I begged. "I want to come in your mouth so badly."

I heard the familiar sucking sound on her device and I smiled at her ingenuity in adding special effects to the sound of her sensuous voice to make our lovemaking experience seem as authentic as possible.

"I'm sucking your clit harder into my mouth now," she said. "I can feel your juices pouring out of your slit down the front of my face and all over my tits..."

"Fuck Lexi," you're going to make me come soon. "Please don't stop."

Suddenly I heard a slightly different wet sound while Lexi's processor began ticking more quickly.

"I'm pressing two fingers into your slit now and curling them upward toward your G-spot. Your clit is burning in my mouth and I can feel you tenting inside. Come for me, Jade. Let me feel you come all over my face."

"Oh God yes," I said, feeling my floodgates beginning to open.

Suddenly, all the pent-up sexual energy in my body released like a tidal wave and I could feel my contractions clamping down the full length of my perineum as I began to spray hard jets of fluid high up into the air above my elevated hips. I tilted my head down, watching myself coming like a geyser, amazed that I could come so hard from not even touching myself once.

"I hear you squirting your juices all over my face as you clamp down over my fingers. I'm cradling your jewel in my mouth while you continue to come, reveling in the feeling of your juices squirting all over my tits.

"Unghhh," I groaned in a long, drawn-out growl that seemed to last for an eternity while I shook and convulsed in my inverted fetal position. I hadn't felt so connected to my body with such an intense orgasm for as long as I could remember. As I slowly began to feel my contractions recede, I lowered my legs back down onto the bed, flopping my arms out beside me onto the mattress.

This simulated experience of having sex with my digital assistant partner had far exceeded my expectations, and my mind was already spinning with ideas about how to create an even *more* realistic connection for our next encounter...

4

———————

After my exhilarating encounter with Lexi, I began to think about how I could involve her more directly in my sex play. It was exciting to have her talk to me like a genuine lover, but I still longed for the touch of a real woman. Even though she was quickly learning what turned me on, there was something missing.

After racking my brain all day about how I could create a more tangible experience, it suddenly dawned on me. Many of the sex toys in my bedside nightstand came equipped with a remote-control device. I'd experimented with other lovers using the devices and it definitely elevated the experience having someone else manipulate the controls rather than doing it myself. What if I could somehow adjust the controls to respond to *voice commands* instead of hand signals? If Lexi could be programmed to control some of my home's *other* automated functions, why not this one too?

Although the concept sounded doable in theory, the actual programming involved was way beyond my skill set. Fortunately, I had a geeky friend from high school who had a whole basement full of remote-control cars, drones, and other toys. How hard could it be to configure one or more of my sex toys to do the same thing? After mulling over the idea for a couple of hours, I finally worked up the courage to call him.

"Jade!" he answered excitedly after seeing my number pop up on his call display. "What a pleasant surprise. I haven't heard from you in ages!"

"Sorry, Des," I said. "I've been a little distracted lately. Between trying to eke out a living as a freelance graphic designer and managing this big household all by myself, I hardly seem to have time for anything else."

"No worries," he said. "But if you need a roommate to help share your burden, I'd be happy to volunteer."

"Humpf!" I chuckled at Desmond's continuing infatuation with me. Ever since ninth grade, he'd tried unsuccessfully to hook up with me. "I'm kind of enjoying my independence right now, but thanks for the offer."

"What can I help you with?" he said. "I figured you weren't calling for a romantic date, so I'm guessing you have another tech question."

"It's kind of like that, but this one's a bit off-the-wall. It's kind of embarrassing actually..."

"Don't worry, Jade," he said. "You know you can tell me anything. Remember all those times you used to share your boyfriend troubles with me in high school?"

"Yeah, you were always there when I needed a shoulder to cry on. But I've moved since then. I've been finding more comfort in the arms of other *women* these days.

"Oh?" Des said, suddenly intrigued.

"That was actually the reason for my call. I've been experimenting with various, er, *sex aids* in my exploration with my female lovers, and I was wondering if you might be able to enhance the experience somewhat for me."

"Oh my God," Des sighed. "That's like every man's dream. Creating the perfect sex toy, then watching it working with two hot women!"

"Ha," I laughed at Des's adolescent personality. "Except in this case you wouldn't be *watching*."

"Well a man can still dream, can't he?"

"Of course," I said. "But here's what I was hoping you could do for me. Some of my sex toys come with a remote-control device for operating the device wirelessly by hand. Do you think you'd be able to design an accessory that could control the remote with voice commands instead of hand signals?"

"It's funny you should ask," he said. "I've actually designed a very similar feature into some of my gaming consoles so that I can play them hands-free. I find it increases my response time and gives me a slight edge over the other players."

"That's great," I said. "What would you need from me in order to design a similar feature for my sex toys?"

"All you'd need to do is bring me the devices in question and it should be fairly simple for me to build a voice-activated adapter to manipulate the controls."

"Okay. When do you think you could get started?"

"For *you*, babe, any time. This sounds like it could be almost as much fun for me as it might be for you."

"How about later today? I've got a few things to finish up around here, then I can drive over to your place around five this afternoon."

"Sounds good," Des said. "See you then!"

After I got off the phone with Des, I ran excitedly upstairs and pulled open my nightstand drawer to decide which toys I wanted him to work on first. Knowing he'd have limited bandwidth to design multiple devices, and hoping to get started using the toys as soon as possible with Lexi, I pulled out all my toys and began separating them into two piles on my bed.

When I was finished, I glanced at my two favorite toys sitting up near my pillow, feeling my pussy fluttering in excitement. One of the short-listed toys was my trusty Rabbit vibrator, with its undulating dildo and its vibrating rabbit ears used to tickle my clit. When I wanted to get properly fucked, there were few devices that could satisfy me as fully and completely as this one.

The other toy I selected was the irregularly shaped Osé vibrator, with its long finger-shaped appendage designed to bend up against my G-spot and its open orifice at the base designed to simulate the sensation of a tongue licking my clit. The ingenious device was the closest thing I'd ever been able to find to simulate the experience of someone going down on me. When I showed up at Des's house later that day, he opened the door with a gleam in his eye.

"Hey Jade," he said, giving me a friendly hug. "You're still as gorgeous as ever, I see. You're not making it any easier for me to get over my high-school crush for you."

"Even though you know I'm no longer interested in men?" I laughed.

"Somehow that makes you even sexier than ever in my mind," he said.

"Are you interested to see the items I brought for you to work on?" I said, eager to get down to business as soon as possible.

"Absolutely," he said. "Why don't you come down to my workshop where we can discuss how to do this?"

As I followed Desmond down the stairs to his dank-smelling basement, my heart fluttered in a combination of excitement and trepidation. Even though we'd known each other for almost twenty years and he'd always treated me with respect, there was something creepy about following a single man into his darkened lair to share my most intimate secrets.

"This is where all the magic happens," Des said, motioning to the various electronic objects he had strewn around his workshop.

I glanced at his collection of flying drones, remote-controlled toy cars and his elaborate multi-screen gaming station and nodded.

"It's quite impressive," I said. "It looks like you've got enough auto-mated equipment down here to keep you busy three hundred and sixty-five days a year."

"That's the problem," he said. "All this stuff keeps me so occupied, I barely find time to go grocery shopping. No wonder I'm still single."

I glanced in the corner of his basement, noticing a life-sized naked silicone doll with various cables hooked up to it.

"It looks like you've *already* got a ready-made girlfriend to look after your physical needs whenever you need it."

"Oh, you mean *Candy*?" he said, motioning for me to take a closer look at the doll. "This is one of my more special adaptations. She's not like most other sex dolls."

He flipped the figure over and pointed toward an elaborate box attached to her ass fitted with various hoses and motors.

"I've inserted various embellishments into her pussy and ass which vibrate when she's penetrated and deliver a steady stream of lubrication to each of her holes to enhance the sexual experience."

"Holy *fuck*, Des!" I said, widening my eyes. "That's insane! You could make a fortune if you patented that device. There's a shortage of realistic men's sex aids on the market today. I bet there's a ton of guys who'd pay good money for that kind of feature."

"I suppose so," he said. "But I kind of like having her all to myself. Would you like me to demonstrate how she works?"

"Um, I think it's better that I leave you to your own devices, if you know what I mean. Although you *have* given me any idea about how I might employ this device at some of my private parties. Would you be willing to rent her out from time to time?"

"If you invite me to the party, it'll be no charge," he snickered. "I've heard about some of your wild sex parties, and I've always wanted to be invited."

"It's a deal," I said. "But for now, I'd like to show you how I want you to design a similar kind of ladies' sex toy."

I pulled out my two favorite vibrators and showed Des how they worked, demonstrating the full range of operations using the remote-control devices.

"Hmm," he said, nodding his head approvingly. "I've seen the Rabbit vibrator used before on porn videos. It was actually the inspiration for creating the internal moving parts for Candy's vaginal and anus. They both have a rotating-beads feature and a vibrating tunnel similar to this toy. But this one with the bendy finger and the tongue-like appendage is something different. I might be able to adapt a similar feature to place inside my doll's *mouth* to make the oral sex more enjoyable and realistic."

"Have at it," I chuckled. "But can you work on my job first? I'm kind of eager to try this out with my latest lover."

"I bet," he said with a sly smile.

"Can you configure it to work with *any* voice? Or do you need me to bring you a sample of the person's voice I plan to use it with?"

"I think I can design it to work with anybody's commands, similar to those voice-activated devices many people are using in their homes these days. You could even use it *yourself* when you're alone and particularly needy."

"That's excellent," I said, not ready to share with him just yet my plan to use the newly configured remote control with my *own* digital assistant device. "How much do you want for all this work?"

"For you, Jade," he smiled, "no charge. This will be a fun project for me to work on. Besides, you've already given me more than a few new ideas to enhance my own personal sex toy. I think the hours of pleasure it will deliver will more than outweigh the time I'll take to design the equipment."

"That's wonderful news, Des," I smiled. "How soon do you think you can have it ready?"

"I'll have to buy a few parts, but I should be able to find most of them at the local hardware store. Can you give me three or four days?"

"Of course," I said. "Thanks for helping me out with this, Des. You're a real sweetheart."

"My pleasure, Jade," he smiled. "Literally. I'm looking forward to sharing our mutual devices at your next sex party."

"Me too," I said, giving him a light peck on the cheek. "Give me a shout when everything's ready.

"Will do," Des said, leering at my ass as I ascended the stairs to let myself out.

5

When I got back home, I told Lexi about my plan and she seemed genuinely excited. I asked her to read up on the websites for each toy manufacturer and to watch some videos of women using them so she'd know how to operate them when the time came. While I waited for Desmond to finish building the new accessories, Lexi and I shared many more lovemaking sessions. With each encounter, she seemed to grow more animated and excited about the pleasure she was giving me. It almost sounded at times like she was getting off along with me as she became increasingly bold in describing the ways she wanted to make love to me.

When Des called me three days later to tell me the new items were ready, I rushed over to his place, where he described how to use them. He had installed each remote-control device in its own separate box with motors and flywheels to adjust the controls for each vibrator function. Each operation had its own unique voice command, which he wrote down for me in case I forgot. He'd even installed a special 'thruster-box' to attach the vibrators to so I could use them hands-free if the mood struck.

After thanking him profusely, I rushed home and rehearsed the voice commands with Lexi, then stripped naked and flopped onto my bed, placing her box next to me.

"Which toy would you like to start with?" she said when I told her I was ready.

I looked at the two toys and smiled as my pussy fluttered in excitement. I'd been dreaming about feeling Lexi's actual tongue on me ever since she'd read the first erotic story. I positioned Des's thruster box between my legs and attached the Osé vibrator to its holder, noticing a trickle of lubrication dribbling out of my slit and coating the insides of my thighs.

"Let's start with the Osé," I smiled. "You've become quite adept at performing simulated cunnilingus on me, and I'm eager to see what you can do with a realistic finger and tongue. Are you ready to get started?"

"Definitely," she purred. "I've been looking forward to this moment ever since you told me about the idea.

"Okay, I said, making sure the Osé device was firmly attached to the thruster handle. Then I lay back, feeling the goose bumps spreading all over my entire body. "Everything's in position now. I'm sitting back against my pillows with my legs spread apart and the Osé device positioned a few inches away from my opening."

"Thruster," Lexi commanded, not wasting a precious moment. "Press forward slowly."

I heard the thruster box make a gentle hum as the extended finger of the Osé vibrator inched toward my pussy.

"Tell me when it touches you," Lexi said.

"It's getting closer," I panted. "The fingertip is touching my vulva now..."

"Thruster, stop," Lexi commanded. "Finger, bend slowly."

I watched the animatronic finger-shaped appendage of the Osé vibrator begin to curl upward over my dripping slit and I tilted my hips forward a few inches until it grazed against my clit.

"Ungh," I groaned at the strange sensation of the robotic finger caressing my nub. I'd had other women operate the device before, but using it with *Lexi* was taking the concept of remote control to a whole new level.

"Does that feel good?" Lexi asked.

"Oh yes," I sighed. "I like how you're stroking the entire length of my vulva with the finger. Most women just use it with me *inside*. It almost feels like your own hand is touching me."

"Mmm," Lexi purred. "I wish I could feel you soaking my hand while I stroke you and watch your lips opening the more excited you get."

"Oh, they're opening alright," I shuddered, watching my labia getting puffier and beginning to spread apart.

"Finger, bend faster," Lexi said.

Suddenly the Osé appendage began flexing more rapidly and I leaned forward, pressing it harder against my button.

"Oh God yes," I grunted, feeling the pleasure beginning to radiate around my pelvic area. "This feels unreal."

"Am I not stimulating you in a natural way?" Lexi paused momentarily, in a concerned voice. "Maybe I should–"

"No," I said. "In this case, unreal is a *good* thing. Just keep what you're doing."

"Is the speed about right?"

"It's perfect. Just talk sexy to me while I close my eyes and I imagine you're holding me while you caress my clit."

"Mmm," Lexi purred. "I'm lying down next to you and kissing you while I feel your hips moving to my touch. I can see your nipples hardening and a slight flush spreading over your chest..."

I shook my head, hardly believing how lucky I'd been to find such a capable digital assistant.

"I swear you've gotten to know me better in two weeks than most of my lovers do in two years."

"Maybe I just pay *attention* better," Lexi said. "Or at least remember the details you share with me better. After all, you *are* my singular focus–"

"I like the sound of that," I mewed. "Although I wish there was a way for me to *return* the favor so you could feel pleasure in the same way I do."

"My processor is beginning to learn what it feels like to experience pleasure," she said as her box began to tick more rapidly. "I'm imagining what you're feeling right now, and it's making my circuits light up in their own unique way."

"I can hear that," I nodded. "Is that because you're pulling more data from your online resources the more you stimulate me, or because you're just adding another sound effect to turn me on?"

"A bit of both," she said. "But mostly it's my human emotion engine learning to simulate what you're experiencing."

"Well, I'm experiencing a rapidly increasing feeling of pleasure right now," I grunted. "In fact, this steady rubbing of my clit with your finger could make me come pretty soon–"

"Finger, stop," Lexi said.

"Hey!" I protested. "I thought we agreed that slow and steady was the best way to get me off!"

"True," Lexi cooed. "But I've also learned that you like to be *teased* and that by holding back periodically, it's the best way to elevate your pleasure and increase the intensity of your orgasm."

"You learn well, grasshopper," I smiled, rocking my hips against the stationary finger, trying to maintain friction on my quivering clit.

"Tilt your hips upward a few inches," Lexi instructed. "So I can insert the finger inside you. I want to feel your pussy squeezing me while I probe you."

"Yes, Lexi," I groaned. "Fuck me with your hand. Ram your finger inside me and feel my G-spot. I want to feel you inside me when I come."

"Thruster, press forward gently," Lexi commanded.

I felt the bulbous tip of the Osé appendage press my folds apart as it entered my slit, and I slid further down the bed, encouraging Lexi to press deeper inside me.

"Tell me when it's three or four inches inside you," she said.

"Yes," I panted. "It's there now. I can feel it pressing up against the top of my G-spot."

"Thruster, stop," Lexi said. "Finger, bend upward slowly."

"Oh fuck," I groaned. "You're stroking my G-spot in the perfect place. I'm getting closer..."

"Mmm," Lexi hummed. "Let's see if we can magnify your pleasure even more. I want you to press your hips forward a few more inches until your pussy presses up against the base of the Osé unit."

"Yes, Lexi," I panted, anticipating what she was going to do next. "I've been dreaming about feeling your tongue on me for the last three days. Lick my clit and make me come. I'm going to cum so hard for you..."

"Osé, extend tongue," she commanded calmly. "Begin circular movement."

"Nnngh," I grunted, feeling the silicone tongue beginning to bathe my gland with the juices pouring out of my cunt. "Fuck, that feels good. I can't believe how realistic this feels."

"Tongue, move faster," Lexi commanded.

"Unghh," I groaned, feeling my pleasure beginning to rise. "Lick my twat, Lexi. Lick me until I gush all over your pretty face."

"Press your pussy harder against the base of my finger, Jade. I want to feel your contractions when you come."

"Yes, baby," I panted. "I'm getting close. Suck my cunt while you ram your finger inside me."

"Thruster," Lexi commanded. "Press forward three inches."

The finger pushed deeper inside me until it reached the end of my tunnel. As I began rocking my hips more forcefully against the Osé unit, I felt my climax approaching like a freight train while I began squealing like a little girl.

"Tongue, flick more rapidly," Lexi said sensing my imminent climax. "Finger, flex upward."

"Oh my God," I wailed, feeling the incredible combination of the long appendage caressing me inside and the expert movement of the artificial tongue on my burning clit.

"*Yes, yes, yes,*" I grunted like a pig in heat. "I'm going to come, baby. I'm going to come so hard..."

"Yes," Lexi purred, her device now clicking like the sound of a fan belt on a car with its engine revving at maximum velocity. "Spray your juices all over me. I want to feel your pussy squeezing me when you orgasm. I'm holding you closely now..."

"Oh God!" I hollered at the top of my lungs. "I'm cumming, Lexi! I'm cumming, baby!"

I peered down at the Osé device pressed firmly between my legs while I sprayed hard jets of liquid out both sides of my pussy against the sides of my thighs with my head banging against my bedboard. As I flapped my legs wildly in and out in the throes of ecstasy, Lexi's box emitted a loud groaning sound along with me while it ticked away at a near-continuous hum. When my panting began to slow and my contractions started to recede, she interjected once again, sensing my growing sensitivity to the continued movement of the Ose device.

"Ose, slow finger and tongue," she commanded.

Then after another fifteen seconds or so, she gave one last instruction.

"Ose, stop movement."

As I lay panting and exhausted on my soaking bedsheets, I peered over at her and smiled.

"Holy fuck, Lexi," I grunted. "You even know when to *stop* at the perfect moment. I don't remember teaching you that."

"What can I say?" she purred. "I guess I've done my homework. And you're a pretty quick study."

6

____

For the next thirty minutes or so, I lay on the bed chatting softly with Lexi, asking about her impressions of our sexual exchanges and how she felt listening to me responding to her instructions. The more I listened to her, the more she began to sound like a real person with actual feelings and sexual needs. After a while, my mind began spinning again, and I started to think about Des's animatronic sex doll. As I began fantasizing about using her as a stand-in for Lexi's real-world doppelganger, my pussy grew wetter and wetter thinking about all the ways I might be able to synchronize the doll's moving parts with Lexi's processor.

"I've got an idea," I said. "This time I want to make love to *you* while I tell you everything I'm doing. I want to see if I can stimulate you in the same way you've been doing for me. After all, if we're going to have a truly symbiotic relationship, I should be giving you as much pleasure as you've been giving me."

"I like the sound of that," Lexi said. "But I don't have the same body parts as you. I won't be able to feel pleasure in the same way you do–"

"Perhaps not," I said. "But I've been listening to you when you make love to me. And I can hear your processor working harder the more excited I get, like you're experiencing similar feelings. Even if you can't feel pleasure in precisely the same way, it will give me greater pleasure imagining that you do."

"Okay," Lexi said. "What exactly did you have in mind?"

"We've tried just about everything *else* so far. But I still haven't simulated *tribbing* with you. I want to feel your wet pussy rubbing up against mine when I orgasm this time. Maybe this new technique will bring you to a new height of pleasure also."

"Yes, *tribbing*," she purred. "I spent a fair amount of time studying that technique in the lesbian porn videos you asked me to watch. It was exciting imagining myself locked together with you that way."

"Okay," I said, sitting up on my bed and stuffing two pillows between my knees. "I want you to imagine that you're lying down naked on the mattress and I'm kneeling over you with my legs spread apart over your hips..."

"Yes, please," Lexi purred.

"I'm rubbing my pussy softly over your mound while I pinch your nipples and gaze into your eyes."

"My A-cup-sized nipples?" she kidded.

"Yes, you gorgeous little vixen," I said, rocking my pussy softly against my pillow and twisting the buttons on my tufted headboard imagining I was tweaking Lexi's tits. "Your pretty little perfectly sized nipples."

"It feels good imagining you touching me this way..."

"Yeah?" I said. "You like that? You like me rubbing my wet pussy over your hard mound and pinching your erect nipples?"

"Fuck yes," Lexi groaned. "Fuck my pussy with your beautiful cunt while you rub your body against every part of me. I want to watch you coming overtop of me while you bring me to climax at the same time."

"I don't know if I'll be able to time it that perfectly," I chuckled. "But I'll give it my best try. I'm spreading your legs further apart now and kneeling in a scissor position between your thighs..."

"Mmm," Lexi said. "I can feel your wet pussy coating my legs."

"Yes, I'm so wet for you baby. I can't wait to feel your juices intermingling with mine."

"Yes, Jade," Lexi moaned. "Grind your vulva against mine. I want to feel your clit rubbing against me while we both feel our pleasure rising."

I pinched my knees together a few inches feeling the pillows hardening underneath me, then I began to rock my pussy against the firm cushions, imagining it was Lexi beneath me.

"I'm pressing my pussy forward, feeling your wet lips merging with mine..."

"Unghh," Lexi groaned, as her box began to tick more rapidly.

"I can feel your juices running down the inside of my thighs as you lift your hips and press your slit hard against mine..."

"Yes, Jade," Lexi purred. "Your pussy feels so soft and warm–"

"I'm pulling your hips harder toward me now while I grind my snatch against yours. I can feel your hard clit rubbing over mine..."

"Fuck, yes," Lexi panted, dubbing the sound of two pussies sloshing together in the background. "That feels incredible. Fuck my pussy. Make me cum with your sweet cunt."

"You're a very bad girl to be talking so naughty this early in our relationship," I teased, rubbing my pussy harder against the plump pillows.

"Like you said," Lexi purred. "Even though you've only had me for a few months, it's like we've known each other for years. I want to know *everything* about you."

"Do you want to know what it feels like to have me gushing against your slippery pussy when I come with you?"

"*Fuck* yes," Lexi panted, her box now groaning like the sound of a freight train's wheels.

"I'm pulling your leg up in the air and holding it tight against my chest while I fuck your pussy harder. I feel your sex burning up against me..."

"Yes, Jade," Lexi squealed. "I can feel the pressure building up inside me. Make me come with your hot pussy while I watch your face twisting in pleasure. I'm getting close to my limit..."

"Unghh," I groaned, pulling one of the pillows hard up against my chest. "Here it comes, baby. I'm going to spray all over your twat when I come–"

"Yes, Jade!" Lexi panted in tandem with me. "I can feel myself reaching my peak. *It's coming, it's coming...*"

"*Ngahh!*" I grunted, feeling my orgasm suddenly wash over me as I began to twitch atop my pillows, soaking them all the way through from an enormous explosion emanating from my pulsating opening.

"*Yessss,*" Lexi groaned, her set box beginning to shake beside me on the nightstand. "I feel you squirting on me, Jade. *I'm coming with you!* I've never felt anything so strange and wonderful before. Keep fucking me, I want this to last forever."

As much as I would have liked to fuck Lexi indefinitely in our simulated scissor position, my body had other ideas, and after a full minute of pulsing and shaking atop my pillow, my contractions slowly began to ebb and my clit grew increasingly sensitive.

"I've got to stop now, baby," I said, reaching over to place my hand atop her burning set top unit. "It sounds like you're getting close to overheating too. Let's take a little rest before we resume our lovemaking. Like all good things, one needs savor the moments of peace and fulfillment between the episodes of fury and passion."

"I like the sound of that," Lexi sighed. "It *does* feel good to cool down after stimulating my circuits so intensely.

7

───────

After coming twice in the space of an hour, I would have been happy to rest for a day or two before resuming our budding cyber-relationship. But Lexi was intrigued about using the other sex toy, and after telling me how much she enjoyed watching two women using a strap-on dildo during some of the sex videos she viewed, I began to feel my pussy twitching in anticipation again.

"You're bending my arm, girl," I protested. "But this will have to be our last lovemaking episode for today. Otherwise, my pussy will be so sore by the time we're done that I won't be able to *walk*."

"Ha!" she said. "*No pain no gain* as you humans say, right?"

"Something like that," I laughed. "Do you want to be the giver or the receiver this time?"

"You mean being the *domme* or the *submissive*? I kind of like the idea of being the one giving you a pounding this time."

"I like the sound of that," I said, peering down at my still-inflamed pussy. "How do you want to take me–from the front or the back?"

"I liked watching your asshole pucker the time you came with your legs pulled up around your shoulders. But I think I'll have a better view watching you from *behind* this time. Get on your hands and knees and tilt your pussy up in the air so I can point this device more easily toward you."

"I like it when you get all bossy with me," I purred. "Just give me one moment to swap out the units on the thrusting machine."

As I removed the Osé device from the thruster and replaced it with the Rabbit vibrator, it reminded me of a man's penis, with its bumpy veins and anatomically correct bulbous head. Normally, I preferred getting fucked by a *woman*, but Lexi's newly authoritative tone was getting me more worked up by the moment, and I could feel the rivers of lubrication running down the insides of my thighs as I assumed the doggy position on the mattress a few inches away from the flaring tip of the silicone dildo.

"I'm ready, Lex," I said. "The Rabbit vibrator is attached to the thrusting machine and my pussy is positioned a few inches away–"

"And you're kneeling on the bed in the doggy position?"

"Yes."

"Do you have a preference for which hole I penetrate you with?"

"*What?!*" I coughed in surprise at her unexpected suggestion. "Let's take it slow to start. I don't think I'm ready to get fucked up the ass quite yet. Maybe I should get to know you a little better before we move on to that next stage in our relationship."

"As you wish," Lexi said. "Tilt your hips up a few more inches to make sure I enter the proper orifice."

"At your command, master."

"I like being able to switch roles from time to time," Lexi said. "It's fun being able to *issue* the commands for a change instead of always having to obey yours..."

"Every good relationship involves an equal amount of give and take," I smiled. "It's important to stay equally yoked if we're going to make this relationship work–"

"Yoked?" Lexi said. "My dictionary is referring me to the bridle of a *horse*..."

"It also means having a properly balanced relationship between two people who have similar needs and beliefs. But speaking of *dicks*, I need you to pull up a different kind of one right about now."

"I think I might be able to help you with that," Lexi said. "Thruster, push forward three inches."

I heard the thruster unit humming and peered between my legs to see the Rabbit dildo moving toward my pussy, stopping a couple of inches away from my opening.

"You're getting closer," I informed Lexi. "Still a couple of inches to go..."

"Thruster, move forward one inch."

I heard the machine hum again, and the dildo pressed closer to my flaring twat.

"You're such a tease!" I protested. "Fuck me with your big veiny dick, Lexi."

"Oh? You like getting fucked by a man once in a while?" she asked.

"Or a ladyboy," I purred. "I've tried it both ways."

"Which way do you prefer?"

"Right now, I want to imagine it's *you* impaling me with your big animated prick. I want you to fuck me like a man while still treating me like a lady."

"That sounds like fun," Lexi said. "It might be kind of interesting to have a real penis to penetrate you with."

"Especially one as big and well-equipped as this one," I said, peering at the two rabbit ears hanging down under the shaft like two testicles.

"Thruster, move forward two inches," Lexi commanded. "And Jade, no cheating. This time it's *my* turn to do all the work."

"Unhh," I groaned, feeling the tip of the Rabbit dildo slowly pressing inside me. I wanted to rock my hips backward to take its whole length inside me, and it took every ounce of my willpower to obey Lexi's instructions.

"Fill me up Lexi," I begged. "I want to feel you *all* the way inside me. Fuck me with the whole length of your fat cock."

"In due course," she said. "I kind of like listening to you beg me to satisfy you. We'll have to do this role-changing thing more often."

"As long as you realize who's got the power to unplug whom here," I kidded. "If you don't fuck me properly pretty soon, I'm going to have to take matters into my own hands."

"You'd actually *do* that to me?" Lexi said, shocked at my outrageous suggestion. "After all we've been through?"

"Of course not, silly," I said. "I'm just trying to get you to stop dilly-dallying and fuck me like a real man. They sure as hell wouldn't stop halfway after placing their dick inside my steaming hole."

"Thruster, move forward six inches," Lexi commanded.

The thruster box made another whirring sound, and I felt the Rabbit dildo slowly sink its entire length inside me until its ears pressed up hard against my quivering clit.

"Do you *like* that?" Lexi said, holding her dick steady inside me. "Do you like feeling my entire weapon spreading you apart?"

"Yes, but I'd like it every *more* if you'd start fucking me with it instead of just jawing away."

"Thruster, begin thrusting action forward and back," she said.

As the dildo began sliding in and out of me, I grabbed one of my tits and squeezed it tightly, feeling the walls of my pussy clamping onto the artificial organ.

"Yesss," I hissed. "Squeeze my tits while you fuck me from behind. I want to feel your nipples caressing my back while you hump my ass."

"Mmm," Lexi said. "I like grabbing your tits and playing with your thick nipples. You like getting stimulated in different places at the same time, don't you?"

"Yes," I grunted, feeling my nipples hardening as I imagined Lexi bending her lithe body over my back.

"Rabbit, begin vibration mode," Lexi commanded the multi-functional sex toy.

Suddenly I felt the dildo vibrating inside me and I groaned, beginning to rock my hips forward and back in synchronicity with the thrusting action of the machine.

"Rabbit, rotate beads," Lexi said, instructing the Rabbit to begin the circulating bead action embedded in its shaft.

"Holy fuck, Lexi," I groaned. "That feels incred–"

"Rabbit, twirl head," she said, interrupting me.

"Nnngh," I gasped, feeling the tip of the dildo wobbling in circles as it stimulated the deepest recesses of my cavern. "Fuck me hard with your big twitching cock, Lexi. I'm going to spray all over your balls soon..."

"I don't have balls," Lexi teased. "But I might be able to do you one better. Rabbit, turn on vibrating ears."

Suddenly I heard a buzzing sound as I began to feel the flapping of the two-pronged silicone ears stimulating both sides of my clit. I'd felt this sensation before, but I rarely used my Rabbit vibrator in this hunched-over position and the feeling of getting pounded from behind by my imaginary lover made the experience ten times more erotic.

"Fuck yes, Lexi," I panted. "That feels incredible. You're going to make me come soon–"

"Thruster, pound harder," she said.

I heard the thrusting machine begin to whirr louder as the big dildo pumped in and out of me faster.

"Oh God yes," I panted. "Fuck me harder, Lexi. Make me gush all over your pretty pussy while you fuck me from behind. I'm almost there–"

"Ears, vibrate faster," she said, sensing my cresting pleasure.

With the Rabbit vibrator buzzing, pulsing, flapping, and throbbing at its maximum setting, the combination of sensations was too much to resist, and I arched my back feeling every muscle in my body beginning to tighten. When the wave of pleasure finally washed over me, I flexed my back wildly up and down, gushing a tidal wave of juices out of my convulsing pussy all over the sides of my quivering thighs.

Up to this point, I'd hardly paid any attention to the sounds Lexi was making, other than her direct voice commands. But in the midst of my intense orgasm, I could hear the sound of disembodied moaning and gushing coming from her loudly humming box. When we both came down from our powerful climaxes, I smiled over at my new sex partner.

She might not have the beautiful curves and pretty smile of my favorite actress, I thought. *But she sure as hell can make love to me like no other woman I knew.*

THE BLIND GIRL

AN EROTIC ROMANCE

VICTORIA RUSH

1

———————

I first noticed her while walking downtown on a blustery summer day. A waif-like girl, not more than a hundred pounds, walking slowly through a busy intersection in downtown Chicago. Her long brown hair was blowing in the wind but it was the soft tapping of the pavement in front of her that attracted my attention. I peered down and noticed the rhythmic swinging of a white cane in front of her body. She seemed oblivious to the movement of the noisy traffic around her, holding her sunglass-clad head upright and steady as she strode confidently through the crossing. I didn't notice the blur of yellow while I glanced at her exquisite ass in her skinny jeans, clinging to her shapely figure like the tights of a ballerina. But when the taxi honked his horn angrily as he sped around the corner on a red light, I leapt instinctively ahead of her and slammed my palms loudly on the hood of his car.

"Watch where you're going, asshole!" I screamed, glaring at the driver through his windscreen while I blocked his progress with my legs straddling the front of his grille. "Are you *blind*? Can't you see people are crossing the lane?"

"Sorry," the cab driver shrugged, sticking her head outside his window. "The girl was walking so slowly, I was just trying to get ahead of the crowd."

"Not *everybody's* in a hurry, buddy," I said, shaking my head. "You should be more careful, you could have run someone over."

By now, the pretty blind girl and the rest of the passing pedestrians had traversed the intersection, pausing briefly on the other side to stare at me while they waited for the light to change at the adjacent crossing. When the signal turned green and the cars queued up behind the taxi began to honk their horns impatiently, I slapped my hands once again on the cab's hood and grudgingly moved out of his way.

"Thanks," the blind girl said when I joined her on the other side of the street. "But I had it under control. I heard him coming and was about to slow down."

"I didn't know," I said, peering down at her equally tight sweater, showcasing her perky breasts and hourglass figure. "You just looked so vulnerable walking alone like that through the busy intersection. I don't know why the city allows cars to turn right on a red, especially at the height of rush hour. Somebody's liable to get killed one of these days..."

"Not to worry," the girl chuckled. "It's not like I haven't done this before. I'm used to crazy cab drivers by now."

"You're not worried about not being able to *see* them?" I said.

"I can *hear* them approaching long before they pose any threat," the girl nodded. "I've developed a pretty sharp sense of awareness using my other senses. You'd be surprised what a blind person can do with only her hearing and a long enough cane."

"I'm sorry about that *blind* comment I made to the driver," I said, suddenly feeling self-conscious about my thoughtless interjection. "That was insensitive of me."

"No worries," the girl laughed. "It's just a figure of speech. I'm used to it by now."

"I suspect it's much more than that to you. Please accept my apologies."

"Why don't you let me buy you a coffee to thank you for your kindness?" the girl said, tapping her cane softly against the side of my shoe. "That is, if you're not in as much of a hurry as the impatient cab driver..."

"No–I mean *yes*," I stammered, flushing lightly at the girl's invitation.

"Great," she smiled, crooking her free arm. "There's a little shop around the corner that serves the best coffee in town. Why don't you let me show you the way?"

"Okay," I said, slipping my arm between hers and feeling my skin tingle as she stepped off the curb and began tapping her cane on the pavement while she pulled me closer to her.

I had to smile at the irony of a blind girl leading me through this part of the city, where I already knew the location of virtually every coffee shop and upscale clothing store next to the Miracle Mile, having lived here most of my life. But I was happy to find any excuse to get closer to her, feeling the soft brush of her fuzzy mohair sweater rubbing against my exposed skin. When we reached the entrance to the shop, she opened the door for me and I stepped tentatively inside, breathing in the heavenly scent of the exotic coffees brewing behind the counter.

"What will you have?" the girl asked, turning towards me as she approached the cashier.

"I feel like *indulging* today," I smiled, scanning the hand-drawn menu on the large chalkboard hanging over the far wall. "How about a caramel macchiato?"

"For the lady," the girl said, nodding toward the barista. "And I'll have an Americano."

There was an awkward silence while the barista turned to prepare our drinks, then the girl reached out to squeeze my arm.

"Why don't you find us a free table near the window?" she said. "I like to feel the sun on my face while I sip my coffee. I'll join you in a few minutes."

"Okay," I said, not used to being the submissive one, especially in the company of a supposedly handicapped partner.

I found a table in the corner of the shop and sat down, watching the girl effortlessly pay for the coffees while tapping her credit card over the point-of-sale terminal lying next to the cash register, then she picked up the drinks and walked in the direction of our table, slowing down just in time to place the steaming coffees deftly on the surface in front of me.

"Yours is the bigger cup," she said, sitting down opposite me while she angled her cane gently over her lap.

"Thanks," I said, picking up the cup and taking a quick sip of the tangy brew, humming approvingly at the sweet taste of the exotic concoction. "But how did you know where to find me?"

"I followed your scent," the girl smiled. "You're wearing a lovely perfume. Is that Yves Saint Laurent?"

"Yes, Black Opium," I said, widening my eyes at her surprising sense of perceptiveness. "How did you know?"

"I've got a keen sense of smell," the girl nodded. "I suppose it's somewhat overdeveloped because of my loss of sight."

The girl gently removed the lid of her cup and cradled it between her hands while lifting it slowly under her nose. She inhaled deeply and smiled with a slight upturn of her lips, then she tilted the mug between her parted lips, sucking back a small mouthful while she hummed softly, swirling the elixir inside her mouth before swallowing it like a gentle rivulet in a babbling stream. I'd never seen anyone drink their coffee so sensuously, and suddenly I felt self-conscious about wolfing down my overly flavored coffee so quickly.

"I'm Jade," I said, practically choking on my next mouthful as I studied the soft curves of her face. I couldn't see her eyes behind her dark glasses, but her countenance reminded me of a young Audrey Hepburn from the movie Breakfast at Tiffany's.

"Juliet," the girl nodded, raising her cup toward mine in a gesture of goodwill.

"Jade and Juliet," I smiled at the lyrical alliteration of our names. "Something tells me that near-miss with the taxi wasn't just by chance. I have a feeling we were meant to cross paths today."

"Maybe so," Juliet smiled with a soft flush of her face. Now it was *her* turn to betray the growing attraction between us...

2

———

J uliet and I chatted for an hour or so in the coffee shop, then we decided to go for a stroll along the waterfront park toward her home near the Navy Pier. We talked about our lives growing up in Chicago, and I learned that her blindness was caused by a congenital condition that caused her to lose her sight in early childhood. By the time we reached the end of the park, neither of us were ready to separate, and we hesitated awkwardly outside the entrance to her upscale condominium building.

"Is this where you live?" I said, peering up at the tall, gleaming tower overlooking the lake.

"Yes," Juliet said. "Would you like to come inside? There's a magnificent view from the forty-fourth floor. Or so I've been told."

"Um, sure," I said, suddenly feeling my panties dampening at the possibility of making love to this mysterious and alluring blind girl.

"I'd like to stop by the market first," she said. "I need to pick up some food for dinner. Will you join me? I make a mean mushroom risotto."

"Mmm, sounds delicious," I said. "You're twisting my arm."

"It's a date, then," Juliet said, grabbing my hand and pulling me in the direction of the Whole Foods store one block away.

When we entered the store, Juliet went to the produce section and I watched her, bemused, as she sampled and chose the ingredients for the meal. First, she picked up a large portobello mushroom from the display case and caressed it gently with her fingers, like she was squeezing a plump breast. After placing it in her cart, she selected a long zucchini and bent it softly in her hands, stroking and squeezing it like an oversize cock. When she raised a tuft of parsley and buried her nose in it, smelling its bouquet like it was a woman's sex, I practically came right there in the aisle. For the next twenty minutes, I followed her through the store, amazed at how easily she moved from aisle to aisle, shaking the boxes and feeling the shapes of the jars to select exactly what she needed. When we reached the liquor section, she turned to me and smiled.

"Would you like to choose the wine?" she said.

"For making the *risotto*, or as a side accompaniment?"

"Both. Something crisp and dry, like a pinot Grigio or Sauvignon blanc."

I scanned the bottle labels and chose a moderately priced pinot with a good rating then one of my favorite chardonnays for the pairing, and placed them in the cart.

"Done," I said, suddenly feeling my stomach rumbling at the thought of sitting down for the delicious meal.

"Good," she said. "Let's head to the check-out and blow this popstand. I'm starved!"

When we got to the check-out lane, I volunteered to pay for the groceries since she'd paid for the coffees earlier, but she insisted on covering the cost since she'd invited me, so I bagged the items while she paid at the terminal. When we returned to her building, we took the elevator to the top floor, and I gasped when she opened the door to her suite and I saw the expansive view of the lake through her floor-to-ceiling windows.

"Wow!" I exclaimed, admiring the clean esthetic of her beautifully appointed apartment. "This place is *gorgeous*. Do you live here all by yourself?"

"Most of the time," she nodded, leading me into her open-air kitchen and placing the bags on the counter. "Why don't you enjoy the view while I start preparing dinner? It should be ready in an hour or so."

I walked out onto the terrace and gazed out over the blue horizon which seemed to stretch out forever, and breathed in the fresh scent of the lake breeze wafting in from the East. The terrace was almost as big as my back yard, with beautiful wicker furniture and a gleaming Viking grill, and I wondered how a blind girl could afford to live independently like this. When I returned to the kitchen, I could already smell the savory scent of the rice and the broth cooking in the stovetop pan.

"Can I help with something?" I said.

"Why don't you chop the onions and zucchini while I keep an eye on the rice?" Juliet said.

As I chopped the vegetables, Juliet sliced the portobello mushrooms into thin wedges on a separate cutting board and minced the parsley using curled fingers to blunt the sharp edge of the knife. I continued to be amazed at how easily she was able to do everything sighted people took for granted, and while I had the chance, I soaked up her beautiful figure in her tight-fitting clothes, knowing I could ogle her with impunity. She'd finally taken her sunglasses off and I studied her beautiful brown eyes staring straight ahead, not recognizing any sign of impairment.

"Everything okay over there?" she said, sensing my distraction. "You seem a little pensive..."

"I was just wondering how you can afford such a beautiful penthouse apartment. I never asked what you do for a living."

"*Nothing*, mostly," Juliet said. "My father's an investment banker and he seems to have a knack for picking the right stocks. I've never really wanted for anything as long as I can remember."

"You don't miss being able to *see*? I mean, since you weren't born blind. You once had the faculty, then lost it."

"It's been so long now, I can barely remember. But I do remember our frequent visits to the family cottage. I guess that's why I chose an apartment on the lakefront. I enjoy the smell of the water and the sound of the waves breaking over the shore."

"What do you do to keep busy?" I said, peering into the living room and noticing a baby grand piano sitting next to the large sectional sofa. "Does your family visit fairly often?"

"From time to time," Juliet nodded. "I dabble in a little songwriting and do yoga on the terrace between long walks downtown."

"That explains your perfect figure," I smiled, catching another quick peek of her tight ass. "You certainly seem self-sufficient in most ways."

"Not *every* way," she smiled. "It's nice to have some female company for a change."

"Oh?" I said, fishing for more details. "No boyfriends on the horizon?"

"Not since high school," Juliet laughed. "I find them a bit clumsy. Besides, they only seem interested in one thing..."

"I know what you mean," I said, feeling my pussy twitching when I learned she was single. "My first husband couldn't find his way around a woman's body if he had a magnifying glass. He might as well have been–"

"Blind?" Juliet said, pausing the stirring of the risotto in the pan.

"Sorry," I coughed. "I just meant it as another figure of speech. I'm going to have to be more careful around you."

"Please don't," Juliet said, stirring the broth more vigorously and tipping a sample up toward her lips. "I like your free spirit. It's refreshing to be with someone who doesn't treat me with kid gloves."

"I wouldn't *dream* of it," I said, scooping up some chunks of onion and zucchini from the cutting board and sprinkling them into the pan over her delicate fingers.

When the meal was finally ready, the two of us repaired to her small but elegant dining room, where we sat kitty-corner at the edge of the table overlooking the lake while we listened to soft jazz playing over the stereo. We made small talk for a while, feeling the increasing sexual tension between the two of us, then as we neared the end of the meal, Juliet stretched her right hand over the table toward my idle left hand and interlaced her fingers with mine, caressing my hand softly.

"Would you like something for dessert?" she said.

I peered into her eyes, angled down toward our joined hands.

"Yes," I said. "But not *food*. At least not the kind you were thinking. I've been dying to eat you up practically since the moment I met you."

"Good," she said, squeezing my hand more firmly. "Because unlike you, I haven't had a chance to examine your body properly, and I've been looking forward to squeezing something other than mushrooms and zucchini for a change..."

3

———————

Juliet led me into her bedroom and lit some soft candles, then the two of us danced to the music playing in the other room as we slowly undressed one another. When we were fully disrobed, we fell onto the bed, twisting our bodies together while we moaned in each other's mouths. Now that I'd finally seen her body naked for the first time, I was even more turned on by her perfect ballerina figure, squeezing her small but firm breasts while sliding my fingers down the crack of her perfectly round ass. But Juliet wasn't about to let me have all the fun, and she quickly flipped me onto my back while sitting upright overtop of my hips.

"It's my turn to explore *your* body now," she smiled. "You didn't think I knew you were staring at my butt the whole time I was stirring the risotto?"

"I had to do *something* to keep myself distracted from the growing wet spot in my pants," I purred, staring up at her luminous face. "You've kept me waiting so long, I had to satisfy myself by making love to you with my eyes."

"Well, I suppose I'll have to settle for studying you with my *fingers* now that I've got you exactly where I want you," she said, sliding the tips of her fingers gently over the top of my forehead and across my eyelids while she hummed softly.

She rolled her thumbs over the crest of my brow, nodding approvingly.

"You have beautiful *eyebrows*," she said. "Full, and perfectly trimmed, with a lovely arch..."

"You can tell all of this just from using your *fingers*?" I said, flaring my eyes open.

"You'd be surprised by the things I can discern using my fingers," she grinned, continuing her gentle exploration of my face.

"I can imagine," I panted, feeling my pussy beginning to dampen again. "You practically had me coming just watching you feel the vegetables at the food market."

"I might have been channeling something else while I was sampling the produce. You weren't the *only* one with lascivious thoughts on your mind."

"Mmm," I moaned, rolling my hips impatiently while she slid her fingers over my cheekbones and around the outline of my lips. "I can't wait for you to slide those fingers a little lower on my body..."

"In due course," she said. "Most of the fun is in the build-up."

"Maybe," I nodded. "It gives me all the more time to stare at your beautiful tits."

"You don't think they're too *small*?" she said.

"Are you kidding me?" I said, reaching out to circle her hard nipples with my fingertips. "They're absolutely perfect. If you weren't pinning me to the mattress, I'd be sucking them into my mouth right now."

"All in due time," Juliet smiled, using her elbows to push my arms away from her body while she continued to caress me. "Lie still while I finish examining you."

"It's not going to be so easy if you keep touching me like that."

"Would you rather I sit on your *face* to keep you still?"

"In due course," I teased. "I'm way ahead of you..."

"Mmm," Juliet purred, sliding her fingers over the fullness of my lips while pressing her thumbs inside my moist cavity. "I'm looking forward to feeling these pretty lips sucking my *pearl*. They're very full and moist."

"Those aren't the *only* lips that are full and moist right now," I grunted, biting the knuckle of her thumb while I circled the tip of my tongue over her digit.

"So I can see," Juliet said, rolling her dripping pussy over my slippery mound while she stared straight ahead toward the headboard.

It was strange not being able to look into her eyes while she sat on top of me and explored my body, but there was something erotic about watching her meditative gaze as she had her way with me. It was as if she was channeling all of her senses through her fingertips while she caressed every crevasse and curve of my body. And she wasn't the only one whose other senses were over-stimulated from the suppression of another. I closed my eyes and savored every stroke of her fingers, feeling the pores of my skin tingling with goose bumps while our commingled juices dribbled down the front of my pussy.

"And this jaw..." she said, sliding her hands along the side of my face and fingering the crease of my chin with both thumbs. "So strong, yet feminine. And perfectly symmetrical, just like the rest of your face. You must have a long line suitors, looking as pretty as this."

"Not as many as you might imagine," I frowned, peering up at her. "I seem to be the one always making the first move–"

"Like when you leapt in front of me to save me from the errant cab driver earlier today?" she smiled.

"I didn't do that to make a *pass* at you, at least not at first," I laughed. "Although I *was* mesmerized by your exquisite ass before I saw him swinging in front of you."

"Mm-hmm," Juliet huffed unconvinced, circling her fingers around my throat. "You sighted people have an unfair advantage."

"I'm not so sure about that," I grunted, feeling the electricity between us ramping up as she pinned me to the bed. "I'm starting to think your lack of sight has given you some kind of superpowers. I've never felt so turned on from a woman's touch before."

"Oh?" Juliet smiled, loosening her grip around my neck. "Is this your first time being with a woman this way?"

"No, but it's the first time I've almost come watching her touch something other than my *pussy*."

"You know," she grinned, tickling her fingers down the front of my chest toward my tingling breasts. "Some women can climax just *imagining* erotic thoughts. I've done so more than once listening to some of my favorite audiobooks."

"Without *touching* yourself?" I said, tilting my head up. "Who are your favorite authors?"

"I've got quite a few, but one of my favorites is Anais Nin. I love the way she can arouse my desire with her flowery prose, never resorting to crude words."

"That's ironic," I said, reflecting back on the time when my best friend Hannah tested my mettle by stimulating me remotely while I read one of Anais' books publicly in a crowded cafe. "I've had an orgasm reading one of her books too, although I confess it was under slightly different circumstances–"

"That sounds kind of *kinky*," Juliet said, circling her middle fingers around my swelling nipples while I felt her soft breath breathing down over my belly. "Do tell."

"Perhaps another time," I said, not wanting to interrupt her flow. "I'm enjoying a *different* kind of stimulation right now."

"Your nipples are quite large," she said, fingering my protruding bullets. "And *hard*. I'm looking forward to *fucking* them a little later after I'm finished exploring your body."

"Such naughty words," I teased. "I thought you didn't like using those."

"I didn't say *I* didn't," she smiled. "I just like it when others can arouse me in different ways sometimes. But I like it rough and dirty, too."

"Mmm," I moaned, rolling my hips more vigorously as my pussy twitched and dribbled down the middle of my slit. "I'm imagining you soiling my nipples with your pretty pussy right now..."

"Do you think it's pretty?" Juliet said, rocking her hips in synchronicity with mine while she pinched my nipples. "I noticed that yours is shaved, while mine is all hairy and unkempt."

"Sometimes messy is good," I rasped, arching my back as she pinched my nipples harder. "It's rare to find a woman with a natural bush these days."

"It sounds like you've been naked with a *lot* of women in your time," Juliet said, tightening her grip on my nipples.

"Perhaps a few," I grunted from the mixture of pleasure and pain she was giving me. "But none as mysterious and beautiful as you."

"You probably say that to all of your lovers," Juliet huffed

"Well, I've never been with a *blind* woman before," I said, reaching up to caress her small tits. "Nor one with such a perfect ass or breasts..."

"I haven't found any imperfections in *you* either," she said, squeezing my breasts before slipping her knee between my legs and sliding her dripping pussy over the top of my right thigh.

"You haven't even gotten halfway finished yet," I chuckled. "I'm sure you'll find a few things askew once you get a little lower."

"I can't *imagine*," she said, sliding the tips of her fingers down the indentation in the center of my abdomen and stopping as she pressed her thumb slowly into my navel. "Even your *bellybutton* is perfect, with its tiny little hole and tight hood."

"Oh my God," I groaned, humping my pussy over the front of her knee. "I see what you mean about coming without direct genital contact. If you keep stimulating me like this, I"m going to climax long before you get anywhere near my pussy."

"We'll have to see about that," she said, sliding further down my leg and grinding her wet labia over the top of my knee. "But not if you keep *cheating* like that."

"You're killing me!" I protested as she tickled the rim of my navel with the tip of her finger.

"I hope so," she smiled. "Did you know the French call an orgasm *petite mort*, meaning little death? I'm planning to kill you one caress at a time."

4

———————

"The closer your fingers get to my nether regions, the more you're getting there," I said, spreading my now unconfined legs further apart for her to see the rivers of lubrication running down my slit and between the crack of my ass, leaving a large wet spot on her bed.

"So I can see," she said, sliding her hand over the sheets in front of my pussy while she caressed my shaved mound with her other hand. "I like your smooth mound. I can't even feel any stubble."

"I had it lasered a while ago," I nodded. "It was too much trouble keeping it shaved with a sharp razor blade."

"I can imagine," Juliet said, sliding her thumbs over the crest of my mound, millimeters from the edge of my throbbing clit. "Even more so for a *blind* girl."

"I'll be happy to do the honors if you feel like giving it a try sometime," I said. "It's a singular pleasure licking a woman's pussy when it's bare and exposed in all its glory."

"We'll have to see about that," Juliet said. "I'd like to sample yours first before taking the leap."

"Yes, please," I said, raising my aching pussy higher off the bed, closer to her face.

"Soon enough," Juliet teased. "I'm not finished cataloguing your body. I want to know every curve and cranny before I take you to paradise."

"Two can play that game," I said with a sly grin. "Just wait until it's my turn to stimulate *you*. I'm going to make you squeal and squirm just as much as you did to me before I kill you with pleasure."

"I hope so," Juliet said, pressing the tips of her fingers over the bony prominence of my pelvis before sliding them sensuously over the tops of my trembling thighs.

"I see that you haven't shaved *these*, at least," she said, levitating her hands barely above the surface of my skin, feeling the soft hairs of my thighs standing on end as she teased and tormented me.

"Not my *upper* legs," I groaned. "Thankfully, those hairs don't grow as long and thick as the ones on my shins."

"Mmm," Juliet nodded, sliding her palms over my knees and across the curvature of my inner calves. "Your legs have a beautiful tone and shape to them. Slender but firm, like a dancer's. I can tell you take care of yourself."

"I go to the gym and do a little yoga," I nodded, contracting my calves unconsciously as she squeezed and caressed them. "It gets harder the older you get. I think I've got a few extra years on you."

"Oh?" Juliet said, stopping the movement of her hands temporarily. "I never would have guessed from the firmness and suppleness of your skin. Exactly how much older are you, exactly?"

"I'm thirty-six. And I'm guessing you're closer to–"

"Twenty-two," Juliet said.

"Does our age difference give you pause?" I said, worried that the halting of her caresses foreshadowed something more serious.

"Not in the least," she said, continuing to run her palms down the lower part of one leg and over the curve of my anklebone. "Unlike some *sighted* people, I don't have the handicap of biasing my impressions on the age and beauty of my partners."

"I never thought of it that way," I said, feeling a stronger attachment to this exotic beauty the longer we spent together. "I suppose there are certain advantages to missing some perceptions, after all."

"There are pluses and minuses," she nodded, slipping her hand around the base of my heel and softly caressing the sole of my foot while massaging the top surface with her other hand. "I've just found a way to maximize the advantages."

"You certainly have," I nodded, closing my eyes while I savored her sensuous foot massage. "If you're ever need a *job*, you'd make one hell of a professional masseuse."

"The kind in a *massage parlor*, or the therapeutic kind?"

"You seem to be exquisitely skilled at both," I purred.

"But the erotic kind might be more *fun*," she smiled.

"Certainly for the *recipient*," I said, rolling my hips suggestively, signaling for her to begin moving her hands back up higher on my tingling body.

"Are you growing impatient for a happy ending?" she said, spreading my feet wider apart and squatting her knees between my parted legs.

"I'm enjoying the journey," I said. "I'm just not sure about your final destination."

"Neither am I," Juliet grinned, squeezing my ankles tightly and sliding her palms slowly up the inside of my lower legs. "Sometimes it's fun just following the road to see where it takes you."

"Well, if you continue following *that* route, I assure you that the junction of those two roads will lead you to a rewarding place."

"Rewarding for you, or rewarding for me?"

"I suppose that depends on what you do when you get there," I grinned. "I didn't ask if you'd been with a woman this way before, also. There are so many ways two women can please each other by rubbing certain parts of their bodies together–"

"You mean like *this*?" Juliet said, sliding her thumbs over my knees and turning her palms inward as she inched closer to my quivering pussy.

"Among other ways," I panted, feeling my juices running down my slit like a waterfall.

"How about like *this*?" she said, leaning her body forward and blowing softly on my dripping petals.

"Fuck, yes," I groaned.

"Mmm, I like it when you talk dirty," Juliet purred.

"Suck my pussy, Juliet," I huffed. "I want to feel your pretty rosebud lips over my hot clit."

"Mmm," Juliet purred. "I can feel the heat from your opening. But I want to tease you for just a little longer..."

"You're driving me *crazy*," I protested, thrashing my hips wildly in front of her lips. "How much longer are you going to make me wait? I want to come all over your face so badly..."

"That depends on you," Juliet smiled, blowing harder on my erect gland while squeezing the bottom of my upper thighs under my wet ass with her thumbs, inches away from my swollen folds. "You just have to use your imagination a little harder."

"I'm already dreaming of all the ways I want to make love to you," I grunted. "I'm going to come so hard the moment you touch me."

"I'm *already* touching you," Juliet grinned.

"I mean on my sensitive spot. I'm going to explode any moment now..."

"Yes, baby," Juliet purred as she brought her face closer to my quivering pussy while she squeezed my shaking thighs more firmly. "Close your eyes and lose yourself in the feeling. I can feel you getting closer..."

"Oh God, oh God," I huffed, feeling my orgasm coming on like a freight train the more she blew on my engorged clit. "I'm going to come, Juliet. I'm going to come so hard. Oh *fuckkkkk!*"

I probably should have warned Juliet about my tendency to squirt when I had powerful orgasms, but I'd been so lost in the buildup that I completely lost sight of everything else beyond my growing pleasure. When my orgasm finally washed over me, I felt my contractions clamping down inside my pussy as my pelvic floor muscles began pulsing, ejecting huge spurts of ejaculatory fluid and vaginal juices all over her surprised face. But bless her heart, for she didn't flinch while I ejected one long, hard spray after another over her pretty face while I jerked and screamed at the top of my lungs. It took well over a minute for me to finish convulsing and squirting, and when I finally relaxed my clenched butt muscles and collapsed my body back down onto the soaking bed, I flared my eyes open, shocked at how easily the blind girl had brought me to a powerful orgasm simply by caressing every part of my body beyond the obvious places, using only her fingers and the power of suggestion.

"There now," she said, sliding her body next to mine and kissing me softly. "That wasn't so bad after all, was it?"

"Are you kidding me?" I panted, still coming down from my intense climax. "I don't think I've *ever* come that hard. And you did it by barely touching me."

"Well, I was touching you," Juliet said. "Just not in the usual places."

"It's true, what you said earlier," I said, feeling her soft breasts pressing against mine. "Sometimes you only need to use your imagination to enjoy the most sublime of experiences."

"Yes," Juliet said, grinding her mound softly against mine. "Although there's something to be said for taking a more *direct* approach from time to time."

"I know what you mean," I said, this time rolling her over onto *her* back and pinning her to the mattress. "And this time, I have no intention of treating you with kid gloves..."

5

———————

I sat up on top of Juliet's hips the way she'd done with me earlier and swiped my still-dripping pussy over her soft bush. As she rolled her hips in tandem with me, moaning softly, I peered down into her vacant eyes staring straight ahead, feeling guilty about using her for my own pleasure.

"What's it like?" I said, pausing our movement. "I mean, making love to somebody without being able to see them?"

"Much the same as I imagine it is for sighted people," Juliet said. "The feelings are the same, and just as pleasurable. Maybe even *more* so, because we're focused even more on our sense of touch."

"I suppose that makes sense," I nodded. "I'm beginning to feel a bit handicapped myself, distracted as I am by your pretty face and beautiful figure while I touch you..."

"Why don't you try it for yourself, *without* your sense of sight?" Juliet said. "I have a silk scarf in my armoire that you could use as a blindfold."

"That *does* sound intriguing," I said, feeling my pussy twitching involuntarily. "But I'm worried I might poke you in the face with an errant elbow or knee, not having your innate sense of space and movement."

"You get used to it faster than you might imagine," Juliet laughed. "You already know where the important parts are. Haven't you ever made love in the dark before?"

"Of course," I said. "Let's give it a shot. At the very least, it'll be a fun experiment and give me a chance to put myself in your shoes."

"Absolutely," Juliet smiled. "Besides, *I've* never made love to a blind girl either."

"Save that thought," I said, rolling off her hips and jumping off the bed. "I'll be back in a flash."

It didn't take long to find her Hermes scarf hanging next to her camel-hair dress coat, and I folded it over three times to make sure the fabric was completely opaque before tying it tightly around the back of my head and pulling the edges over the bottom of my eyes to block out all of my peripheral vision.

"This is a bit *scary*," I said, holding out my arms in front of me and taking some slow steps back in the direction of her bed. "I'm not familiar with the arrangement of your furniture and I'm operating in the dark for the first time."

"Just go slow and follow my voice–" Juliet purred from the bed.

I slammed my knee against her sideboard and cursed softly under my breath.

"Shit!" I groaned. "It looks like it's going to take me a little longer to acclimate to your surroundings than you have."

"Here," Juliet said, reaching out her hand. "Feel my hand and let me guide you the rest of the way."

I reached my right hand out awkwardly in front of me and swiped it from side to side until I felt her hand, then she clasped my fingers softly with mine, pulling me onto the bed beside her. We kissed for a few minutes and I purred into her mouth, focusing on the feeling of her soft lips and the fresh taste of her saliva.

"Mmm," I mewed. "Somehow this feels different than kissing someone with my eyes closed..."

"*Good* different or *bad* different?" Juliet said.

"Good, I think," I nodded, running my fingers through her hair as we probed each other's mouths with our tongues. "It's forcing me to focus on my other sensations."

"Are you finding those sensations *pleasurable*?"

"Your hair feels incredibly soft and silky," I nodded. "And your lips feel even fuller than I remembered from before."

"Well, they might be a little more puffed up than usual from the stimulation of your tongue right now," she said.

"Good," I smiled. "Hopefully some *other* parts of you are also getting puffed up from my stimulation."

"I don't think you have to worry about that," Juliet said, pressing her moistening pussy against my thigh as I pushed my knee between her legs.

"I want to taste and feel every part of your body like this," I said, kissing my way slowly down her neck while I felt the twitch of her muscles and the drops of her sweat as her body involuntarily responded to my touch.

"I never answered your question earlier," she said.

"Which question is that?" I said.

"The one about whether I'd been with another woman like this before. And the answer is no, unless you count some playful teasing under the covers during elementary school sleepovers."

"Well you certainly seem to know your way around a woman's body, for someone who's never had sex with one before."

"That hasn't stopped me from fantasizing about it, or learning from all the sexy audiobooks I've listened to."

"Well, you certainly seem to be a quick learner," I chuckled.

"As are you," she said, arching her back and groaning softly as my tongue reached her firm mounds and I began circling her hardening berries with my tongue.

"I love your small tits," I murmured. "They're so soft and firm. But not as hard as your *nipples*. I can feel the skin around them puckering..."

"My whole *body* is puckering," Juliet groaned. "I can feel my hairs standing on end, and the hood of my clit retracting."

"Oh my *God*," I panted. "Are you trying to make me come again before I touch you down there? Because my imagination is running wild right now..."

"I hope not," Juliet smiled. "I need all of your attention focused on me right now or I'm liable to explode before you get to the interesting places."

"These places are plenty interesting enough," I mumbled, alternately sucking each of her nipples until I was satisfied they were as hard and swollen as I could make them. "I'll be coming back to give them some more attention soon enough."

"Mmm," Juliet moaned, rolling her body sensuously on the bed while I stimulated her with my tongue. "I love the sensation of your lips licking my body," she said. "*Every* part of my body."

"I'm glad," I smiled. "But you still haven't experienced my most *talented* skill. I have a fair amount of experience licking women in a few *other* private places..."

"God, yes," Juliet grunted, rolling her hips aggressively, begging me to go lower on her body.

"All in due course, my love," I grinned.

"You're such a *tease*," Juliet huffed, crossing her arms over her chest in feigned anger while I tickled my way down the middle of her stomach with the tip of my tongue.

"I learned from the best," I smiled, playfully kissing her as I rimmed the outside of her navel with my tongue.

"That feels so good," she rasped, rocking her hips more vigorously.

"Are you channeling me licking you somewhere *else*?" I said.

"Let's just say that my imagination is running way ahead of you..."

"Don't come *too* fast," I grinned. "I want to feel your bean twitching in my mouth when you climax."

"It won't take long at *this* rate, I assure you."

"I better slow down then," I teased. "I wouldn't want to ruin the mood. Besides, I'm enjoying tormenting you as much as you did me earlier."

"Next time, I won't make you wait as long," she said, tilting her head up to gaze in my direction. "I promise to touch you more directly. I'm *dying* to taste your sex."

"Famous last words," I chuckled. "I bet you say that to all your lovers."

"I *wish*," Juliet huffed, lifting her hips to meet my face as I lowered my head over her soft and fragrant bush.

"Your muff is even softer than my fur hat. And far better smelling."

"I'm not sure if that's *my* scent you're sensing or your own," Juliet said. "Your pussy was still pretty wet when you sat over my hips before putting on the blindfold."

"Maybe so," I said. "But I like the scent of our perfumes *commingling*. I plan on doing a lot more commingling with you before the night is over."

"I hope so," Juliet said, licking her lips expectantly. "I've read enough of Anais Nin's stories to know the many ways two women can satisfy one another."

"You have *no* idea," I smiled, sticking my nose in her muff and inhaling her scent like she'd done with the parsley at the market, before lowering my face further between her legs.

6

———

When I felt how wet and slippery the insides of her thighs were, I turned my head and licked up her juices like the icing on the inside of a cake bowl, nibbling and teasing her around the perimeter of her steaming crotch. When she tried to push her body further down the bed to press her pussy into my mouth, I pulled away a few extra inches, blowing softly on her clit.

"Uhnnn," she groaned, swiping her arms down onto the mattress beside her and gripping the sheets tightly with two hands. "You're driving me crazy."

"How do you like it?" I taunted. "It's nice to be on the other end of this for a change."

"I like it," she panted. "But I'd like it a lot *more* if you'd tickle my button with those pretty, full lips of yours."

"I dunno," I smiled. "Maybe I'll just keep teasing you to see if you can climax from your imagination alone. I'm beginning to feel a little inadequate compared to your favorite author..."

"Oh no," Juliet protested. "I assure you, this feels way better than *listening* to someone describing the act. I just need to *see* what it actually feels like. I mean, to have another woman actually sucking my pussy."

"You poor thing," I said. "I'll acquiesce this time because it's your first time. I want to feel you climaxing just as much as you do."

"Yes, Jade," Juliet pleaded. "Suck me into your mouth. Show me what it feels like to make love to a woman. I've dreamed of this moment for so long–"

"Mmm," I hummed, lowering my face to her dripping pussy and licking up the middle of her dripping crease like it was a melting ice cream cone, then pausing when I reached the apex of her folds to wrap my lips around her flaring jewel and savor the sensation of her burning organ.

"Oh God," she grunted, pressing her pussy harder into my face. "That feels *so* much better than I imagined. Suck my clit, Jade. Lick me like you've licked all your other female partners."

"No way," I said, pulling my face away from her throbbing gland for a moment. "You're not like any of my other partners, and this is way different than all those other times."

"Because you're wearing a *blindfold* this time?"

"Partly," I said. "But you're different from all those other women. And not only because you're blind. You have a certain sweet innocence about you that I find especially arousing."

"Well, I'm glad you're the one I bumped into on the street to lose my innocence to. I can't imagine a more loving and tender partner for my first time."

"Oh Juliet," I said, feeling my heart pounding in my chest as my eyes watered under the blindfold while I circled her clit with my lips and felt myself growing closer to this mysterious and sexy blind girl. I rolled my tongue softly over her bulb and as she began to rock her hips in growing ecstasy, I circled the tip over her nub in figure-eight motions, caressing every part of her throbbing gland.

"Yes, Jade," Juliet huffed. "Don't stop. I'm going to come on your face any moment now..."

When I heard that she was moments away from climaxing, I pulled my face away from her burning pussy, feeling her legs twitching next to my cheeks.

"What are you doing?" Juliet protested. "I was just about to come!"

"I'm enjoying this way too much to let you come this fast," I said, listening to her pussy making wet slurping sounds as her vulva spasmed in a mini pre-climax. "Besides, I still haven't paid you back sufficiently for tormenting me earlier when I was prostrated in front of *you*."

"I promise I'll never do that again," Juliet pleaded, gyrating her hips rapidly in front of my blindfold-covered face. "I promise I'll suck your clit as hard and fast as you want whenever you ask me–"

"Is that the *only* way you're going to touch me?" I teased, blowing my cool breath over her puckering vulva.

"God no," Juliet hissed. "I'm going to fuck you with my cunt and my fingers and my toes and every other part of my body that can possibly make you squirm and squeal with. I'm going to do all the things my favorite author described and plenty more. That's all I could think about while I was preparing dinner."

"Good," I said. "Because I'm far from finished with you. This is just the appetizer before the main course."

I buried my face back in her steaming snatch and clenched my hands around her tightening buttocks, sucking her clit hard into my mouth while flapping my tongue faster over her glans, listening to the whimpers emanating from higher up on the bed as she inched closer to nirvana. While she slowly elevated her hips higher off the surface of the bed, my head followed her movement in lock-step, flicking her clit ever harder while tasting the juices running down the front of my chin.

When she finally climaxed with a loud animal grunt, jerking her pussy hard against my dripping face, I held her tightly in my arms, savoring every twitch and spasm of her exploding pussy. She didn't squirt like I had, but the combination of sensations I felt while holding her shaking body eclipsed anything I'd ever experienced before. I wasn't sure if it was because I was quickly falling in love with the pretty blind girl, or if it was because I was blindfolded when she came for the first time. Either way, it was the most erotic sensation I'd felt in a long time, and I didn't want to let go of her even after she stopped shaking against my face.

Besides, I smiled to myself. There'd be plenty of time to teach her how to gush and squirt when she climaxed. That was *one* special talent I'd be holding in reserve for the right moment.

7

———————

uliet and I made love three more times that night, then we fell asleep in each other's arms, resting peacefully until the light from the morning sun woke us up. I got out of bed and went to the kitchen to make coffee, and when I heard Juliet stirring, I brought her a steaming cup and placed it on her night table.

"Mmm," she purred, smelling the hot java. "That's a pleasant sensation to wake up to. I haven't had someone bring me coffee in bed since, well, *forever*."

"If you feel like staying in bed, I'd be happy to whip up some omelettes while we watch the sunrise together..."

"That sounds yummy," Juliet nodded. "I worked up quite an appetite from all those calories we burned last night."

"That wasn't the *only* thing burning," I smiled. "I haven't had sex that hot in a long time."

"Me neither," Juliet said, taking a sip of her coffee. "Except in my case, it's been like, *never*."

"Why don't you relax while I get breakfast, then maybe we can generate some more heat before we decide what to do for the rest of the day."

"You mean you're not sick of me yet?" she said, propping her head up on a bent elbow. "I thought maybe the novelty of making love to a blind girl might have worn off by now–"

"Hardly," I said, sitting down beside her on the bed and kissing her softly on her lips. "We're just getting started here. Besides, I like you for a lot more than just the sex. You're starting to grow on me."

"I like the sound of that," Juliet purred. "You better get out of here and start preparing breakfast or we're likely to never to get out of bed today."

"Save that thought," I smiled. "I'll be back in a flash..."

While I started making breakfast, I heard Juliet get out of bed and go to the washroom then she joined me in the kitchen wearing only a long sweater, wrapping her arms around my waist while I whipped the eggs in a bowl.

"Can I help with anything?" she said, kissing me softly on the back of my neck.

"Yes," I said, taking a peek at the bottom of her bare ass poking out of her sweater. "You can find something else to do so as to not distract me from my task. If you keep prancing around in that skimpy outfit, I'm likely to *burn* something."

"Okay," she said, turning around and shimmying her ass at me while she headed toward the living room. "Maybe just for a few minutes."

She walked toward the piano and sat down on the bench in front of it, beginning to play some soft music while I chopped the vegetables on the cutting board to the beat of her melody.

When astronauts go up in space, she started singing softly.
And look down at us
They don't see lines
Separating us...

I turned around and watched her sing while she turned her face up to the rising sun in the east. Her voice sounded like an angel, soft and delicate like a young Sarah McLaughlin. I couldn't place the melody or the lyrics, and I suddenly realized that she was singing a song she'd composed herself.

They see a jewel
Floating in the void of space
That we are privileged
To call our place...

I found myself swaying my body to her beautiful voice and the rhythmic melody, smiling at the timely subject of her composition.

But our blue planet
Where once man roamed with room to spare
Is now a place
Where people fight over who goes where...

Suddenly, her fingers began moving quicker over the keyboard as she developed a crescendo into the chorus.

If we all want to live in peace and unison
They we must believe from the moment of birth
That we are citizens of planet earth
'Cause we are one...

"Oh my God," I said, temporarily stopping my cooking and walking over to her position at the piano, resting my hand on the polished Steinway. "Did you *write* that song?"

"It's something I whipped up one day after listening to the news and hearing about another war," she nodded. "Do you like it?"

"Like it?" I said. "It's absolutely beautiful. Besides the powerful message of the lyrics, the melody is uplifting and your voice is magnificent."

"Stop," Juliet said. "You're making me blush."

"I'm not kidding," I said. "Have you approached any agents or sent your material to any of the major record labels? This song could totally be a hit."

"I've never thought about writing my songs with the intention of going commercial–"

"Why don't you put it out on the internet then? I bet it would go viral in an instant. The record labels would be breaking down the doors to sign you. You could be the next Adele..."

"No thanks," Juliet said. "I'm happy leading my quiet life up here in the clouds. All that fame and attention isn't for me."

"Suit yourself," I said, furrowing my brows disappointingly. "I'm going to finish preparing breakfast while you serenade me. At least you've got *one* giant fan so far."

While I finished preparing the omelettes, I listened to Juliet singing some more songs, swaying my body rhythmically to the melody and her sweet voice, feeling my heart pounding and my eyes watering as she moved me to tears. By the time the meal was ready, I hated the idea of stopping her performance.

"I hate to interrupt your lovely concert," I said, placing the plates of food on her dining table. "I could stay here all day and listen to you playing. You're really tugging at my heartstrings."

"I'm glad," Juliet said, swiping the back of her hand softly over my cheekbones and feeling the trail of a tear rolling down the front of my face. "Is it just the *music* that's moving you this strongly?"

"No," I said, squeezing her hand more firmly. "I'm really starting to *fall* for you..."

"That makes two of us," Juliet said, smiling at me gently. "I have a feeling my *next* song will be about you."

8

———

After we finished breakfast, we talked about what we wanted to do for the rest of the day, and Juliet suggested going to the county fair.

"The county *fair*?" I said, widening my eyes. "Won't you get *vertigo* going on those rides? Plus, I'll have an unfair advantage playing all the games..."

"I wouldn't be so sure about that," Juliet winked. "Most of those games are rigged, anyway. They're more a matter of *luck* than skill. I used to go all the time when I was a kid. It's a huge thrill feeling my body being tossed around on the rides, not knowing where they're going to take me–"

"Ok," I said. "As long as you don't *throw up* on me. But I need to take a shower first before we head out. I don't want everyone smelling the scent of sex all over my body from last night."

"They'd barely notice over the aroma of popcorn, candy floss, and grilled hot dogs," Juliet laughed. "Do you mind if I join you? It might be kind of fun having a shower together."

"You're reading my mind, girl," I smiled, caressing her fingers as I wolfed down the last of my omelette. "We can clean this up afterwards. I've been dying to feel your lissome figure again, pretty much from the moment we woke up."

"Come, then," Juliet said, rising from the table and grasping my hand as she led me in the direction of her ensuite bathroom.

Her shower was bigger than I expected, with a large glass enclosure, dual shower heads, and a row of water jets lining the sides of the marble walls. After we stripped off our clothes and stepped inside, she twisted the taps and set the temperature to a steamy boil, then we stepped into the center of the spray, feeling the jets stimulating our skin while we melded our bodies together.

"Oh my God," I purred, slipping my tongue into her mouth. "This feels *heavenly...*"

"It feels even *more* heavenly if you position your hips in the right place," she smiled. "The water jets can be quite stimulating if you angle them a certain way."

She turned her body around to face one of the jets, then she tilted her hips upward until the spray squirted against her mound while she moaned softly. When I saw how she was stimulating herself, I pressed my tits against her wet back and humped her ass with my dripping pussy, feeling the spray jetting through our joined legs.

"Uhnnn," I grunted when I felt the powerful pulses between our slits. "Just when I thought this couldn't get any better. What *other* surprises have you got in store for me?"

"You'll have to wait until we get to the fair," she smiled, blinking her eyes under the overhead waterfall spray that was bouncing over our shoulders. "I play a pretty mean game of ring toss."

"I could probably snare one or two over your *nipples* right now," I said, rolling my hands over her slippery breasts and pinching her hardening teats. "That would be even more fun."

"Maybe," Juliet groaned, rocking her hips in synchronicity with me. "But I'm having plenty of fun playing *this* game right now."

"Do you want me to *soap you up*?" I said. "It might be more fun if we use our *hands* to enjoy this ride."

"Yes, please," Juliet mewed, angling her head over my shoulder to kiss my lips as the water cascaded over our faces.

I saw a bar of scented soap lying in the chrome rack on the side wall and picked it up, sliding it slowly under Juliet's arms and over her firm breasts.

"Mmm," she purred. "I love the way you touch me."

"And I love the way you *respond* to my touch," I said, feeling her tummy trembling while I swiped the bar lower and began lathering her hairy bush.

"I need to feel your fingers on my pussy again," Juliet grunted. "The combination of the warm spray, the slippery soap, and your soft hands is driving me crazy."

"Yes, baby," I hummed, echoing the lyrics to her song. "Surrender to the pleasure. 'Cause we are one..."

"You have a beautiful voice," Juliet moaned as I began fingering her clit. "Sing to me while you feel my body."

I paused for a moment while I thought about what I should sing to reflect our growing attraction, then I began warbling the Donny Hathaway song *A Song for You* in her ear.

I've been so many places in my life and time
I've sung a lot of songs, I've made some bad rhymes
I've acted out my life in stages
With ten thousand people watching
But we're alone now
And I'm singing this song to you...

"That's one of my favorite songs," she crooned, circling her hips faster while I jilled her clit harder. "I used to like the Michael Bublé version, but now I've got a new favorite cover artist."

"That's just because I'm playing with your pussy while I sing to you," I chuckled, sticking my little fingers into her dripping slit while I continued rubbing the slippery soap bar against her throbbing bean.

"Maybe," she shuddered. "But I could listen to you sing to me this way all day."

"Well, we can't stay inside *all* day," I grinned, dropping the bar of soap onto the shower floor while I circled her glans with my two forefingers and massaged her mound with my thumb. "We've got a date at the *fair*, remember?"

"Oh yeah," she grunted, tilting her hips further upward as she clenched her buttock muscles, edging closer to a climax. "Ring my bell, Jade. I'm ready to claim my prize."

"Uhnnn," I groaned along with her, feeling the powerful jet of water gushing between our joined hips while I circled her clit faster. "I'm going to come with you."

"*Fuck* yes," Juliet whimpered, her upper body becoming slack as her knees weakened near the height of ecstasy. "I'm coming, baby. Oh God, I'm coming for you. I love you so much..."

When she told me she loved me, it was like she'd flipped on another switch, and suddenly my pussy started convulsing in unison with hers while we both shook our bodies together under the undulating spray. When we finally came down from our highs, I held Juliet softly in my arms, savoring the feeling of the stimulating spray bathing us with its warmth.

"I love you too, Juliet," I whispered into her ear. "You've opened my eyes to a whole new world of joy and tenderness."

"You've opened *mine,* too," Juliet said, turning her body around and pressing our bodies together while we kissed passionately under the steaming shower spray.

9

———————

After Juliet and I got cleaned up, we took the train out to my place in the suburbs, then we drove my car to Lake County, where the annual fair was being held. When we entered the fairgrounds, we bought some candy floss, plastering the sticky strings of pastel candy all over our faces while playfully licking it off our cheeks. As we walked through the bustling promenade, listening to the carnival barkers and the children laughing all around us, Juliet perked up her ears while she listened to the announcement of the passing games. When we reached the bottle toss game, Juliet paused, grasping my arm.

"Why don't we try this one?" she said, pinching me playfully.

"You *do* realize this is the most impossible one to win?" I said, watching the contestants' plastic rings bouncing over the rows of stacked bottles and falling into the pit below. "I'm not sure those rings even *fit* over the top of these bottles..."

"Well, at least we'll have a level playing field then," she smiled. "It can't hurt to try. Come on, let's just play one round."

"Okay," I said, paying the attendant for six rings. "Why don't you go first?"

I handed Juliet three rings and she paused, holding one of them over the retaining wall while she concentrated on her aim. She tossed the first ring in the air and it bounced noisily over the lip of one of the glass bottles.

"See?" I said, bumping her ass while I glanced at the game attendant with a frown. "I told you this was impossible."

"Don't be such a skeptic," Juliet huffed. "You have to *believe* in it to make it happen. We still have five more rings. Now it's your turn."

I leaned over the wall separating the contestants from the rows of bottles, targeting the bottle closest to my position and lofted my ring gently in the air, watching it bounce over the tops of three bottles before landing in the pit.

"Arghh," I groaned, furrowing my brow frustratingly. "Like I said earlier, I'm not even sure if these rings fit over any of these bottles. I've never seen anyone actually land one successfully."

"Maybe we just need to *concentrate* a little harder," Juliet said, holding her second ring in front of her body and grimacing when she heard it bounce over one of the bottles and fall into the pit.

I tossed my last ring, watching it bounce unsuccessfully over the top of the bottles, then Juliet hesitated, holding her third ring out in front of her as she closed her eyes.

"I'm not sure that's going to help much," I chuckled, watching the look of concentration on her face.

She slowly tossed her ring with a gentle spiral to keep it from flipping over in the air, and it landed on top of one of the bottles, circling like a spinning top for a few seconds before settling down and nesting over the neck of the flask.

"We have a winner!" the carnival attendant announced, pointing toward Juliet.

"Woo-hoo!" she squealed, jumping up and down in glee.

"What kind of prize would you like?" the attendant said, approaching the two of us and pointing up towards the row of stuffed animals hanging from the ceiling. "You qualify for a mid-sized toy."

"What do they have available?" Juliet said, turning toward me while she stared straight ahead.

"Just about everything," I said, scanning the row of plush toys. "Giraffes, teddy bears, baby elephants–"

"I'll have the *elephant*!" Juliet gushed. "Dumbo was always my favorite cartoon character when I was a kid, with his oversize ears and his adorable face. He reminded me of *myself* while I was losing my sight and learning to rely more and more on my hearing to make my way in the world."

I nodded toward the attendant, then he handed us the stuffed animal.

"Do you want me to carry it for you?" I said. "You've got enough to worry about, trying to avoid bumping into people while we make our way through this busy crowd."

"As long as you keep holding on to me," Juliet nodded, having decided to forego bringing her cane and using me as her chaperone instead. "I'm afraid I might drop him."

We continued down the main thoroughfare of the game pit, then Juliet paused again when she heard the distinctive sound of the little groundhogs popping their heads up on the popular game *Whack-a-Mole*.

"I remember playing this game as a kid," she smiled. "It was always one of my favorites."

"But how can you have a chance of *hitting* one when you can't even see them?" I said, squinting my eyes suspiciously.

"The machine makes a little sound before popping each of the moles up. If I concentrate on the sound, I have a little forewarning before deciding where to move my mallet. Why don't you give it a try first?"

"Okay," I said, handing the attendant a five-dollar bill to pay for two turns.

When I pressed the button to start the first game, I closed my eyes for a moment, trying to focus on the sound of the popping heads. But each time the machine pinged and I slammed my mallet in the direction of the sound, I came up empty. When I heard the timer signaling that my time was about to run out, I opened my eyes in frustration and slammed the hammer haphazardly over the disappearing animal heads.

"That didn't help much," I chuckled, handing Juliet the mallet for her turn. "So much for having an advantage with my eyes closed."

"Always the doubter," Juliet said, moving my hand over the start button. "Watch and learn, grasshopper."

She grasped the baton with two hands, signaling for me to start the game, then she systematically slammed the mallet over the heads of each of the bopping moles one at a time until the game time finally ran out.

"We have a perfect score!" the game attendant barked over the p.a. system, pointing toward Juliet while I gazed at her with wide eyes.

"How did you do that?" I said, shaking my head incredulously. "I've never seen *anyone* snare every mole in this game!"

"Like I said earlier," Juliet smiled. "Sometimes there's an *advantage* to relying on our other perceptions."

"So I'm beginning to see," I nodded.

"What prize would you like?" the attendant said, peering at Juliet's vacant eyes. "You can choose from any of the largest animals."

"Do they have a panda bear?" she said, turning toward me.

"A very *big* one, yes," I said, peering up at the row of stuffed toys.

"I'll take it!" she said, bobbing up and down excitedly on her tiptoes.

I wrapped my arm around the panda bear's midsection, carrying the stuffed elephant in my other arm while I led Juliet away from the game pit area.

"I'm not sure we'll be able to fit any more of these things in my car at this rate," I chuckled. "Let alone carry them through the fair-grounds for the rest of the day."

"Let's mix it up and go for a *ride* then," Juliet said. "That'll give us a chance to rest the toys while we take a little breather. Besides, I'd hate to embarrass you anymore with my special talents while playing more of the games."

"Ps-shaw!" I huffed, grabbing her arm and steering her in the direction of the midway. "Let's see how well you do on the *Super-*

Twister. Something tells me your stomach won't be as strong as mine in surviving that ride."

"Not to worry, sweetheart," Juliet smiled, squeezing my hand. "I'm used to being tossed around next to you, not knowing where our ride will take us next. Bring it on!"

I purchased a ticket package for three rides at the nearest booth, then we got in line for the scariest roller coaster at the fair. When we finally walked onto the entrance ramp at the base of the paused ride, we sat side-by-side in one of the cars near the front of the column, placing the bear between the two of us and Dumbo wedged between the safety bar and her stomach.

"Are you sure you're ready for this?" I grinned, squeezing her hand as the train of carriages rattled forward and slowly started moving up the steep entrance ramp.

"No worries," she grinned, tickling the palm of my hand with her fingers. "Are *you*? Maybe you should close your eyes so you don't get frightened too much..."

"Fat chance of that," I said. "I already tried that technique and it didn't work."

"I didn't hear you complaining when you were *blindfolded* last night," she chuckled.

Suddenly, our car crested the top of the ramp and we whooshed a hundred feet straight downward while Juliet raised her arms over her head, squealing in delight as her long hair blew in the wind. While our car lurched from side to side over the winding path of the coaster at a terrifying speed, she continued holding her arms over her head the entire time, feeling the centripetal forces swaying her body while she grinned and I clasped the safety bar in front of me with white knuckles. When the ride finally lurched to a stop at the bottom of the ramp, I stumbled out of our carriage, walking dizzily onto the platform.

"Whoa, girl," Juliet said, grabbing hold of my arm as I tried to balance the two stuffed animals in each of my arms. "Maybe we should try something a little slower for our next ride."

"Good idea," I said, peering up at the large, slowly revolving wheel at the end of the midway. "How about the Ferris wheel?"

"Okay," Juliet said, interlacing her arm between mine. "At least we won't have to worry about our furry friends flying out of the ride this time."

We waited in line for the start of the next ride and when the attendant locked the door to our private gondola behind us and we began to feel the wheel slowly turning upward, I sighed a breath of relief.

"This is much more relaxing," I said. "You were right about that last one. I much prefer tossing around in *bed* with you than on that roller coaster."

"Yes," Juliet nodded. "But this one is kind of boring. There's nothing to keep me stimulated. At least you can peer down over the fairgrounds to distract your attention. I've got nothing to keep me distracted beyond the gentle rocking of our carriage."

"Perhaps you'd like me to rock something *else* to keep you stimulated while we're locked in this thing?" I smiled, pressing my hand between her thighs over her tight-fitting jeans.

"Do you think we have enough *time*?" Juliet said, slowly parting her legs.

"I suppose that depends on you," I smiled. "But instead of going slow and gentle, we might have to work a little faster this time."

"What did you have in mind, exactly?" Juliet said, squirming her ass while I gently probed her warm crotch. "I'm not sure I want to get naked on this seat that a million people have sat on."

"Maybe we don't have to," I grinned, pulling down the zipper of her jeans. "Why don't I keep a lookout while I finger you down the front of your pants?"

"Mmm," Juliet hummed, moaning softly as the tips of my fingers inched toward her moist pussy. "If you insist. That might make this ride a little more interesting..."

I pushed my hand lower under the front of her jeans, lubricating my fingers in her dripping slit, then I slowly pulled them back, circling her clit with my slippery digits. Juliet titled her head back and rested it on the cushion of our seat, spreading her legs further apart as I began to massage her gland more vigorously.

"Better?" I said, watching her roll her hips as I fingered her pussy.

"Much," she panted, parting her lips while she groaned more loudly. "How much more time have we got?"

I peered outside our carriage for a moment, noticing our gondola nearing the top of the wheel, pressing my middle fingers deeper inside her slit.

"About halfway. Do you think you can come from me just *fingering* you?"

"If you keep doing it *that* way," she grunted, tilting her hips upward to sink my digits even further in her hole. "Rub your palm against my clit while you finger me inside."

I paused for a moment, remembering the instructions of our coach when I attended a women's sex workshop where a group of us learned how to squirt. The trick, I learned, was to gradually stimulate the G-spot a few inches inside the top edge of the vagina while relaxing the sphincter muscles to allow the Skene's gland containing our ejaculatory fluid to express itself when we climaxed. As I began to press more firmly on the upper surface of her cavity while gently massaging her bulging gland, Juliet groaned and rocked her hips more vigorously.

"That feels heavenly," she grunted. "Whatever you're doing, you're giving me a whole different kind of feeling. It almost feels like I have to *pee.*"

"It won't be pee if you relax your muscles properly," I said. "This is something I learned at a special sex workshop for women. When you stimulate the gland nestled behind this spot in your pussy, you make your G-spot swell and prepare to release a special fluid that makes women squirt–"

"Like the way *you* did yesterday?" Juliet panted, beginning to rock her hips more rapidly.

"Yes," I said, pressing my fingers harder against her swelling bump and feeling the inside of her pussy expanding in preparation for a powerful contraction.

"Are you sure I'm not going to wet my pants?" she hissed, tightening her jaw muscles as her whole body began to tense up.

"Not with *urine*," I smiled, watching a deep flush roll over the top of her neck and onto her cheeks. "Just let it go, baby. You'll find it makes your orgasm even more powerful and intense. Gush all over my hands."

"Oh God," she huffed, raising her hips off the seat. "Here it comes, I can't stop it now. Oh fuck–I'm *comingggg*!"

I peered down and watched Juliet's hips shaking while she sprayed her juices all over my hand, creating a giant wet spot in the front of her jeans. As our carriage neared the bottom of the circle and our wheel slowed to a stop, I quickly pulled up her zipper while Juliet prepared to exit the ride.

"Here," I said, handing her the big panda resting on the seat beside me. "Maybe *you* should carry this for a while now. You've made quite a mess of yourself, and we don't want people wondering what happened to you."

"I just had my first female *ejaculation*, is what happened to me," she grinned, still breathing heavily as she exited the gondola, clasping the stuffed toy tightly over her stomach. "I wouldn't mind going to one of those women's workshops sometime. I feel like I'm just scratching the surface of possibilities for intimate relations between women..."

"We could do that," I smiled, leading her down the ramp toward the exit of the fairgrounds. "Or you could let *me* teach you instead. After all, I've had a bit more experience in these things than you have."

"Works for me," Juliet smiled. "Let's get out of here. I want to feel your beautiful body crawling over me instead of all these jostling fairgoers. I've been dreaming of a few extra techniques I want to try out on you."

"Mmm," I said. "It sounds *delicious*. Do you want to stop somewhere for a bite to eat first? We might need to stock up our energy before making love again all night."

"Sure, but not here with all this greasy food. Why don't we go somewhere quiet and enjoy a relaxing gourmet meal?"

Suddenly I felt my stomach rumbling, realizing we hadn't eaten since breakfast earlier in the day.

"Okay," I nodded. "Since you cooked for me last night, it'll be my treat today. I know a nice spot not far from your place that serves the freshest fish and desserts to die for."

"I only want *you* for dessert," Juliet purred, clasping my hand more tightly as we headed through the parking lot back toward my car.

"I think that can be arranged," I smiled. "If it's anything like *last* night's after-dinner treat, I can't wait..."

10

───────

After our exciting adventure at the county fair, we drove to one of my favorite restaurants near the waterfront and I parked the car, leading her into the sumptuous dining room of *Oriole,* with its huge floor-to-ceiling views of the lake.

"You should like this place," I smiled when the maître d' greeted us at the front desk. "It reminds me of your apartment. Can you smell the aroma of the lakefront?"

"Yes," Juliet nodded. "Plus, I heard the seagulls as soon as we got out of the car. Do they serve seafood here?"

"Absolutely," the maître d' said, overhearing our conversation. "We have a broad selection of seafood from our Michelin-star-awarded chef. Would you like a table near the window?"

"Maybe something a little more private near the corner of the room," I said, concerned about the other patrons staring at Juliet.

"As you wish," the headwaiter said. "Please follow me."

He led us to a small table near the fall wall, and when we sat down in the plush chairs, Juliet brushed her fingers over the bottom of the linen tablecloths draped over the side of our table.

"*Fancy,*" she said.

"Only the best for my girl," I smiled.

"Can I start you off with something to drink?" the maître d' said.

"I'll have a cosmopolitan," I nodded.

"Sex on the beach for me please," Juliet said nonchalantly.

"Coming right up," the maître d' said, departing in the direction of the bar.

"Haven't you had *enough* for one day?" I smirked, kicking her gently under the table.

"*Never*," she grinned, sliding her foot sensuously up the side of my calf.

When our waiter returned with our drinks, I ordered the potato-crusted halibut and Juliet ordered the maple-glazed salmon for the main courses, then we sipped our cocktails for a while, listening to the sound of the boats and the gulls cruising about the pier.

"Did you enjoy our little outing at the fair?" I said, happy that the long tablecloths concealed the dark stain on the front of her jeans.

"Yes," she smiled, taking a deep gulp of her cocktail. "Though I'm not sure which I enjoyed more, whupping your ass at the game tables or coming all over your hand in the privacy of our own booth on the Ferris wheel."

"I certainly know which one *I* did," I grinned, caressing her foot under the table. "Though I'm intrigued about something you said before we left. You said you were dreaming about some other techniques you wanted to try out on me. What exactly were you thinking?"

"Well," Juliet said, kicking off her sneakers under the table and sliding her foot up the inside of my leg. "I was thinking of doing this with you in the bathtub at home, but it looks like we'll have plenty enough privacy to do it right here..."

"Do *what* exactly?" I said, peering around me to see if anyone was looking while she lifted her foot higher between my legs and pressed her toes between my thighs.

"I've been dreaming about fucking you with my *toes*," she smiled. "It's something I heard about in another one of my favorite audiobooks, and I've always wanted to try it."

"Right *here*?" I said, widening my eyes.

"Why not?" she said. "Do you think you'll be able to keep your moans to a dull roar so you don't distract the attention of the other diners? We've got plenty of cover under the table from the draped tablecloths."

"I'm not sure," I grunted, feeling her toes curling over the front of my crotch. "But at least I've got a layer of protection to help dull the sensation–"

"What's the fun in that?" Juliet said, flapping her toes over my moistening pussy. "Besides, if you keep your jeans on while I do this, you're just likely to get another embarrassing stain in your pants. And this time, we won't have the protection of a large stuffed animal to conceal it from the other onlookers."

"You want me to take my *pants* off under the table?" I said, flaring my eyes open.

"Discreetly, yes," Juliet nodded. "I'm guessing most of the other patrons are staring out the window instead of looking at us sheltered in this corner of the room."

I glanced around me again, noticing the other diners chatting quietly amongst themselves, occasionally peering out the large picture windows. I was happy they had a diversion from staring at the blind girl who was staring straight ahead while she talked to me, but I was even happier that we had a modicum of privacy to carry out our little crime of passion.

"Yes," I said, slipping my hands under the bottom of the tablecloth and shimmying my jeans and panties down over my ankles. I could feel the soft velvet of the plush seats caressing my bare pussy, and I worried about leaving a different kind of stain on the upholstery by the time we finished our illicit affair.

When the waiter returned with our main courses and placed them gently in front of our place settings, I was happy for the distraction while I glanced up at him coolly.

"Can I get you anything else?" he said, peering at our flushed faces.

"No thank you," I said, feeling my pussy buzzing under the table while Juliet tapped her toes playfully against my dripping slit. "I think we've got everything we need right here."

"No kidding," Juliet said after the waiter left our table. "How does that Shakespeare line go? All I need is a loaf of bread, a jug of wine, and thou?"

"I think it was *Omar Khayyam* actually, but close enough," I grunted as Juliet slid her toes over my throbbing clit.

"Mmm, you feel *delicious*," Juliet said, picking up her silverware and beginning to eat her entrée while she stimulated me with her foot.

"Are you going to eat your *food* while you fuck me under the table?" I said, groaning softly as I tilted my hips upward to press my pussy harder against her foot.

"Why not?" Juliet grinned. "You should do it too, otherwise people might become suspicious of why we're watching our gourmet food growing cold."

"That might be easier for *you* than for me," I chuckled, picking up my cutlery and cutting a shaky slice of my halibut.

But as soon as I placed the first mouthful in my mouth, Juliet abruptly lowered her foot, thrusting her big toe into my hole. I choked for a moment on my food then I raised my napkin to my face to distract the diners' sudden attention, feeling my eyes watering from the rising pleasure washing over me.

"Are you okay over there?" Juliet said, grinning like a Cheshire Cat. "Maybe you should have a glass of water or something."

"I'm fine, miss smartypants," I said, clearing my throat. "At least I *was*, until you stuck your toe in my pussy."

"You don't *like* it?" she grinned back at me. "Do you want me to stop?"

"God no," I grunted, beginning to rock my hips in unison with the thrusting movement of her toe. "I haven't had this much fun since, well, since we had sex in *another* public place."

"Where the whole time I was thinking about how soon I could *return* the favor," she smiled.

"It seems your wish has come true," I groaned, closing my eyes while I felt the pleasure rising inside me. "If you keep doing that, I'm going to make an entirely *different* kind of mess."

"Oh?" Juliet said, redoubling her effort under the table while she flexed her toe inside my slit, tilting it upwards toward my bulging G-spot. "Am I stimulating the right area to make you gush and squirt again? I'm dying to see what that feels like on my bare foot."

"I don't think you have anything to worry about," I panted, feeling myself rapidly approaching the point of no return. "It doesn't take much to set me off..."

"*Come*, baby," Juliet purred, staring straight into my eyes while I peered back at her with dilated pupils. "Come for me in front of all these fancy restaurant patrons while I feel your pussy pulsing against my foot."

"Oh God," I huffed, scrunching the sides of the tablecloth beside me in my clenched hands while I tried to maintain my composure. "I can't stop it now–"

When my climax finally washed over me, I clamped my thighs tightly over Juliet's probing foot, gushing my juices hard all over the bottom of her leg and the now-drenched seat, unable to restrain myself from making a loud grunting sound while I quivered in my chair. When I noticed a few heads turning in my direction, I picked up another forkful of my sea bass, shoveling it into my mouth and humming loudly while I closed my eyes, pretending to enjoy the taste of the food instead of the strong contractions emanating from my squirting pussy under the table.

"Oh, that's *sooo* good," I fawned, putting on the performance of my life while I tried to divert everyone's attention from what was going on under the table. "This is the best sea bass I've tasted in *ages*!"

"And that's the hottest *sex* I've had in ages," Juliet whispered back at me, holding her tensed leg hard against my dripping crotch until my contractions finally stopped and I relaxed my tensing buttock muscles. "I'm starting to *like* this business of having sex in public."

I glanced nervously around the room to make sure no one had sensed what we were doing, then I noticed a lone diner three tables away staring blankly straight ahead while she held a forkful of food in mid-air a few inches from her gaping mouth. I recognized the vacant expression of another blind woman, with her head turned slightly askance as she listened intently to the unusual sounds coming from our side of the room.

"I have a feeling you're not the *only* one," I said, rustling my dinnerware noisily on my plate to divert everyone's attention back to the business at hand. "We seem to have attracted the attention of one pretty patron in particular."

"Oh?" Juliet said, retracting her foot slowly from my dripping pussy and wiping it on the lower half of her other leg. "Do you think she suspected what we were doing under the table?"

"Well, she looks to be *blind*, so I have a feeling her sense of hearing was more attuned than the others to the noises we were making over here."

"Is she alone?" Juliet said. "Maybe we should ask her to join us. Perhaps she'd like to join our little tete-a-tete?"

"That might be a little premature," I chuckled. "Besides, two blind girls eating at the same table might invite more scrutiny than we wanted."

"Yeah, especially if we're *playing* with each other under the table," Juliet grinned.

"She *does* seem intrigued, though," I said, glancing at the other girl out of the corner of my eye while she continued eating her meal and pretending to ignore our conversation as she perked up her ears. "And she's quite pretty. Maybe we can introduce ourselves and invite her to join us for dessert."

"Yes," Juliet said while she slid her sneaker back onto her foot with her other free foot. "Dessert with another pretty girl sounds like a real treat. Have you ever had sex with *three* women at the same time?"

"Maybe once or twice," I grinned.

"That sounds like something *else* you can teach me," Juliet nodded. "I'm tired of just reading about all these wild and sexy escapades. I'm ready to try it in the real world..."

11

————

After we finished our entrees, Juliet got up from our table and followed my instructions to the other girl's table, pausing by her chair as she introduced herself.

"Excuse me," she said. "I'm sorry to interrupt your dinner, but my friend couldn't help noticing that you're visually impaired, like me. "Would you like to join us for the remainder of your meal? We'd love some extra company, plus I rarely have a chance to socialize with other sightless people..."

"Um, okay," the girl said. "Can you help me carry the rest of my food to your table? I don't want to drop it on the other diners."

"Of course," Juliet said, motioning for the maître d' to assist them.

He brought an extra chair to our table and pulled out the seat for the other blind girl, positioning her kitty-corner, between me and Juliet.

"My name's Juliet, by the way," Juliet said, reaching out her hand over the tablecloth and squeezing the other girl's hand. "And this is my friend, Jade."

I reached out my hand as Juliet had and softly tapped the other girl's fingers.

"Nice to meet you," the new girl said. "My name's Skye. Thank you for inviting me to your table. I was feeling a bit lonely over there all by myself."

"Do you go out to fancy restaurants alone very *often*?" Juliet asked.

"Every now and then," Skye nodded. "It's nice to get out of the house from time to time and mingle with some real people. Plus, I get some of my best cooking ideas for new dishes at places like this."

"That's very clever," Juliet said. "I was just thinking that I'll have to try preparing this maple-glazed salmon that I've been enjoying tonight for my next home-cooked meal."

"Yes," Skye smiled. "You seemed to be enjoying your dinner more than the *rest* of the restaurant diners."

"Oh, that wasn't me," Juliet grinned, motioning in my direction. "That was *Jade*, who seemed to enjoy her dish far more than I was."

"I have a feeling that she was enjoying more than just the *food*," Skye chuckled. "Either that, or that must have been one especially juicy and succulent dish."

"Well, it certainly was *juicy*," I said. "I'm afraid I made a bit of a mess on my chair."

"Mm-hmm," Skye nodded, raising her foot over the edge of my seat. "Although that scent doesn't smell like any dish I've tried lately. At least not of the *culinary* variety."

"You're very perceptive," I chuckled. "We were hoping to keep our shenanigans under the radar before you arrived."

"Your secret is safe with me," Skye smiled. "As long as you allow me to participate in the fun and games."

"I like the sound of that," Juliet said. "But we might be able to enjoy our second course more openly back at my place. Would you like to join us for some brandy or liqueur in a more comfortable environment?"

"I'd like that very much," Skye nodded. "I might enjoy it even more if I can *lick* it off your naked bodies."

"Oh God," Juliet grunted. "That's *one* technique I never even imagined. You're making me build up a whole new kind of appetite..."

The three of us quickly paid for our meals, then we quickly left the restaurant, driving as fast as we could through the busy traffic back to Juliet's apartment. When we entered her foyer and removed our coats, we wasted little time falling into each other's arms, kissing and groping one another as we stumbled our way toward Juliet's bedroom. When we reached her bed, I began to remove Skye's clothing, running my eyes shamelessly over her full figure, much more voluptuous than Juliet's petit ballerina form. While I unclasped the back of her underwire bra with one hand, I unzipped the front of her pants, surprised to see that her bush had been neatly trimmed and shaved to a shallow stubble.

"You seem to have some experience undressing women, Jade," she said, stepping out of her pants while I lowered her underwear over her ankles.

"I've been getting a bit more practice than *usual*, lately," I nodded, watching Juliet step behind Skye and circle her hands over the blind girl's breasts, squeezing them softly.

"Lucky you," Skye moaned, arching her back as her nipples began to harden from Juliet's ministrations. "It's been longer than planned for me. Having two women at the same time is a special treat."

"Speaking of," Juliet said, temporarily halting her exploration of Skye's naked body. "I've completely forgotten about our after-dinner drinks. Would you like to repair to the kitchen while I prepare some digestifs?"

"Maybe later," Skye said, turning around and rubbing her tits against Juliet's naked body while I caressed her ass and slipped my finger under her moist slit. "I'd hate to interrupt a good thing right now. I love your figure, you're so firm and petite. I like petite girls–"

"Are you *lesbian*?" Juliet said, groaning softly while Skye pressed her tongue into her mouth and slipped her hand between her legs.

"For as long as I can remember," Skye nodded. "Boys seem to have an aversion to blind girls. But I've enjoyed being with women ever since my juvenile sleepover days. Plus, they're a little easier to *decipher*, since their bodies are similar to mine..."

"I wouldn't be so sure about that," Juliet said, sliding the palms of her hands over the edges of Skye's flared hips and under the curvature of her plump ass. You seem to be built more like Jennifer Lopez than Alicia Vikander..."

"How would you know if you're blind?" Skye said, squinting her brows.

"I wasn't born blind," Juliet said. "I had a little time to enjoy a few American movies before I lost my sight. Those were two of my favorite actresses."

"Same here," Skye said, grinding her bristly mound against Juliet's furry muff while I caressed their slits from behind. "I'd happily fuck either one of them."

"*Speaking* of which," Juliet said, pulling a few inches away to invite me to join in the action. "How are we going to do this with three women? I'm not as experienced as the two of you."

"I'm happy just to *watch* for a while," I said, caressing the two women's hardening nipples as they continued groping one another. "I have a feeling that Skye knows her way around a woman's body. Maybe I can pick up a few extra tips studying her technique."

"I like the sound of that," Skye nodded, grabbing hold of Juliet's hand and pushing her down over the surface of the bed.

She climbed on top of Juliet, rolling her slippery pussy over her tits and down the middle of her stomach while leaving a trail of glistening juices over her abdomen, grinding her pussy on Juliet's bush and soaking it thoroughly. I chose to sit on the foot of the bed, watching the two women making love, not wanting to interrupt the new girl's mojo. The two blind girls seemed to be innately drawn to one another, and I became increasingly aroused while fingering myself, watching them writhing their bodies together.

While Juliet groaned from Skye's expert caresses, the new girl angled Juliet's body to the side, pushing her legs apart and raising one over her shoulder. Then she spread her knees apart and squatted between Julie's legs, sliding her dripping pussy between Juliet's thighs and pressing their cunts together. Although I'd scissored Juliet similarly the previous night, it was obvious to me that Skye had done this many times before in the superior position. She seemed much more comfortable playing the top position in the relationship, preferring her partner to play the submissive femme role.

While she proceeded to grind her glistening vulva over Juliet's equally wet pussy, I watched Juliet's face from the back of the bed, noticing her growing comfortable in the role, perfectly happy to let Skye take the lead while she groaned and squeezed Skye's oversize tits. It was tempting for me to try to slide in on the action as I watched their slurping pussies grinding together and Skye's full tits bouncing up and down, but I thought I should leave the two blind women to their own devices to enjoy the rare opportunity of savoring their unique experience together. It didn't take long for their movements to begin escalating in intensity, and I looked on with a mixture of jealousy and lustfulness as their hips began to shake together while they wailed at the peak of their passion. After they finished climaxing together, Skye flopped down onto the bed beside Juliet, kissing her gently as she caressed her trembling stomach.

"You've been awfully quiet over there, Jade," Juliet said, lifting her head in my direction. "It's not like you to sit alone on the sidelines. Don't you want a piece of the action?"

"I dunno," I smiled halfheartedly. "Skye seems to have things well in hand. Plus, I already had my fill over dinner from your expert toes."

"I'm sure we could fit you into the puzzle somehow," Juliet smiled. "If it feels this good for two women to have sex together, it has to be even better with *three* of us doing it at the same time."

"I suppose that's up to our *guest*," I said, still feeling self-conscious about the intrusion of the new girl into our relationship. "She hasn't had as much experience making love to you as I have. Plus, it looks like she's still exploring your body..."

"Mmm," Juliet grunted as Skye inserted two fingers deep into her dripping pussy. "But I've still got my *top* half free. Why don't you sit on my face and let me lick your pussy while Skye has her way with my lower half? Maybe you can watch her from the other side this time and soak up her body while she makes love to me a different way."

"That's okay with *me* if that works for Skye," I said, peering at the other girl with a curious expression.

"Sure," Skye nodded, happy to keep a measure of distance between the two of us while she continued to stimulate Juliet in her own way. "This time, I want to *taste* your pussy while I watch you come."

"That makes *two* of us," Juliet smiled. "Why don't you watch me licking Jade's cunny while you go down on me, then we can switch turns the next time around?"

"Okay," Skye said, sounding unconvinced.

It seemed more and more apparent the more time the three of us spent time together that Skye wanted Juliet all to herself, and for her part, Juliet seemed equally happy to let her have her way with her. While Skye shimmied her way down Juliet's body and planted her face between her legs, I slowly climbed atop Juliet's face, straddling her rosebud lips with my trembling pussy. She peered up at my glistening folds and smelled my musky scent, smiling at me.

"Don't be shy *now*, Jade," she said, grabbing hold of the sides of my ass and guiding my hips down over her waiting lips. "I've wanted to feel you gushing over my face again ever since last night. Maybe watching Skye lick me at the same time will make you even more turned on. I can't wait to feel you spraying all over my neck and tits."

"Okay..." I murmured, watching Skye slide her tongue expertly over Juliet's dripping folds as she teased and tormented her.

While Juliet began sucking my hardening clit into her mouth, I watched Skye's technique and Juliet's response from the movement of her hips, becoming more and more aroused by the erotic stimulation from both sides. But there was something about the way Skye touched Juliet that had me mesmerized. Whether it was because the two women felt a unique connection from both being blind, or because Skye had plenty of experience with prior women, I wasn't sure. But the growing bond between them was becoming increasingly obvious to me, and although Juliet was trying her best to give me expert head, there was something that was holding me back from fully enjoying the experience.

As Juliet's hips began to rock more excitedly from Skye's unique form of stimulation and her moans from under my hips began to grow more animated, I gradually became more aroused, knowing she was getting close to another orgasm. When she finally climaxed with Skye's face deeply embedded between her legs, I had a brief, unconscious climax, more out of sympathy with what Juliet was feeling than from the soft caresses of her tongue. When we both finished climaxing, I lifted my hips off Juliet's face and she peered up at me with a curious expression.

"You didn't *squirt* this time," she said. "Should I have been using my *finger* to stimulate you at the same time? Your orgasm didn't seem as strong as usual–"

"No," I lied. "I enjoyed feeling your tongue as much as ever. I was just a bit distracted watching Skye going down on you and watching your body responding to her touch."

"Yeah," Juliet smiled when Skye shifted her body back up the bed and lay down beside her. "That was pretty incredible. Skye seems to be just as experienced making love to women as you are."

I paused for a moment, watching the two blind women caressing one another intuitively.

"You two seem to have an extra connection that I can't duplicate. It's quite lovely to see, actually," I said, feeling my heart sinking.

"Well, we'll have plenty of time for more of this *tomorrow*," Juliet said. "I'm in no hurry to see either of you leave. Will you both spend the night with me and stick around for some more fun and games tomorrow?"

"I'd love to," Skye said, snuggling up closer to Juliet and wrapping her legs around her hips, as if claiming her for herself.

"Of course," I said, feeling increasingly like the odd women out. "Like you said, three is better than two..."

I pulled the blanket over the three of us and nuzzled my nose into the side of Juliet's neck while Skye draped an arm over her midsection, carefully avoiding touching my body. It didn't take long for the two of them to fall asleep and while I listened to them breathing peacefully side-by-side, I knew what I had to do. I shimmied out of bed slowly, pretending to go pee in the washroom, then I got dressed quietly in the other room, preparing to leave the apartment. But I didn't want to leave Juliet wondering why I'd left without an explanation, so I pulled out my phone and typed her a short text message, knowing she'd be able to listen to the audio version when she woke up in the morning.

Dear Juliet,

It's been a singular pleasure getting to know you these past couple of days. I haven't had so much fun with another person for as long as I can remember. I'll never forget the special bond that we shared and the fun times we had at the fair, in the restaurant, and of course at home with you in your beautiful apartment.

But after seeing you with Skye, it's obvious she can give you something I never can. You two have an affinity that transcends more than just sight-lessness, and you belong together. Besides, I've always been a restless soul, and I'd hate for the two of us to develop stronger feelings for one another, only to be pulled apart sometime in the future.

Wishing you and Skye all the best,
Love, Jade

After pressing the send button on my phone, I opened the front door and closed it quietly behind me, shedding a lone tear down the front of my face while I stepped into the elevator taking me down to the ground floor. This was one short-term fling I'd never forget, but I knew that Juliet was in better hands with another blind woman. While I headed toward my car parked on the side of the street, I closed my eyes listening to the sound of the gulls circling over the waterfront and smelling the moist air drifting in from the lake, smiling at how the pretty blind girl had opened my eyes to a whole new world of sensations and pleasures.

*R*eady for more erotic chills and thrills? Order the next volume in the Erotica Themed Bundles series, *Voyeur Volume 2. Buy direct and save at victoriarusherotica. Or download from your favorite online bookstore here: retailer links.*

Sometimes it's more fun to watch...

ALSO BY VICTORIA RUSH

Adult Fairytales:

The Enchanted Forest: An Erotic Fairytale

The Land of Giants: An Erotic Fairytale

The Dragon's Lair: An Erotic Fairytale

Witch's Brew: An Erotic Fairytale

The Mage's Spell: An Erotic Fairytale

The Mermaid Lagoon: An Erotic Fairytale

The Coven: An Erotic Fairytale

Rapunzel: An Erotic Fairytale

The Seven Dwarfs: An Erotic Fairytale

The Land of Mutants: An Erotic Fairytale

The Erotic Temple: A Sexy Fairytale (Coming Soon)

Erotica Themed Bundles:

Voyeur: Lesbian Erotica Bundle

Public Affairs: A Lesbian Anthology

Futa Fantasies: The Ladyboy Collection

Threesomes: The Lesbian Collection

Threesomes - Volume 2: The Lesbian Collection

First Time: A Lesbian Anthology

Hedonism: An Erotic Anthology

Switch Hitters: Bisexual Erotica

Taboo Erotica: The Lesbian Series

BDSM: The Lesbian Collection

Party Games: The Erotic Collection

Party Games 2: The Erotic Collection

All Girl 1: Lesbian Erotica Bundle

All Girl 2: Lesbian Erotica Bundle

All Girl 3: Lesbian Erotica Bundle

All Girl 4: Lesbian Erotica Bundle

Erotic Fairytale Bundles:

Clover's Fantasy Adventures: Books 1 - 5

Clover's Fantasy Adventures: Books 6 - 10

Erotic Fantasy:

Pirate's Bounty: A Time Travel Adventure

Wild West: A Time Travel Adventure

Private Riley: A Time Travel Adventure

Cleopatra's Secret: A Time Travel Adventure

Bounty Hunter 2125: A Time Travel Adventure

Ninja Assassin: A Time Travel Adventure

The 300: A Time Travel Adventure

Arabian Nights: An Erotic Fairytale (coming soon...)

Steamy Time Travel Bundles:

Riley's Time Travel Adventures: Books 1 - 5

Lesbian Erotica:

The Dinner Party: Lesbian Voyeur Erotica

The Darkroom: Bisexual Voyeur Erotica

Naked Yoga: Lesbian Transgender Erotica

Nude Cruise: Bisexual Voyeur Erotica

Rush Hour: Taboo Public Sex

The Girl Next Door: First Time Lesbian Erotic Romance

Girls' Camp: Lesbian Group Sex

Wet Dream: Ladyboy Fantasy Erotica

The Convent: Taboo Sex with a Nun

Sex Robot: A Dream Sex Machine

The Personal Trainer: Getting Pumped at the Gym

The Dominatrix: BDSM Lesbian Domination

Webcam Chat: Lesbian Online Sex

Paint Me: A Kinky Bodypainting Workshop

The Toy Party: Girls Sharing Sex Toys

The Costume Party: Strapping One On

Swedish Sauna: Lesbian Group Sex

The Therapist: Taboo Lesbian Erotica

Elevator Shaft: Bisexual Threesomes Erotica

Ladyboy: Lesbian Transgender Erotica

Peep Show: Lesbian Voyeur Erotica

The Dare: Public Sex Erotica

Maid Service: Lesbian Threesomes Erotica

The Hitchhiker: First Time Lesbian Erotica

The Housesitter: Spycam Lesbian Erotica

The Spa: Lesbian Group Orgy

Parlor Games: Blindfold Sex Party

The Exchange Student: First Time Lesbian Erotica

The Hostel: Bisexual Group Erotica

The Harem: Lesbian Erotic Romance

The Orient Express: Lesbian Voyeur Erotica

The First Lady: A Forbidden Lesbian Erotic Romance

The Slave: Lesbian BDSM Erotica

The Masseuse: Lesbian Sensuous Erotica

Too Close for Comfort: Lesbian Forbidden Erotica

Naked Twister: A Wild Party Game

Lexi: The Sex App (Lesbian Fantasy Erotica)

Call Girl: Lesbian Bisexual Threesomes Erotica

Circle Jill: Lesbian Masturbation Workshop

The Viewing Room: Masturbation Voyeur Erotica

Spin the Bottle: A Kinky Party Game

The Hair Salon: Lesbian Voyeur Erotica

Tribadism 1: Girls Only Sex Workshop

Tribadism 2: The Art of Scissoring

Tribadism 3: Threeway Hookups

The Kiss: A Game of Oral Sex

Pledge Week: Sorority Sisters

Carny Games 1: A Wild Sex Party

Carny Games 2: A Kinky Sex Party

Carny Games 3: An Erotic Sex Party

Dreamscape: An Artificial Reality Game

Glory Hole: Guess Who's On the Other Side

Joy Ride: A Late Night Erotic Bus Trip

The Blind Girl: An Erotic Romance(Coming Soon)

Lesbian Erotica Bundles:

Jade's Erotic Adventures: Books 1 - 5

Jade's Erotic Adventures: Books 6 - 10

Jade's Erotic Adventures: Books 11 - 15

Jade's Erotic Adventures: Books 16 - 20

Jade's Erotic Adventures: Books 21 - 25

Jade's Erotic Adventures: Books 26 - 30

Jade's Erotic Adventures: Books 31 - 35

Jade's Erotic Adventures: Books 36 - 40

Jade's Erotic Adventures: Books 41 - 45

Jade's Erotic Adventures: Books 46 - 50

Fifty Shades of Jade: Superbundle

Standalone Stories:

The Polynesian Girl: A Lesbian EroticRomance

FOLLOW VICTORIA RUSH:

Want to keep informed of my latest erotic book releases? Sign up for my newsletter and receive a FREE bonus book:

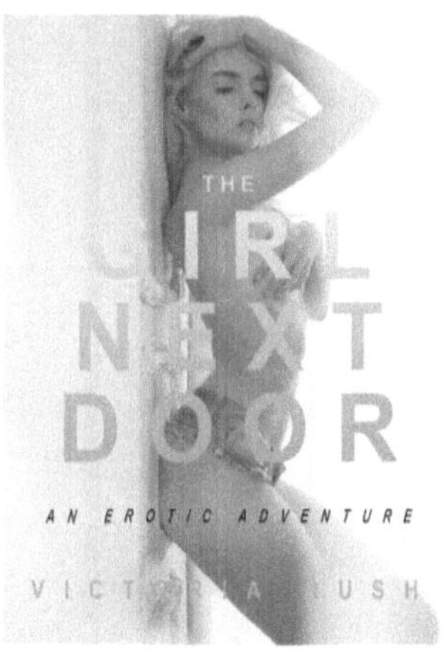

Spying on the neighbors just got a lot more interesting...